Praise For Eva Crocker And *All I Ask*

Winner, BMO Winterset Award · Longlist, Scotiabank
Giller Prize · Finalist, ReLit Award for Novel

"A wickedly funny, sexy, joyous novel, threaded through with sadness, uncertainty, and emotional risk." — *Toronto Star*

"Funny, hot, and heartfelt." — *Xtra*

"Crocker pulls off an ending that brings the drama full circle in a way that is both unexpected and satisfying." — *Quill & Quire*

"A carefully crafted, observant novel, whose dialogue and scene composition retain an intimacy and immediacy." — *Montreal Review of Books*

"*All I Ask* is a wonderful character study and an encapsulation of a particular time and place.... Crocker is a writer we will be talking about for a long time." — *Newfoundland Quarterly*

"Eva Crocker's stunning debut eloquently depicts a generation struggling to gain self-determination in a climate steeped in societal deprivation, violence, and greed. Her characters, informed by progressive ideals and the optimism of youth, labour to overcome precariousness in all aspects of their lived experience. Housing. Employment. Love.... *All I Ask* is precise and fervent storytelling." — Megan Gail Coles, author of *Small Game Hunting at the Local Coward Gun Club*

T0050076

Praise For Eva Crocker And *Barrelling Forward*

A *National Post* Best Book of the Year · Winner, Alistair MacLeod Prize for Short Fiction · Winner, Canadian Authors Association Emerging Writer Award · Finalist, Dayne Ogilvie Prize for LGBTQ Emerging Writers · Finalist, NLCU Fresh Fish Award for Emerging Writers

"An intimate and fascinating read." — *This Magazine*

"A fine and enthralling collection that will excite and seduce readers." — *Toronto Star*

"*Barrelling Forward* comes at you in about the same way as her title would suggest: brazen, but entirely enthralling. Crocker may well be our modern Munro, or at least something close when it comes to Canada's greatest storytellers."
— *National Post*

"Eva Crocker is a remarkable stylist; her impressive stories crackle with life and originality."
— Zoe Whittall, author of *The Best Kind of People*

"Honest, funny, smart and so, so well-crafted, *Barrelling Forward* is a feast for those starving for the real thing in fiction. This is the work of a debut writer already at the top of her game."
— Alexander MacLeod, author of *Light Lifting*

"Eva Crocker is a bright new misfit in CanLit."
— Heather O'Neill, author of *Daydreams of Angels*

Back in the Land of the Living

Also by Eva Crocker

Barrelling Forward
All I Ask

Back in the Land of the Living

A Novel

Eva Crocker

ANANSI

Copyright © 2023 Eva Crocker

Published in Canada in 2023 and the USA in 2023 by House of Anansi Press Inc.
houseofanansi.com

All rights reserved. No part of this publication may be reproduced or
transmitted in any form or by any means, electronic or mechanical, including
photocopying, recording, or any information storage and retrieval system,
without permission in writing from the publisher.

House of Anansi Press is committed to protecting our natural environment.
This book is made of material from well-managed FSC®-certified forests,
recycled materials, and other controlled sources.

House of Anansi Press is a Global Certified Accessible™ (GCA by Benetech)
publisher. The ebook version of this book meets stringent accessibility
standards and is available to readers with print disabilities.

27 26 25 24 23   1 2 3 4 5

Library and Archives Canada Cataloguing in Publication

Title: Back in the land of the living : a novel / Eva Crocker.
Names: Crocker, Eva, author.
Identifiers: Canadiana (print) 20230180558 | Canadiana (ebook) 20230180566
ISBN 9781487009779 (softcover) | ISBN 9781487009786 (EPUB)
Classification: LCC PS8605.R62 B33 2023 | DDC C813/.6—dc23

Cover design: Alysia Shewchuk
Cover image: (fishnet) MicroOne/stock.adobe.com
Typesetting: Greg Tabor

*House of Anansi Press is grateful for the privilege to work on and create from the
Traditional Territory of many Nations, including the Anishinabeg, the Wendat, and
the Haudenosaunee, as well as the Treaty Lands of the Mississaugas of the Credit.*

With the participation of the Government of Canada
Avec la participation du gouvernement du Canada | Canadä

*We acknowledge for their financial support of our publishing program the Canada
Council for the Arts, the Ontario Arts Council, and the Government of Canada.*

Printed and bound in Canada

For Emily Fearon,
a lighthouse in the big city

One

Fall 2019

1

Marcy arrived in the city on the first of September at night, close to midnight. She'd found a room to sublet after weeks of scrolling through Facebook housing groups. She got a cab from the airport to drop her in front of an apartment in the Mile End. The driver had his window down and a cool, damp breeze filled the car as they hit the highway. In the city there wasn't much traffic. On Saint-Laurent people were smoking in groups outside of bars. The storefronts glowed, the mannequins inside were dressed in fluorescents and pleather. There were mazes of pylons wrapped in messy swirls of caution tape on almost every corner. The driver cruised smoothly around them.

"Almost there," he told her as they turned onto a darker street. Fat garbage bags sat at the bottom of tall, curved staircases.

The cab stopped, and the driver got out and jogged around back for her suitcases.

"It's okay, I got it," she said, reaching for the bigger bag, but the man got hold of the handle first. He swooped it out of the trunk and over an eddy of dust-coated, disintegrating litter that hugged the curb. She lifted her smaller bag out.

"Okay?" the driver asked before climbing back into his car.

"Yeah, thank you."

She dragged her bags up to the building and rang the bell. Maybe no one would open the door. It was possible she'd sent rent into the ether and now she would be alone with her suitcases and have to find somewhere else to stay. She didn't know anyone in the city well enough to ask if she could crash at their place.

Someone with shoulder-length blue hair pulled open the door. "Marcy? I'm Al."

Marcy followed their narrow back up a steep set of stairs to a door that opened on to the kitchen. Marcy had a long suitcase handle in each hand and the bags thumped up the steps behind her. In the kitchen something was frying and white froth was bubbling over the lip of a saucepan.

"Are you hungry?" Al rushed to the stove and lifted the pot off the burner as streams of bubbles slid down the sides and hissed on the red element.

"I'm okay," Marcy said, even though her stomach was clawing at itself. It seemed rude to eat immediately, although maybe it would have been friendly.

"I just got home from work around nine and then I was answering some emails and now I haven't eaten and it's almost midnight. This always happens to me."

"I think it's after midnight."

Al lifted a pork chop out of the pan with a fork and flipped it.

"I was vegetarian for six years. This is my first time making a pork chop, I don't really know what I'm doing."

"It smells good, what did you put on it?"

"Just salt and pepper and garlic."

"That's perfect," Marcy said, undoing her boots.

Al smiled down at the pork chop.

"Your room is right there, if you want to put your stuff away." Al pointed to an open door off the kitchen. The lights were off so Marcy couldn't see in.

"But you're welcome to hang out too," Al said.

Marcy pulled her suitcases close to the couch and sat down. There was a rangy plant on top of the fridge, and its vines had been thumbtacked so they wrapped all the way around the small kitchen.

"I'll hang out for a little bit. You're a DJ, right?" Marcy asked. She'd learned that from Facebook but the flyers taped down the side of the fridge reminded her.

"Yeah, what about you? Do you DJ?"

"No." Marcy had never been asked that before.

"You're going to school?" Al strained the pot over the sink and Marcy saw they were making spiral noodles.

"No, I guess I'm kind of just hanging out. I'm looking for work, if you happen to know of anything. I'm looking for a long-term place after this too, I mean just if you hear of anything," Marcy said.

"I'll keep an ear out. I'm going to eat these with some pesto from the jar. I normally I make my own but this was on sale." Al untwisted the lid and sniffed. "This stuff is actually pretty good, I think anyway."

They scooped a tablespoon of grimy sauce out of the jar and swirled it into the noodles.

"You know what I just remembered? The couple who's renting Arnina's room for the month, they get here on the tenth. They're from Newfoundland, maybe you know them?"

"It's a small place," Marcy answered. "How old are they?"

"A little older than us, like early thirties, I guess. Lesbians. They have a dog, I hope that's okay, I should have mentioned the dog, sorry."

"I love dogs."

"Is it weird for me to ask if you know them? Cause they're from Newfoundland?"

"No, it's a small place, I probably do know them," Marcy repeated. "But I can't think of who they could be. I know all the queer people there. I mean, basically."

"You don't want a little bit of pasta?" Al asked, lowering their pork chop onto a plate.

"I would have a little bit," Marcy said. "If there's enough."

"Should I put on some music for us?" Al clicked on their keyboard and ambient music poured out of speakers anchored to the wall above their heads.

Marcy insisted on doing the dishes after they'd eaten. Al shovelled the leftover pasta into a large, cloudy Tupperware. When the cleanup was done, Marcy wheeled her suitcases into the bedroom. She could hear Al running the taps in the little bathroom down the hall. She felt the pasta sitting in her stomach, a comforting warm greasy lump.

Someone had built stilt legs for the bed so that things could be stored underneath it. Three mattresses were piled on top of the rough wooden frame and a sea of mason jars huddled beneath it. Some had dark liquids labelled with strips of masking tape. *Valerian, Mugwort, Thistle, Skullcap.*

There was a narrow desk with a chair pulled up to it and a dressmaker's mannequin. The top mattress was level with Marcy's collarbone. She did a hop and tried to swing one leg up. Her heel caught but she slid back down, dragging the crocheted bedspread with her. The third time, she managed to belly-flop herself up there. She slept curled above the potions in her new princess-and-the-pea bed.

WHEN MARCY WOKE up, Al was in the kitchen drinking coffee from an aluminum stovetop espresso maker and eating a piece of toast smeared with butter. They showed her a roommate ad for an apartment in Little Italy with a move-in date at the end of the month. They flipped from an Excel spreadsheet on their screen to another tab to show Marcy the ad. She felt touched that they'd kept the ad open for her until she woke up. The photos were from the spring, there was a big balcony with tomato plants growing in plastic buckets and the bedroom had stained glass in the windows.

"You can tell them you know me," Al said.

"Thank you so much," Marcy answered, already composing a response to the ad on her phone.

"There's still some coffee," Al said. "Oh, and there's two loaner bikes locked to the fire escape. Keys are in the drawer of that hutch near the front door. I think the pink one should fit you."

Marcy got herself a mug and sat on the burgundy couch that separated the apartment's foyer area from the kitchen. It was the type of couch she associated with Montreal; carved wooden armrests and a prickly upholstery in a pattern of vines and flowers. While Al typed in their spreadsheet, Marcy worked on her roommate pitch.

Outside the narrow kitchen window, the sky was already intensely blue. Marcy tapped Send on her smeared phone screen.

Eventually Al closed their laptop and began collecting things from around the apartment. They were going to a cafe to do work with a friend. Marcy felt a pang of loneliness at the thought of the big empty day ahead of her. She had no plans except scrolling through job postings.

She stepped out onto the fire escape and tasted exhaust in the humid air. She saw the two loaner bikes, a slick black frame for someone tall and a chunky fuchsia mountain bike with thick tires. She was instantly in love with the mountain bike. It felt like a physical manifestation of her personality, or, more, who she hoped to become in Montreal. She got the key from the hutch, lifted the bike frame onto her shoulder, clutched the handrail, and went down the steep fire escape. When she sat on the seat she could just reach the ground with the tips of her sneakers.

FOR THE NEXT few days, she and Al ate breakfast together in the little kitchen. One morning Al was at the table writing in a journal when Marcy got up.

"I'm heading out soon," they said.

Marcy got a mug from the cupboard; it had a pixelated photo of two women wrestling in an inflatable pool filled with mud. One woman had a splash of mud down the centre of her body and speckles of mud all over her face. Marcy had been using the same mug each morning, the ritual of it felt good. She was wearing a big T-shirt and a pair of soccer shorts, no bra. She noticed that she was savouring the days until the empty bedroom at the end of the hall was filled. She liked it being just her and Al.

"Have you heard of *The Artist's Way*?" Al asked.

Marcy shook her head. "Is it okay if I use some of your oat milk? I'm going to pick some up today."

"Oh my god, anytime. It's this book from the seventies, I haven't read it but my friend was telling me about it. There's all these exercises to, like, foster creativity or just help you be in your process, kind of. One of them is you free-write four pages every morning, even if it's, like, blah blah blah, you fill the pages. That's what I was doing. I just finished."

Al flipped their journal closed and put a flat palm on the cover.

"Nice." Marcy had been waking up in the middle of the night with anxiety cycling through her chest; thinking about the end of the month and money. The girl from the ad Al showed her had written to say they found someone who was a better fit for their household but they wished her luck. The first mouthful of coffee washed the bad sleep headache away; fresh start, new day.

"I do feel like it's really productive." Al wiped a finger through some peanut butter on their plate. "You get into a kind of flow state. It's meditative."

"I should try it," Marcy said.

"The other thing, which I haven't started yet but I'm going to, is that you take yourself on artist dates."

Now Al was collecting their things, sliding them into their bookbag.

"Maybe if I get up earlier we can do it together sometime," Marcy said.

"Well, the whole thing about the artist date is you do it alone. The idea is you go on your own and try to be kind of like attuned to the world around you, look at it through your artist eyes."

"Oh, I mean the free write."

"The Morning Pages."

"Yeah," Marcy said.

"Sure, we could do that. I'm trying to think what to do for my first artist date. I might go look at the fountain in the Desjardins Mall."

"What's that?"

"It's just a fountain but it's a really good one. There's a light show and jets, it's very atmospheric. I was thinking I'd get a pretzel and look at it."

Al moved into the porch area and started lacing their boots, saying, "Okay, anyway, I'm late, have a good day, see you later, mwah, bye."

A gust of wind howled in the stairs and then the front door slammed shut. Marcy didn't tell Al but basically her whole life since arriving in Montreal felt like an artist date. She spent most days wandering around alone, trying to make the awe she felt about her surroundings outweigh her loneliness.

That night she decided to take herself to Dollar Cinéma, a cheap theatre Al had told her about, and tried to think of it as an artist date. She relished the long train ride to Namur station. She'd applied for a number of tutoring jobs that afternoon, lying on her belly in her tall bed, tediously typing the same message again and again on her phone.

On the metro, two preteen girls with bookbags sat down across from Marcy and pressed their heads together for a selfie. They instantaneously transformed their giggling faces into empty-eyed, parted-lip stares for the camera. It was wild to imagine growing up in a place with a subway, regularly travelling so far and fast at that age.

Outside the metro station Marcy walked along the highway, her hair whipping in the backdraft of the rush of cars. A mother with a toddler and a baby in a stroller approached her on a narrow bridge above another highway, the basket in the bottom of the stroller stuffed with Walmart bags. At the last moment Marcy stepped into the road to let the family pass and a PT Cruiser blared its horn as it sailed by her.

She followed the blue light of her Google Maps avatar to a strip mall. She took a long walk around the exterior until she found an entrance beside the parking garage, with the Dollar Cinéma logo and an arrow printed on a sheet of paper taped to the inside of a glass door.

She saw one stooped, older man leaving the mall as she arrived; other than that, the first floor was deserted. Many of the stores were closed down. Empty clothes racks stood in the carpeted rooms, naked mannequins stared through the plate glass windows. The few stores that had merchandise inside were locked with cross-hatched metal gates and fat padlocks.

It was still bright inside the mall, though. Plastic plants reached stiffly out of their pots. The floor was shiny and sticky, just a few salty boot-prints marring a recent wax job. Al had said Dollar Cinéma was on the second floor, so Marcy boarded a skinny escalator.

Afterwards she'd tried to remember if she noticed the smell first. Ammonia and fur and warm breath; the smell of animals living inside. There were a series of cages arranged in front of a block of empty storefronts. The enclosures were of varying heights. Two emus stood with a fence just under their bald chins. They stared at Marcy and lifted and dropped their feet in an angry dance. A laminated sign hanging off the fence said *Ne touchez pas aux émeus*, and below it, *Do not touch the emus*, even though the height of the fence seemed to invite it.

The biggest pen held a mother pig with four piglets snuggled against her. There was a tall, narrow enclosure with a fake tree inside. Marcy scanned the identical leaves for a long time before seeing the dopey face of a live sloth between them, its arms and legs embracing a brown plastic branch.

She looked around, first for an attendant and then for any other witnesses. There was a group of teenagers on the other side of the foyer. They pulled open the door below an illuminated sign for Dollar Cinéma and disappeared. The emus were still stamping their feet and now they'd also begun jerking their heads back and forth on their long necks. Marcy found herself hoping Al would be home when she got back so she could describe the scene to them.

In the Dollar Cinéma lobby a wall of leather massage chairs were set up opposite the concession counter. You could drop toonies into the arm of the chair to make it rumble to life. Marcy bought a ticket to *Hustlers* and a bag of bright yellow popcorn at the long glass counter. She had decided not to spend any more money than the metro fare, the movie ticket, and the beer she'd picked up at the dep on the way but when she smelled the popcorn she wanted it so badly. She decided it was worth giving up something else later.

She asked the man behind the counter about the animals.

He refused to acknowledge that anything about the abandoned petting zoo was unusual.

"It's closed for the night." He passed her the popcorn and turned to help people she hadn't noticed lining up behind her.

There was one couple sitting in the centre of the theatre where Marcy's movie was playing. She sat two rows ahead of them. She heard them speaking to each other in French and worried for the first time that the movie might be in French. She decided that if it was, she would sit through it, and she might even understand some of it. She had some French from junior high. When the ads that ran before the previews started, they were in English with French subtitles and Marcy relaxed in her seat. She cracked the beer during an explosion in one of the trailers, absurdly worried the couple might rat her out to the skinny old man behind the concession stand.

When the movie ended Marcy found herself trying to think of how she would describe it to Al. She'd been excited about the prospect of a film that included both a heist plotline and sexy dancing — *Hustlers* delivered everything it promised, but it was a mistake to go alone. She wished she'd picked something broodier, like a movie about someone trying to get out of the mafia. She heard the couple behind her leave and stayed in her seat. The beer had made her tired and she didn't want to face the cold walk to the metro.

WHEN SHE GOT home Al wasn't there. Their bedroom door was open and the lights were off. Marcy stirred two tablespoons of CBD oil into a cup of valerian tea before going to bed. Sometimes this concoction let her sleep through the anxiety that made her lungs feel tight at night. She needed to find an apartment and a job. In the daytime she was pretty good at being in the moment, being distracted by her surroundings. Sometimes she got caught in a bad loop of thoughts but she almost never got the constricted feeling in her chest in the daytime.

She left her jeans on the floor and hauled herself up into the tall bed. She streamed a reality show filmed in the States at the height of the housing crisis about people digging through "abandoned" storage lockers for things to sell. She slept a deep dreamless sleep.

The next day Marcy woke late and when she got up Al had already left the house. She'd just turned off the shower when she heard voices on the stairs, a clamour of boots.

"Put the muzzle on her," one of the voices said.

"We left it in the car."

"For fuck's sake."

"She'll be fine."

There was a pounding on the inside apartment door. Marcy was heading for her bedroom, but she froze midway across the kitchen, barefoot in a towel.

The knock came again. Marcy knew the door was unlocked and she watched the handle turn. A black dog bounded into the room followed by two women with duffle bags slung over their shoulders. Ashley Whiteway. Of course, Marcy had known her forever. She was a couple of years older, and she'd lived at Pleasant Street when lots of Marcy's friends were cycling through the old downtown house. The other woman was thin and tall with straight blond hair.

"Romeo!" Ashley yelled. The dog hopped on the couch

and turned a circle, bucking its back legs like a horse. "She's
a puppy."

The dog ran at Marcy and slapped her paws on Marcy's
chest. Marcy clamped her arms tight to her sides to stop
Romeo from dragging her towel down. She stepped backwards and the dog fell and then leapt on her again. Its curved
nails left eight short red welts on her chest.

"Romeo, down! Marcy, oh my god. Imagine, you live
here? That's wild. Newfoundlanders, see? We find each
other. This is Melissa, my girlfriend."

Ashley grabbed the dog by the collar and stooped to hold
her until she sat beside her leg, shivering with excitement.

Ashley beamed at Marcy. Marcy knew what the look
meant—Ashley had gone out into the world and found a
girlfriend, and now she was bringing her back to the island.
What all the Newfoundland queers dreamed of. Ashley was
being smug about it.

"Nice to meet you," Marcy said. "I'm just going to get
dressed."

"We're dropping off our stuff and the dog and then we're
going to get lunch. Did you eat? Want to come with us?"
Ashley asked.

Marcy scrambled for an excuse, but nothing was coming
to her. She was just going to lie on her bed in the towel
looking at Instagram. And she was hungry.

"Sure, I'll be quick."

As soon as Marcy closed her bedroom door Ashley called
out to her.

"Yeah?" she said, trying to keep the irritation out of her voice.

"Do you know which room?"

Marcy opened the door, the towel around her was damp

and her hair was dripping cold water down her back. She pointed to the empty bedroom from the threshold of what was starting to feel like her room, in spite of her limited time there.

WHEN MARCY EMERGED dressed, Ashley was sitting at the table and Melissa was pouring her tea. Romeo had curled herself into a circle on the couch, her wet nose resting on the tip of her tail, eyes closed.

"See? Now she's passed out. That's what puppies are like. Some sweet when she's like that," Ashley said. "We're just having a quick cup of tea and then we'll head out. Sit with us."

Marcy knew it was absurd, but it grated on her how comfortable Ashley seemed in the apartment.

Marcy pulled out a chair. "Have you been to Newfoundland before, Melissa?"

"No, but I've seen pictures and heard Ashley's stories about it. It sounds really special there."

"That's one word for it."

Melissa placed a teacup in front of Marcy and poured. She took Al's oat milk out of the fridge and put it on the table. Marcy didn't like the idea of Al coming home and seeing their milk out like that, but she thanked Melissa for it anyway.

"Are you moved up here now?" Ashley asked her.

"Yeah."

"How long have you been here?"

"Like ten days," Marcy said.

"Oh, so barely at all, you haven't had time to start missing home yet," Ashley said.

"I'm not going to be missing it." Marcy tipped some of Al's milk into her tea.

"You don't like it there?" Melissa asked.

"Where did you grow up?" Marcy asked her.

"San Francisco."

Marcy nodded like "gotcha," locking eyes with Ashley. "It's just really small."

"Sometimes you gotta get out, it's good to get out," Ashley said. "But then you gotta go back. You never lived away before, have you?"

"San Francisco seems like such a cool place," Marcy said.

"Yeah, well it's ruined now by tech gentrification."

"Where should we eat?" Ashley asked. "I haven't been here since 2014."

Marcy led them up the street to a falafel place Al had told her about.

"It's really cheap and good," Marcy said, pulling the door open.

When the wraps were ready they sat in the window and ate them. Marcy kept glancing sideways at Melissa and Ashley to see if they were enjoying their falafel and they seemed to be enjoying it. Al walked by the window on their way home and Marcy waved. Al stared for a moment and then waved, a big smile breaking across their face as they continued on towards the apartment.

"Should we get a beer after this?" Ashley asked.

"Yeah," Marcy said, feeling light and bubbly already. She was enjoying being part of a little group.

The three of them ended up in a small, dark karaoke bar. The floor was carpeted and a row of VLT machines burned bright in the back corner. When they arrived a woman in skin-tight light denim was singing an emotional anthem in French. She stood with her legs wide apart and held the mic with both hands. The people sitting at the bar had twisted around on their stools so they could take in her performance. It didn't feel so different from karaoke at the Georgetown Pub in St. John's.

Ashley wrote *MMMBop by Hanson* on a slip of lined paper and brought it to the host. Melissa went to the counter and bought them a pitcher.

Ashley and Melissa kept buying beer. Soon Ashley and Marcy were putting on thick Newfoundland accents for Melissa's benefit. It wasn't the way Marcy talked normally but she could put it on for an undiscerning ear. She found herself enjoying the little improv session. She quizzed Melissa on a string of words mainlanders wouldn't know; sook for someone who's moping, streel for someone who goes around dressed sloppily without a care in the world, buster instead of grinder for the tool you use to break up your weed.

"I know most of those from Ashley," Melissa said. "Except streel."

"Streel's a good one," Ashley said.

"How long are you here for?" Marcy asked.

"Until the end of the month, then we're driving back home."

"Forever?" Marcy asked.

"We signed a year-long lease. It's on Barnes Road and there's a chicken coop in the backyard. We need a roommate, though, if you change your mind about sticking it out."

"I'm not going back," Marcy said. "Not for a long time, anyway."

. . .

IN JUNIOR HIGH Marcy had been mostly left alone. She ate lunch with a group of punk girls and Steve Dempsey, who wore a trench coat and 1940s aviator-style goggles in his hair. Steve turned out to be gay, but Marcy didn't learn that until much later when they met as adults in a pizza place in Halifax late at night. He was making out with his boyfriend in the window while they waited for their slices. Once she saw it, it made so much sense. Of course Steve Dempsey had been gay, continued to be gay. She'd hugged him in the steamy pizza shop. She and Steve Dempsey and his boyfriend ate their slices outside, standing on the corner. A drip of the red sauce had dribbled down the front of Marcy's jacket and she didn't notice it until the next morning when it had hardened on and stained the fabric.

In junior high they'd spent most of their lunch hour in the graveyard alongside the school, or in winter they'd hung out in the heated lobby of the real estate office down the street. Often, she and her friends got harassed, and once they even had bricks from the torn-down convent behind the school flung at them, but no one ever really picked on her in particular.

Except for one afternoon when she'd been walking to school alone. A girl with blond streaks in the front of her hair had stuck her face close to Marcy's and asked, "Did your friend call my cousin a skank?" Marcy vehemently shook her head no, and surprisingly the girl seemed satisfied with that.

That day she'd had a doctor's appointment in the morning. There was a scaly rash behind her knees and the doctor prescribed her a tube of antifungal cream. That rash would go on to haunt her from there on out, appearing under her breasts and in her armpits whenever she was broke or on the brink of a breakup or overworked.

She'd stopped into the Red Circle convenience store to buy a pizza bun and a tin of Pepsi on her way to school. She'd missed the crush of adolescents that crowded the store just after noon every weekday, and by some miracle there were still pizza buns left. The woman behind the counter microwaved the white bun for her. It had a smear of tomato sauce, two slices of pepperoni, and a square of mozzarella. If it got too busy, they refused to microwave your bun, so Marcy felt lucky.

She unwrapped the sandwich and stepped out into the snowy road. She had her headphones in and she was listening to a CD Steve Dempsey had made her with his dad's new CD burner — the first she'd ever heard of. The sky was bright blue. The doctor had said her rash would be gone in three to seven days. She smiled recognizing the beginning of "The Love Cats" by The Cure.

She was licking a glob of warm tomato sauce off the side of the golden bun, getting ready to take the first soft bite, when she was yanked backwards. The zipper of her jacket dug into her neck. Her heels skidded along the ground until her tailbone smacked against the pavement. Her Discman bounced on the slushy ground and sprang open. The disc with Steve's Sharpied inscription slid across the pavement, shiny side up. She'd involuntarily clenched her fists, mangling the pizza bun between her fingers. Three girls gathered above her. Marcy's cheeks burned with embarrassment. She shook the pizza bun off and wiped her hands on her pants. She held her clean hand up, thinking the girls had stopped to help her off the ground.

"Get up."

Marcy recognized the girl from Home Ec. They'd even shared an assignment where you were given a budget and a flyer and had to plan a meal based on what was advertised. The girl's blond hair was straightened, stiff and shiny. She had a pale face and dusty yellow makeup above striking green eyes.

Marcy reached for her Discman. She snapped it shut and wrestled it into the pocket of her coat before standing. Her whole butt was numb and pain radiated through her lower back. The CD Steve had made her was still a few feet away, sending winks of rainbow light onto the white plastic siding of the house across the street. A distress signal.

"We got something for you," the girl from Home Ec said, moving behind Marcy. She didn't recognize the other two but all three of them were wearing the puffy windbreakers that were popular with kids from the junior high in Shea Heights that had amalgamated into theirs after a fire a month or two before.

One of the girls stepped forward and brandished a stick from behind her back like a bachelor with a long-stemmed rose. There was something scrunched on the tip, opaque plastic with a yellow ring at the bottom. A used condom. Marcy felt a hand tighten on each of her biceps.

"Open your mouth," the girl from Home Ec said.

"What?" Marcy said.

"You're a dyke," the girl said.

"No, I'm really not." Marcy was relieved to have a charge to refute.

The girl with the stick seemed to be considering the plea but the hand on Marcy's left bicep squeezed harder, trying to hurt her. Marcy looked towards the convenience store.

The woman working there had a newspaper spread out on the counter. She was bent over it, engrossed.

"We know you are. Stick it in her mouth!"

Marcy crouched down. It wasn't an elegant or courageous move, but it loosened their grip on her arms and for a moment she was free. Then an electric jolt of pain across her scalp. They had her by the hair. Marcy stood and her head was forcibly craned backwards. She felt the stick jab between her lips and scrape her clenched teeth.

"Open your mouth, you're going to swallow it." Another tug on her hair that sent pain down her neck. Then a horn blared behind them. She was released. The stick fell to the ground and the girls casually crossed the road and kept on walking towards the school at a lolling pace. The car horn blared again and Marcy stepped onto the opposite sidewalk.

She watched the car glide over Steve Dempsey's CD. The tires just missed it. She stuck her tongue out and wiped the taste away with her sleeve. Then she scooped a lump of exhaust-soaked snow from the hip-height bank in front of the store and rubbed it across her face. She chewed some of the dirty snow and spat it into the road. The tomato sauce in her mouth turned her spit pink. She was ashamed of squatting down. Of not yelling in their faces or kicking them in the shins. Or in the crotch. She had always suspected that she was spineless and now she knew for sure. When she bent to pick up her CD, pain fanned across her lower back. She wasn't going to school, but she didn't want to go home.

She'd spent that afternoon alone in the heated lobby of the real estate firm. She'd listened to Steve Dempsey's CD until her Discman died, then she'd walked home.

2

After Al's, Marcy moved into a sublet room in an apartment above a chandelier showroom in Little Italy. The ground-floor windows were filled with a crowded display of ostentatious light fixtures. Most were hanging sculptures made of stainless-steel tubes with bulbs protruding at uneven intervals. She liked the older-style models strung up in the back of the warehouse, the ones with dangling jewels and metal vines curled around them. The showroom splashed chandelier light all over the sidewalk in front of the building in the evening and she liked walking through it.

Sometimes she would cross paths with chandelier customers in the lobby. She took a freight elevator with fake wood panelling up to her place on the third floor. The hallways were wide, covered in scuff marks and lit by fluorescent lights in mesh cages. She lived alongside jam spaces and artist studios, a haircutting salon and tattoo parlour, a venue that hosted punk bands and poetry readings. She sometimes caught peeks of the other lofts when neighbours were on their way in or out. The lofts were all differently shaped, with various DIY renovations made to accommodate whatever purpose they served.

The guy who lived across the hall had a long grey ponytail. One of Marcy's new roommates, Kathleen, said you could tell he was Quebecois from the kind of music that washed through his walls and into their apartment. Lounge-lizard, psychedelic rock with a trumpet. Once, when he was signing for a package, Marcy got a luxuriously long look into his loft. Crates of records lined one wall and stretched almost to the top of the fifteen-foot ceilings. There were two PAs set up on either side of a big-screen TV playing a muted video of a Samoyed puppy stumbling through a grassy field. There were string instruments in stands and hung on the walls, beautiful things with long necks and polished wood bodies. Heavy curtains with swirls of bright pink, dark purple, and sky blue kept the afternoon sun out of the apartment.

HER ROOMMATES, SHARON and Kathleen, were siblings from the Prairies. They'd been living in Montreal for almost a decade. Marcy was intimidated by them. They both played music. Sharon DJed almost every weekend, she wore sports bras with mesh panels and leather pants when she went out dancing. She'd gone to art school and had a studio a few blocks away where she made abstract wooden sculptures as well as practical items like salad tongs and interesting coat hooks. Sharon used clippings from the plants that filled the apartment to make salves and tinctures and teas. She had this calm demeanour that felt almost religious to Marcy.

Kathleen was in a metal band with a couple of guys in their fifties. She sent a polite note to the roommate chat asking for permission for KIDNEY to jam in the apartment every so often. Kathleen could make conversation with anyone, it was a combination of being genuinely good-natured and a skilled charm that Marcy assumed she'd learned bartending. She realized she didn't know for sure but she thought they must both be at least a little queer.

TWO WEEKS AFTER Marcy moved in, the sisters got a short job trimming weed in the apartment down the hall for a couple of days. On their second day, Marcy sat in the kitchen while they got ready to go. They were both wearing black T-shirts and jeans. Before leaving, Sharon picked a sticky sheet off the lint roller and rubbed it over her front like she did before her waitressing shifts at a Greek restaurant on Saint-Viateur. Marcy often didn't notice the dirt around her until someone else started cleaning it; she envied Sharon's tidiness.

Sharon held the roller out to Kathleen. "Can you do my back?"

Kathleen moved the roller down the slope of her sister's back, stopping at the hem of her T-shirt and starting again at the base of her neck. She held the roller up and examined the yield. Then stroked it down the length of her back again. Looked the roller over, ripped the sheet off and stuffed it through the revolving lid of the garbage can. She rubbed her sister's side with the fresh sheet. Sharon giggled, maybe because it tickled, and Marcy laughed too. There was something comical about how stiffly Sharon stood in front of Kathleen to be de-linted for a day of weed trimming. Marcy was always on the periphery of their intimacy, she tried not to be awkward about it.

Kathleen had been living in the apartment the longest. She had been part of the original group of roommates who'd put up the walls that created three separate bedrooms within the loft's 1,500 square feet. Sharon had joined her two years ago after a bad breakup.

The walls were just sheets of Gyproc that didn't reach the ceiling in some places.

Two plywood walls had been erected in one corner of the main living area. A door had been cut into one of the walls, which locked with a hook and eye. The toilet, sink, and bathtub were inside. The fridge was pressed up against the outside of the wall, not too far from the kitchen table. This meant that everyone could hear you taking a shit and you could hear everyone else. There was just no way around it. If there was a noise, a fart or a splash, sometimes her roommates laughed. Marcy had been raised to never acknowledge the fact that people shit, she felt the bathroom situation was forcing her to grow as a person.

There were small holes in the sheet of drywall that separated Marcy and Sharon's bedrooms. The whole time Marcy lived with them, she had never heard Sharon and Kathleen argue, not once. Later, when she was mostly living with Leanne, she would think about how calm it had felt in the loft.

. . .

FIVE MINUTES AFTER they left for weed trimming Kathleen came back. "They need another person, do you want to come?"

"Oh, I can't, I have stuff to do."

"Okay, just checking." Kathleen closed the door and Marcy heard the key in the lock. She grabbed the handle and tugged it open again before Kathleen could flip the deadbolt.

"Actually, I'll come, thank you." Marcy stomped into her sneakers and stepped into the hall. Kathleen locked the door.

"Do I need anything?" she asked, patting her empty pockets.

"No, you're good."

You could always smell the weed at this end of the hallway; it hung around the door like woodsmoke. Inside, the smell was warm and wet and more vegetal than being in a room where people were smoking.

Marcy took her shoes off on a square of grey carpet that had been sliced into a mat with an exacto knife. There was an industrial sink mired in a plywood counter. A platform close to the ceiling was stuffed with loose rolls of thick plastic. About twelve people were gathered around two long tables. Mostly men, and everyone seemed to be white except for a Black woman and an Asian guy.

Behind them there was a messy living room area. A collection of mismatched chairs surrounded a low coffee table with some skateboarding magazines on it and a couple of takeout coffee cups.

Sharon patted an empty seat next to her and Kathleen sat on her other side. Marcy's roommates introduced her to Hannah, the woman on her right. She was wearing glasses with lilac-tinted lenses that made it surprisingly hard to read her expression. Someone handed Marcy latex gloves with fine powder inside and a pair of scissors.

There were three plastic containers filled with weed plants spread down the centre of the table. Sharon showed Marcy the system: drop leaves and stems into a black garbage bag duct-taped to the edge of the table, carefully trim the buds and drop them into a smaller bin in front of them. The buds were covered in a sparkly sap, crystals that built up on the scissors and eventually made it hard to keep clipping. There were a couple of razor blades that people passed around to skim along the scissors when they got too gluey. Everyone had a little square of wax paper that they cleaned the razor blade with, gathering a personal glob of residue they were allowed to take home with them. Once a pile of trimmed buds accumulated in the small bin, you could shake them into a larger container. Marcy found it very satisfying.

Time passed weirdly. It was overcast in the morning but towards the afternoon it started to clear. Marcy guessed that most people were Anglo like her roommates, and for the better part of the morning people were silent except for one guy who talked on and on about travelling, not letting anyone else get a word in edgewise, and then switched things up just before lunch by trying to engage Laura, the Black woman, in a conversation about Bob Marley that she clearly didn't want to have.

SHARON NUDGED MARCY and said, "It's interesting to see the view from this side of the building."

"Ours is better," Marcy said.

"We have the mountain," Sharon said.

Marcy got lost in the view. You could see the McDonald's from this loft. Her fingers were still sawing away at a bud. "Imagine it's a Christmas tree," Sharon had told her when she first started trimming. She realized she was high, a body high, hitting the way edibles do. The sky was hazy purple.

"Look at the colour of the sky," Marcy said. "It looks eerie, or is that just me?"

She meant to say it just to Sharon but everyone at the table turned. At first she was embarrassed, but they all thought the sky was strange too. Someone said it looked like an alien movie.

The guy in charge stood up and said, in a mix of French and English, that after lunch he was going to need people to trim faster than they had been.

Marcy, Sharon, and Kathleen trooped back to their own apartment for the thirty minute lunch break. Kathleen invited Hannah to join them as they were leaving. Hannah pointed out a trail of weed crumbs Kathleen had left on the hallway floor when she'd come back to the apartment to grab Marcy.

"Like Hansel and Gretel," Hannah said.

Hannah and Kathleen went to get sandwiches at the new deli on the corner and Marcy heated up some stew she'd made earlier in the week.

"Hannah seems cool," Marcy said. She'd cranked the burner up and bubbles of steam were bursting through the thick orangey-red liquid.

"She can be kind of harsh but she's sweet when you get to know her," Sharon said.

Hannah and Kathleen got back from the deli with

sandwiches wrapped in checkered paper. Marcy poured her soup into a bowl even though she knew the potatoes would still be cold in the centre. They all complained about the obnoxious guy at the end of the table, lamented that none of them had attempted to shut him up.

"Have you done a lot of this kind of thing?" Hannah asked Marcy.

"Weed trimming? I've never done it before."

"What kind of work do you do?"

"I'm looking for work. I worked at a like bar-slash-cafe in St. John's before I moved here. But I don't speak French."

"I think it's time to head back," Kathleen said before Marcy had a chance to ask Hannah about her work.

The second day of weed trimming passed more quickly than the first, with Marcy even more deeply stoned than on the first day. When she got home, Marcy wandered around the apartment aimlessly until she fell asleep on the couch with all her clothes on. When she woke up, three envelopes had been pushed under the door, each with one of their names scrawled on it. There were two $100 bills in her envelope and a little packet of pineapple-flavoured weed gummies. She took the envelope to her bedroom and closed it in the drawer of her desk. She was groggy but the money made her happy. She'd been so focused on finding this place that she had let the job hunt slip and had been burning through the money in her account.

Marcy looked out the window. She had no idea where her phone was, but the pale yellow sky suggested early morning. Across the street from her building there was an eight-foot plywood barrier with scaffolding on the outside of it. Often the line of people waiting to get into the Glitz, the bar across the street, stretched from the door into the scaffold-tunnel that ran alongside the bar. Outside the scaffold there was an erratic formation of orange pylons, a mix of cylindrical and cone-shaped. Sometimes a truck would come at dusk to rearrange the pylons. Sharon had told her all the construction in the city was owned by the mob. They rented out the pylons for a dollar a day as part of a money-laundering operation. This morning Marcy watched as a group of young men in yellow vests hopped out of the pickup and erected a blinking sign on tall skinny legs that said *Ralentir*.

KATHLEEN HAD A little soldering station set up in a corner of the loft, where she was teaching herself to do repairs on small electrical appliances. Her desk was a mint-green collapsible card table that faced the wall. At that desk she'd fixed a toaster oven for their neighbour and was rewiring a seven-foot-tall vintage floor lamp Sharon had brought home from a yard sale. Marcy watched her peel back the plastic coating on the old cord with a paring knife to reveal a burst of frayed wires.

"Are you going to charge people?" Marcy asked.

"I'm just learning, it's fun trying to learn. I spent, like, hours reading Reddit forums."

"I bet you could make money off that, if you wanted." Marcy leaned against the door frame.

"I wouldn't charge friends. Or like the neighbour, you know?" Kathleen said.

"Yeah, not friends. But you could advertise fixing vintage lamps online, people with money would totally pay for that."

"Yeah probably." Kathleen didn't sound convinced.

"Or I mean, I guess you could just enjoy it."

"Yeah, I don't know. Sorry, I just have to check something." Kathleen tapped her phone, unmuting a YouTube video where someone held up a mangled twist of wires.

Marcy sauntered into the kitchen even though she didn't need anything in there.

KATHLEEN FINISHED WORKING on the lamp about a week later, one evening after supper. She put its homemade shade, a sheet of lace stapled around two wire hoops, back on, and then brought it to the living room area, where Sharon and Marcy were projecting the world figure skating championships on the wall. Kathleen dragged the lamp into the middle of the room and Marcy hopped up and shut off the projector. Kathleen slid the shade on and invited Sharon to reach inside and tug a string hanging from the gasket. The lamp cast shadow vines on the wall. Sharon's hand knocked the bottom of the lacy shade as she let go of the cord and the shadow vines swayed.

Kathleen put her hands on her hips. "Not bad, right?"

Sharon hugged her sister. Marcy looked at the shadow vines shivering on her bedroom door.

Kathleen said, "Where should we put it?"

The question was meant to pull Marcy back into the event. The sisters were always so careful to make sure she wasn't left out of anything.

MARCY'S PHONE LIT up in the bed next to her that night. Hannah had Facebook-messaged her an ad seeking participants for a paid study at McGill. *Just signed up for this — thought you might be interested.* The study was about training AI to recognize misogynistic hate speech in online comments. Participants would be paid $200 for a six-hour training session on recognizing and sorting hate speech. After the training you were paid by the phrase for up to six months. Standing just inside the front door with her boots on, Marcy filled out a digital form that asked about her sex, age, race/ethnicity, and citizenship. She clicked Submit.

When she'd finished, she saw that Hannah had sent her another link. *The pay's not great but there's always contracts here, just email Janice, you can say you're a friend of mine.* This company subcontracted people to edit the closed-captioning on workplace training videos. Now she had an apartment secured for at least two more months, an acquaintance, and two gigs.

Things were coming together. Marcy slid her carry-on suitcase out from under the bed. She took out her Magic Wand vibrator and unravelled the cord for the first time since she'd moved in. When she plugged it in, the green light on the handle shone bright in her dark bedroom. Pass go, collect $200.

IN THE MORNING the hate speech people had written with an advertisement for another gig. This one was twenty hours a week for a minimum of three weeks with a possible extension, at seventeen dollars an hour. The email was hard to decipher but it said something about sorting phrases related to mental health. Marcy immediately filled in her information, in case there were limited positions. She got an automated response seconds later saying her application was being considered. She forwarded the email with info about the study to Hannah. It felt good to be able to reciprocate. Probably Hannah had already received the same email, but anyway, it was about the gesture.

Hannah invited Marcy to go see *Parasite* at Cinéma du Parc. In St. John's there was just the Cineplex in the mall and the Sobeys Square theatre, and both of them only showed blockbusters. When an interesting trailer came on people would lean over and whisper in your ear, "That'll never come here."

Marcy walked the forty-five minutes from her house to Cinema du Parc. She almost never took the bus, she was afraid of accidentally getting carried beyond her stop and not knowing how to make her way back. Plus she liked the long walks, they reminded her how big the city was.

She and Hannah got Vietnamese food from the food court above the movie theatre. They carried their trays across the food court and sat at a table bolted to the floor. A girl at the table next to them was studying. She had handwritten notes on loose-leaf splayed out beside a glossy textbook.

"Did you go to school? Like university?" Marcy asked.

"Yeah, I did some courses, I didn't finish."

"Do you ever think about going back?"

"No, university is a scam. Plus if I want to learn something I'm not going to go to some racist, classist institution. I'll go to the library. I'm not going to ask delusional rich weirdos who've spent the last twenty years in this insular institution completely disconnected from the real world."

"Yeah," Marcy said.

With Hannah sitting right across from her at the little table,

Marcy worried she was looking into Hannah's face too much. Hannah had very bright brown eyes. Even in their short time together that evening, Marcy had noticed several people checking Hannah out. She tried looking at her plate more.

"Do you want to go back?" Hannah asked her. "You went to school, right?"

Marcy saw Hannah pour the little plastic cup of sauce over her meal and she did the same. "I did sociology. I didn't finish either. Sometimes I think about it. All those things you said are true, but I guess I was thinking it could be a way to meet people."

"Sure, I mean maybe if it wasn't so expensive. I'm still in debt from the last round and that was six years ago. Even if it was free, though, I don't know. I do kind of think it's bullshit. Like right now, I'm teaching myself coding from YouTube. There's so much information on there for free."

"Fair," Marcy said. "Did you see the email I sent about that other study? I read it but I didn't totally understand, it's about mental health? What does that even mean? In this context."

"I've done mental health ones before. There's tons of those apps now. It's just like the hate speech thing, you're teaching AI to sort phrases. Did you go to the training yet?"

"I have it on Tuesday," Marcy said.

"They're both just about sorting phrases so the algorithm can understand them when they encounter them again. For the mental health ones you usually sort them based on the degree of risk the clients pose to themselves or others. They call them clients, the people who use the app. It's one of those therapy apps. Do you ever get the ads for them on Instagram?"

The girl next to them was filing her notes away in a
plastic folder that tied shut with a little bit of string. She
slammed her textbook closed and put it in her bookbag.
Marcy checked the time.

"We should go soon," she told Hannah.

"It's obviously fucked, in that people should have access
to publicly funded therapy. Also, why are people turning
to an app like this in the first place? Because the capitalist
hellscape we're living in is impacting people's mental health.
It's circular, right?"

"Yeah," Marcy said, shovelling her meal into her mouth.

"Sorry. Am I being too much? I know I'm a downer
sometimes."

"No, you're just telling it like it is. I guess I still don't get
like, are these real people's sentences we're sorting? The hate
speech ones definitely feel like real people wrote them."

"Those are from Reddit comment sections. I don't
know where they get the phrases for this mental health
one, maybe they're generated by programmers or maybe
they did a trial run. Sometimes they cull things from
the internet. I've done work for these kinds of mental-
health-therapy apps before and I've had to quit, it's
exhausting, it's dark shit. Basically, you're supposed to
help the algorithm understand when someone can be fed
a computer-generated platitude and when they absolutely
need to interact with a real person. Which is supposed to
be a last resort because then they have to pay real, licensed
humans. Do I have time for a cigarette?"

"I mean —" Marcy could see people crowding onto the
escalator that descended into the basement theatre. She
didn't want to be late for the movie.

"You want to see the previews? Why don't you save me a seat? I'll just be five minutes."

Marcy sat through a car commercial and an ad for Skittles dubbed into French, then a promotion for a Latinx film festival that had a French voiceover but English subtitles. The first preview was in English, it was for an indie family drama about a young woman who'd been hospitalized because of an eating disorder. People stood up one at a time to let Hannah down the row to sit beside Marcy just as the preview's melodramatic score swelled to its climax. Hannah leaned in to whisper in Marcy's ear, "Thanks for coming to this with me."

She smelled of fresh air and cigarettes. Hannah leaned close again. "I don't know if I told you, like all my friends moved away this fall. That's the thing about Montreal. People leave, Anglo people especially. A lot of them come for school and then they leave."

She'd begun in a whisper, but as she went on her voice rose to its normal volume. Marcy could feel the people behind her glaring, but she also liked Hannah's voice so close to her ear.

THAT NIGHT AFTER the movie, Marcy sat alone in her bedroom above the chandelier showroom, sorting hate speech. The three categories to choose from were Hate Speech, Reclamation, and Not Hate Speech. The sentences appeared on the screen without any context so it felt impossible to tell whether or not something might be "reclamation." She mostly hit Hate Speech over and over again. After a while it felt easy to click through the sentences that made up the bulk of the phrases, the ones that simply named the violent acts the writer would like to perform. It was the phrases that described carrying out acts in more specific detail that stuck in her head.

When she closed her laptop Marcy noticed the sky looked the way it should an hour after sunset. It felt much later. She checked the time: ten thirty p.m. Out the window a handful of white pinpricks were visible through a mauve haze. Three steady stars and one that crawled deliberately through the darkness, slow enough that it took Marcy a moment to recognize it was a satellite. Instinctually the too-bright sky felt bad, not right. She thought maybe it was some kind of solar event triggered by the climate crisis. An apocalyptic eclipse. Then she remembered light pollution and felt the first pang of homesickness since arriving in Montreal.

She'd left stars behind. Even on nights when fog blocked out all the stars she'd got a lot of comfort from darkness. Now a phone company's ugly fucking CGI gecko stared into her window from the billboard across the street with his hand on his hip. *You made your choice.* She thought about closing the curtains on him. Instead she put her laptop down on the floor, rolled onto her stomach and pressed her face into her pillow.

She thought about what people might be doing at home. It was an hour and half later and a weeknight, so maybe nothing. Probably the staff at Destruction were closing up for the night. That made her feel a bit better. She pictured walking through the Battery. The brine in the air cleaning out her sinuses and curling her hair. She tried to remember each house and pothole. The silver mailbox that was actually a tampon disposal receptacle from a public bathroom someone had screwed into their door frame. The one lawn that was crowded with plywood cut-outs painted like Disney characters from the nineties. The narrow cement stairs enshrouded in mile-a-minute that led past the house where Linda had lived with Scott O'Neil for a summer. Marcy fought an urge to dig under the pillow for her phone, to write Linda or Brittany. She had decided it would be easier to never speak to any of them again. Instead, she pictured the outcropping of navy blue rock where three or four cormorants gathered every day looking out at the Narrows. She thought about the cracked-open sea urchin shells that littered the grass along the path. Birds picked the urchins out of the ocean, flew up high and dropped them so the shells split and the birds could peck at the jelly inside. The sun dried the shells until the prickly spines fell off and you could take them home and use them to decorate your windowsill. Marcy tried to focus on the sound of cars passing through the intersection outside. The building noise of a car approaching and the decrescendo of it carrying on into the night sounded sort of like waves crashing on the beach and sucking back out into the bay. She pulled the blankets over her head to block out the light.

MARCY HAD BEEN in the room above the chandeliers for a month and a half. The guy who lived there before, a friend of Al's named Mark, had sublet it because he'd gotten work on a film set in B.C.

She had spent those first six weeks sleeping between his sheets, surrounded by his things. Mark's pale pink salt lamp glowed on the bedside table, illuminating a huge drawing of a chandelier on translucent sketch paper he'd pinned to the wall at the foot of the bed. Marcy imagined he'd found it abandoned in the freight elevator or maybe tossed in the dumpster alongside the building.

One afternoon she came home to find Sharon on the couch in the living room. Marcy had been at Rossy in Parc-Ex buying towels. She'd chosen two of the cheapest full-size bath towels. They were made of stiff acrylic fabric and covered in a pattern of crabs and sandcastles. She'd bought the towels because the one towel she owned had developed a musty smell and a soft but greasy texture. She'd put it through two rounds in the washer at the laundromat down the street and it still didn't come clean.

Marcy crossed the living room without taking her shoes off and regretted it when she saw the footprints she'd left on the floor. "I'll clean that."

"Mark isn't moving back in, his girlfriend came by and took his records."

"Oh no." Marcy smoothed the bright stack of towels in her lap. The little peaks of stiff fabric tickled her palms. The sound of jackhammers in the pit across the street bleated against the windows. The noise and dust from the surrounding construction was almost constant and never faded into the background. Marcy swept the apartment every morning and never became less surprised by the small hill of grey dust that had found its way in.

"And we have to find another roommate now," Sharon said. "Unless you want to stay."

"I would love that." Marcy worried she might have answered too quickly, too enthusiastically, but Sharon surprised her by leaning across the couch to hug her.

That night Marcy gathered Mark's collection of crystals and put them in a garbage bag under the bed. She unpinned the chandelier drawing, rolled it up, and slid it in alongside the trash bag. After weeks of living out of her wheelie suitcases and a collection of tote bags, it felt good to settle into the room permanently. Sharon and Kathleen were boycotting Amazon and even though she agreed with that, Marcy ordered a set of microfibre sheets and a matching duvet cover from the site because they were so much cheaper than anywhere else. She hoped her roommates would be out when the package arrived.

THAT WEEK, SHE made chicken cacciatore and bought a bottle of red wine, and a baguette for mopping up the sauce. She casually offered to share it with them, and they obliged. She didn't say it out loud, but she was thinking of it as a celebration of their new, permanent roommate-hood.

After supper the three of them opened another bottle of wine and watched a documentary called *Anthropocene: The Human Epoch*. Kathleen lifted the projector down from above the shelf filled with oils and vinegars and plugged it into Sharon's computer. Then Marcy helped Kathleen drag the couch into the centre of the room while Sharon found a torrent.

"Everyone settled?" Sharon asked before hitting play. Kathleen and Marcy, settled into the reoriented couch, lifted their wine glasses for yes.

Fire lashed across the white wall in front of them, the same orange as the flames that had shot out of the barbeque when Marcy's uncle squeezed a stream of paint thinner on the coals at her twelfth birthday party. The whispering sound of a fire amping itself up poured out of Sharon's fancy speakers and filled the big room. The flames expanded, then wavered thin, allowing pockets of black smoke to form between them before busting out wide and tall again. The fire was reflected in the dark windows that lined the wall to the right of them.

"It's scary," Sharon said, curling in next to Marcy on the couch.

"If anyone looks in the window they're going to think our building is burning."

"I'd be scared if I looked up and saw that," Kathleen said, leaning forward in her armchair to pass Marcy a joint.

After the movie Marcy got between Mark's sheets and fell deep asleep beneath the left-behind comforter.

LATER THAT WEEK Marcy and Hannah rode the metro to Namur station to go to the big Value Village out there. In the thrift store Marcy trailed behind Hannah watching her rub fabric between her fingers and fling clothes into the growing pile in her cart. As soon as Hannah chose a piece of clothing Marcy could see why it was special. Hannah honed in on vintage cuts made from expensive fabrics. Marcy noticed she had five leather coats in the cart at once. But she also picked up newer and cheaper things in garish, clashing colours. When Hannah lifted them off the rack they transcended mundane ugliness into sublime ugliness. Marcy shuffled through hangers a couple of feet behind Hannah, until Hannah eventually said, "How about we meet at the change rooms for a fashion show in a little bit?"

Marcy realized she'd been crowding Hannah. She wandered into the men's section and stroked basketball jerseys and big floppy hoodies. Hannah was moving slowly down the long rack of dresses at the back of the store, her pile towering above the sides of the cart. Marcy picked a pair of knee-length forest green Adidas shorts and a red sweatshirt with *Lifeguard Atlantic City* on the front before moving back into the women's section, where she found a tiger-print turtleneck and a short corduroy skirt that buttoned up the front.

Hannah veered her cart over to Marcy. "You ready?"

"I found some things." Marcy held up the lifeguard hoodie. "Is this cool?"

"It'd be hot if you cut the sleeves off."

They chose changing stalls next to each other. Hannah came out in a low-cut polyester shirt with feathers gluegunned around the wrists. She twisted and turned in front of the mirror with the door to her stall open.

"You should try this," Hannah said, peeling it off and standing in her sports bra and jeans in front of the changing stalls.

"Are you sure?"

Hannah flicked the shirt at her.

Marcy took it into her stall. Even in the scratched-up narrow mirror she could see the shirt was tight in all the right places.

"It's so good," Hannah said when Marcy opened the door. Hannah had pulled a red baby-doll dress on over her jeans.

"It's eight dollars, though," Marcy said.

"Worth it. It's crazy, the sleeves?"

"I have nowhere to wear it." Marcy could see her cleavage did look good.

"Wear it on a date."

"I haven't been on a date in a really long time, since way before I moved here." Marcy pulled the shirt off over her head and put it on her "maybe" pile.

"Why? Are you asexual?"

"What? No." Suddenly she was self-conscious about being outside the stall in just shorts and a sports bra, even though it seemed natural when Hannah did it.

"Okay, some people are. Just asking."

"Yeah, I didn't mean to react like that. I like sex. A lot, usually. Or sometimes I do, in the right context I do. You know what I mean?" She thought about explaining what had happened before she left, but she wanted Hannah to know her better first.

"Are you depressed?" Hannah asked.

"I don't think so. I mean, I don't think that's why."

"Okay, well I think you should get laid. It's good for you. You should go on a date, it's important to meet people. Even if you don't like each other or hook up, it's good practice." Hannah was doing up a pair of pants. "There are so many queer people in Montreal, isn't that why you came here?"

"Those fit you perfectly."

"These are my pants," Hannah told her. "Imagine if you said you hated them."

At the checkout, the cashier pointed the little laser gun at each price tag and the numbers appeared on a digital screen that was swivelled towards Marcy. She breathed heavy through her nose. The final price was over sixty dollars. It made her sick. She tapped her debit card on the screen. It wasn't that she didn't have the money at the moment — she still had some of the money she'd brought from St. John's — it was that the way she'd acquired it made it feel important to spend it wisely. And it was unlikely she would have this kind of money again. She didn't want to feel used to spending money this way. She would stay up extra late sorting hate speech. If she stayed up until three that night and the next one, it'd be like she'd never gone to the thrift store.

Outside, the sun was shining. There was a guy waiting at the bus stop in shorts.

"This could be the last summery day we get. Are you hungry?" Hannah asked. "There's a really good Caribbean place that way."

Marcy was hungry. She hadn't recognized it as hunger until Hannah mentioned food but she had the spacey and queasy feeling she got when she went too long without eating. "I'm really tired, I think I gotta go home."

"Okay, well I think I'll get some." Hannah extended her arms, a thin plastic bag stuffed with clothes dangling from each clenched fist. Marcy stepped into her arms, it felt so good to be hugged.

"I'll come with you," Marcy said.

"It'll be quick, it's like two blocks that way. Then I'll metro with you."

She and Hannah split a half-chicken meal and a beer. It felt nice to go sip for sip with Hannah.

When she got home, she laid the red lifeguard hoodie out on the kitchen table, arms spread wide. She carefully removed the sleeves with a pair of scissors from Sharon's shelf in the bathroom.

3

Marcy went on her first Tinder date with a woman who did administrative work at an art gallery. Marcy had biked an hour across the city to meet her at a cafe in Verdun.

She hadn't realized how far away the cafe was until she started biking. She locked her bike on around the corner from the cafe and opened the app to see if the woman had written.

I'm getting my hair cut in the van in the driveway door's open

There was a cube van in a skinny driveway that looped around the cafe. The back doors of the van were flung open. Big scrawls of cursive graffiti decorated the hood. As she got closer she saw the sliding doors on the side were also open.

Marcy paused at the top of the driveway. She loosened the damp fabric that had bunched in her armpits and wiped her nose with the back of her glove. It was getting cold for biking. She walked up to the van and knocked. The smell of weed hung around the vehicle.

There were two guys sitting inside, one on a milk crate and the other on a space heater. The woman from the app was in a barber's chair and a sinewy guy with a long blond ponytail threaded through the back of his trucker cap was snipping her hair. They were all white with a B.C. grown-up skater dude vibe.

"Hi, I'm Marcy." She realized she'd forgotten the woman's name.

She felt the three men appraise her. Then they looked at the woman in the chair, gauging her reaction to Marcy.

"Pass me my glasses," the woman said. She shook her head, and the barber drew the scissors away from her. The woman held her hand out in front of her but stayed sitting, saying, "I'm covered in hair."

Marcy stepped on the tailgate of the van and hopped up. She shook the woman's hand.

"I need to take these off again," the barber said and lifted the glasses off her face.

One of the men stood up and offered Marcy his milk crate.

"You're sure?" she asked.

"Oh yeah, please, go for it. A friend of Elise is a friend of ours."

Someone passed Marcy a joint and she smoked it. Usually weed made her talkative.

"You know what movie I love?" the hairdresser asked, swishing clippings off the woman's shoulders with a thick, circular brush. "*Raising Arizona.*"

"I love that movie too," Marcy piped up from the milk crate, she didn't want to be silent and weird.

"I watch it every night, I find it comforting." The barber was swirling the brush against his palm, working the woman's hair out of it.

The woman extended her hand again and the barber placed her glasses in them.

"Carl always cuts my hair. I was living in Ottawa for a while, and I would just wait until I visited Montreal to get a haircut. No one cuts my hair but Carl."

The barber smiled. Marcy couldn't tell if he found the woman obnoxious or if they genuinely had some kind of friendship. The man on the space heater was rolling another joint.

"How did you meet?" Marcy asked.

"At his shop," she said.

"I used to have a shop." The man was untying his apron.

"I like the van though," the woman said.

"The van's cool," he said.

"It's got character," Marcy chimed in.

"Yeah," he said, but the adult skater sounded downtrodden; he wanted a shop, not a van. Now he had to watch *Raising Arizona* every night to soothe himself to sleep. Marcy felt a pang of sympathy, imagining his eyelids fluttering on a drool-stained pillowcase while Nicolas Cage stalked around in an undershirt on the TV.

The woman stood and brushed the hair out of her lap and onto the floor. "Can I get you something to eat? They have really good food in the cafe."

The cafe was also a record shop with a set of turntables in the centre. Lots of people drank their coffee standing up but there were a few seats. All the conversations happening around them were in French. The Barista left his station to flip the house record that was playing. They sat in a booth in the window. Marcy took in the new haircut — the woman was about the same age as her but the cut struck

Marcy as a very middle-aged look; short with a swooping bang in the front.

The woman ordered them both affogato, which Marcy had never had before, and halloumi grilled cheese sandwiches.

"Dessert first, what do you think?" the woman asked the waiter in French. Marcy could understand her without knowing exactly what she'd said.

"Why not?" he answered. "Same for you?"

"Yes, please," Marcy said in English.

Marcy was fully stoned now and it was easy to talk about herself. She rambled on about Newfoundland. How it was sort of like Quebec in that everyone there also hated Canada. Except they also hated Quebec.

"Why did you leave? Because you're gay?" the woman asked, swatting at a little clump of hair on the lapel of her blazer.

The waiter sat a teacup with a palm tree on the side in front of each of them. Inside, a shot of espresso had been dumped over a swirl of soft serve. Marcy dug into the dessert with the teaspoon balanced on the edge of her cup.

Marcy nodded. "Exactly." And maybe, that was sort of a part of it? If she was being very generous with herself.

The halloumi sandwiches arrived. They had pesto in them and oil dripped down Marcy's chin when she bit into hers. She didn't mind, she pulled a napkin from the dispenser on the table. The woman was on a roll about her workplace; everyone there hated her, didn't respect her opinions, they edited her grant reports without asking. It had happened to her at her last job too. Marcy thought it was possible that was true but more likely the woman was a pain in the hole. Marcy knew she didn't want to date her but she felt immensely happy to be sitting in the warm, sunny window, both stoned and buzzing from the espresso, eating her greasy sandwich, nodding along to the woman's increasingly vitriolic rant. Hannah was right about dating.

On the walk home Marcy's phone died and she got lost. She found herself biking along a busy four-lane road, not sure if she was heading towards home or away from it. Her hands stung with the cold. She had a horrible feeling in her chest. She thought of her ex-girlfriend Brittany. In a scenario like this she would have found a way to call and Brit would have picked her up and fit the bike in the trunk of her beat-up Toyota Corolla.

Brit had first approached Marcy at a Docs4Change screening of *Pride Denied: Homonationalism and the Future of Queer Politics*. Marcy and her friend Fred had comprised the whole Docs4Change St. John's organizing team. This time sixteen people showed up for the screening, which was about ten more than usual. In the winter attendance usually went up a little but this was early June. A group of eight people had arrived just as the movie was beginning, almost doubling their audience. Her memory of the evening poured through the lens of everything that happened after, so it was hard to trust. She remembered that she and Fred had scheduled the movie to start at eight, later than usual because the days were getting longer. She had run outside fifteen minutes before the screening to tape a flyer to the door of the church hall so people would know where to go. The sun was just starting to set, heat was still radiating up off the sidewalk. You could smell the stink of sewage coming off the harbour.

When Brit walked in with her small crowd during the opening credits, some of the sunset light flooded in with her. She was wearing cargo shorts and a baggy forest green T-shirt. Her head was buzzed.

Later Marcy would do the buzzing for her in the bathroom they shared. Future-Marcy believed some part of her had known as soon as she laid eyes on Brit that there would be an intense intimacy between them. Maybe not specifically that she would fold over the tip of Brit's ear and hold it with one finger as she stroked the side of Brit's head with the vibrating teeth of the clippers, but maybe. Maybe all that was already inside her.

Marcy and Fred had rushed to the back of the room to collect more grey metal folding chairs. The new guests shook the chairs open, mouthing "sorry" as the hinges screeched and snapped into place. Fred and Marcy shook their heads like no worries. Back in their seats at the front of the room they turned to each other and smiled wide. They were ecstatic about the turnout, their most successful screening since they'd taken over in January.

"The email list!" Marcy whispered to Fred.

He passed the clipboard in his lap to a woman sitting behind him, and when it made its way back to the front there were seven new email addresses on the list.

In the discussion after the film Brit made a representative of the St. John's Pride Board cry by explaining all the reasons cops shouldn't be allowed to participate in Pride and then firmly shutting down their rebuttals. Marcy held her breath when an older woman explained her brother was in the force and it hadn't been easy for him to come out when he did, in Newfoundland, in the '80s, much harder than it was for some of the young people in the room, but he did come out because he felt he had to do it for his community.

"The thing is," Brit said, calm and even-keeled, "it isn't about your brother in particular, it's about the institution of policing which is fundamentally racist, homophobic, and transphobic."

At the end of the screening Marcy and Fred packed away the grey metal folding chairs.

"What will we show next month?" Marcy asked, dragging an armful of chairs across the varnished hardwood floor of the church hall.

"Seriously!" Fred said.

"To keep up the momentum," Marcy said. "We talked about the bee-extinction movie —"

"No," Fred said.

"I know," Marcy said.

"Everyone knows about the bees."

"We need something that ties into a local issue, like we talked about," Marcy said.

"Totally, do you have the keys?" Fred asked.

They collected their clipboard and donation bucket for the Native Friendship Centre. There was one five-dollar bill and a couple of loonies in there. Fred shook the bucket and made the coins rattle together. They put the measly donations in an envelope to bring over to the centre when they'd hopefully collected a more substantial donation.

SHE AND BRIT didn't hook up until a couple of weeks later. They'd seen each other around and exchanged messages in the time before the next Docs4Change screening. In the end, Marcy and Fred had decided on a documentary about the corporate co-opting of breast cancer awareness. It didn't generate nearly as much controversy or excitement but Brit had shown up and she'd hung around as they cleaned up. She offered them both a ride home.

Marcy and Brit had circled through the Dairy Queen drive-thru after they dropped Fred off. They both ordered vanilla cones dipped in chocolate.

"Should we go for a little drive?" Brit asked her. "Up Signal Hill?"

"Yes, please." Marcy bit the tip off her ice cream, crunching through the hard chocolate shell.

It was a foggy drive up the steep hill to a view of the ocean. Marcy put her window down and breathed in the heavy, damp air. Her teeth were aching from the ultra-sweet soft serve. She leaned out and tossed the cone. The wind whipped it from her hand and it disappeared into their backdraft.

"I couldn't finish it." Marcy smirked at Brittany's surprise.

"What if there was someone behind me?"

"There isn't," Marcy said.

When they got to the top, Brit asked, "Do you want to face the city or the void?"

"The void," Marcy said. "Unless you'd rather the other way."

"No, I like the void."

Brit pointed the car at the ocean and clicked the key so the motor shut off but the lights stayed on, illuminating the wall of fog in front of them. Marcy glanced behind her. The back seat was filled with plastic signs on wooden stakes. They'd been collected at the end of a rally in support of the nurses' strike; Brit was dropping them back to the union in the morning.

"I saw a fox up here the other day," Marcy said. "It wasn't shy at all."

"People feed them." Brit popped the bottom of the cone in her mouth.

"I was sitting on a rock, and it nibbled my sneaker."

When they kissed, Brit had the same sweet, milky taste in her mouth as Marcy. Brit had her tongue pierced. A stainless-steel stud that bounced off Marcy's teeth. They were both twisted at weird angles in their seats. Marcy's nubbly black peacoat was open and Brit slid a hand under her sweater and squeezed the chub that hung over the top of Marcy's jeans. She fought the urge to squirm away from being touched in a place she was self-conscious about. Brit bit Marcy's lip and squeezed her tighter. Brittany's hand was so cold it burned, Marcy liked the sting of it. She was getting wet. A car rolled around the parking lot, two streams of yellow light cutting through the fog. The headlights shone right through the windows and illuminated Brittany. Marcy felt a lurch in her stomach like leaving the ground on a Ferris wheel. It felt, at least looking back, like she could see the whole trajectory of their thing in that moment. It was already in motion.

On the way back down the hill Marcy saw a glint of white on the side of the road that she thought was a small bone.

"Roadkill!"

"What?" Brit slowed.

"I think I saw something dead on the shoulder, can we back up? I might take a photo for Fred. He has an art project where he documents roadkill."

Brit started inching the car backwards, Marcy unrolled her window and stuck her head out.

"There!"

Brit stopped the car. It was a paper bag with smushed fries inside. A plastic fork gleamed white in the red tail lights.

"Oh, it's just fries," Marcy said. For a moment it had felt like some kind of omen.

Brit drove her home and Marcy invited her in. She made them both cups of tea and walked slowly up the stairs to her bedroom, careful not to let the hot water slop over the rims. She put the teas on her dresser next to a box of scrunchies. She tried to climb on top of Brit while they were making out but Brit shook her head no. Then she fingered Marcy and made her cum three times. When they fell asleep Marcy was the big spoon and she pressed her forehead into Brittany's shoulder.

The first time Brit shut down Marcy didn't understand it. Maybe Brit didn't either; she said she thought she had mono. In the lead-up to her being bedridden, Brittany's texts became less and less frequent. They'd just started dating and Marcy thought she was being slowly dumped.

Eventually she invited herself over to Brittany's. She told her friends she was going to make Brit say it to her face. When she arrived Brittany's roommate let her in and directed her upstairs. There was music coming from the bedroom, so Marcy opened the door. The heat was blasting in Brit's bedroom, she was kneeling on the floor smoking out the window. She was wearing a pair of light blue, silky basketball shorts and a hoodie with the logo of her mom's work on the front. When she saw Marcy in the doorway she picked her phone off the floor and looked at it.

"I thought you would text before you came," Brit said, dropping the device onto the carpet.

Often Brit invited her to share a cigarette and they leaned out the window together. From Brittany's room they could see the Narrows. Sometimes in the night they'd watch a lit-up boat slide through the mouth of the harbour together.

"I thought you had mono," Marcy said.

"What?"

"Should you be smoking?"

"I shouldn't be smoking, I'm addicted to cigarettes," Brit said.

Marcy sat on the unmade bed and startled when she noticed Brit's budgie bird perched on the edge of a coffee mug on the nightstand.

"The bird is out!"

"I let him out. He likes to be out." Brit ground her cigarette out on the inside of the windowpane. Marcy had never seen the bird out of its cage before but she kept that to herself.

There was a bowl on the nightstand with some soup in it; noodles hardening in a pale yellow broth with half-circles of neon-green grease on the surface.

"You had some soup?"

"I'm really tired," Brit said.

"Do you know where you got mono? You know someone who had it or?"

"The soup's from yesterday, I didn't eat anything yet today."

"You didn't eat anything? It's two in the afternoon."

"I'm really really tired." Brit closed the window. She stood up and threaded her arms through the front pouch of the hoodie. The bird lifted off the mug and flew in lopsided circles around the room. Marcy cowered. She didn't want it to land on her, she was afraid she'd slap it.

"Can I show you something?" Brit said.

The bird swooped determinedly across the room and landed on the dresser. Brit walked to the computer and clicked open a tab of the official music video for Blur's "Song 2."

"I know this song," Marcy said.

"Just listen," Brit said, recuperating some of her usual swagger.

Marcy had a vivid memory of an older cousin explaining that this song was intended to be a joke. He said it was a parody of Nirvana that blew up and Marcy had felt deflated by the news. She thought the grumpy distortion was genuine and that it reflected a frustration she could relate to; she'd felt caught out for enjoying it. When the singer did the first snotty "wee-hoo," ushering in the growly guitar, Brit lifted a finger. "Listen."

It occured to Marcy that Blur taking the piss didn't actually make the song less sincere, it was still detached and moody, just with a sense of humour. The third time the singer wee-hooed the budgie warbled along with him.

Brit swung away from the screen and looked at Marcy triumphantly.

"The girl at the pet store, usually I'd say the woman, but she was a teenager, she really was a girl. Anyway, she said they talk." Brit's face was pale, but her eyes were very animated.

"I don't know if that counts as talking."

"No, I mean it hasn't talked at all, she said they talk the most of any bird."

"Of any bird? What about —"

"Maybe any bird in the store. Anyway, it doesn't talk but it sings along to this song."

"Only this song?" Marcy asked.

"So far only this song."

The bird cooed with the vocals again. Brit came and sat on the bed. Marcy wrapped her arms around Brittany, squeezing her tight. Marcy laid the side of her face on Brit's chest — there was no wheezing or rumbling just long, heavy breaths. Brit apologized and Marcy said, "For what?"

Every couple of months there would be three or four days in bed like that. Marcy learned to recognize the warning signs. Brit got irritable and distant in the lead-up. She stopped being interested in food and slept longer than usual. The news made her cry or slam things around.

Marcy started to hope for the days in bed because they marked the beginning of the end of the worst part. When she was able to get out of bed again, Brit was sweet and gentle. She made creamy shrimp pasta. She wanted to know what Marcy was planning for Docs4Change. She organized protests and email blasts in support of the nurses and against the tuition hike and the new austerity measures. She made carpool trees to get people to meetings about shutting down construction of the Muskrat Falls hydroelectric dam.

When Brit and Marcy decided to move in together they fought about which items to buy for the house. Brit wanted new and matching things. Marcy was happy with scuffed, mismatched things. The plastic kettle was one item they fought about. Marcy was content to boil water in a saucepan on the stove. But Brit picked up the kettle when they were at Canadian Tire getting dishtowels and a plunger.

"Oh look it's on sale!" she said.

"My arms are full, I'm hot, let's go," Marcy said.

"We should get this." Brit dropped it into the cart.

. . .

IN THEIR NEW apartment Brit put her autographed Jodie
Foster postcard on the mantel. It was a gift an ex had
brought back from a trip to Hollywood.

"On the mantel?" Marcy said.

"Yeah," Brit answered, crowding Marcy's plants together
to make room.

Around the time they moved in together, Brit began men-
toring a kid through the St. John's Boys & Girls Club. She'd
pick the kid up in the Corolla and take them for coffee or to
the movies. Once Marcy went with them to play air hockey
at the arcade in the mall.

Brit was so good with the kid, she was gentle but never
condescending — this tone and demeanour seemed to come
naturally to her. Marcy sat in the seat of a broken racing
game, her hands on the steering wheel, watching Brit and
the kid send the puck back and forth across the illuminated
table. She felt deep deep in love. When it was time to go,
the kid almost had a meltdown, but Brit was calm and firm.

"We're going to see each other next week, right?" Brit
asked.

The kid nodded and zipped their coat, suddenly placid.

"Okay, and you can pick the music for the drive," Brit said,
eking a small smile out of the kid.

One night, tipsy after a screening at the Women's Film
Festival, Marcy told Brit she sometimes felt embarrassed
about her moustache. She was opening the oven door to
push around the frozen fries she was making to stave off
a hangover.

"Do you think it's noticeable?"

"I think it's hot," Brit said.

Marcy froze. She had convinced herself that no one could see the moustache.

"It's really pronounced right now, but it gets kind of bleached in the summer," Marcy said.

"Queer people find that hot," Brit told her. "It's part of what made me attracted to you. At first, before I knew you."

"You're just saying that."

"Seriously." Brit lifted a finger and stroked the hairs at one corner of Marcy's mouth.

Marcy felt squeamish, but underneath that there was some pride brewing. "I used to be embarrassed about my treasure trail too, but two people told me they found it sexy," she said.

"It's very sexy," Brit said.

"I'm just saying, I was ashamed of it before. One person said it was the reason they wanted to sleep with me."

"Who?"

"It doesn't matter. I'm just saying —"

"Everyone wants to sleep with you."

"No."

"You were kinda bragging, but okay," Brit said.

"Anyway." Marcy took the fries out of the oven and ate one. The inside was still ice crystals.

"They can't be done yet," Brit said.

Marcy put the tray back in and shut the door.

The next day she cut her hair short — shaggy but short. She'd never had it that way before she met Brit.

. . .

SHORTLY AFTER THEY'D moved in together, Marcy got a
job at Destruction, a restaurant/bar above a fish shop on
Water Street. Her co-workers all wore black baseball caps,
and black hoodies with black high-waisted jeans, and they
partied together after work. Everyone played in bands with
different configurations of the Destruction staff and sometimes with their significant others. They drank in each other's
kitchens till morning and trooped down the hill in pairs to
their shifts.

Marcy began staying out with them after work more and
more often. At first she would call Brit to see if she wanted to
join them but she only did once — "I don't feel comfortable,
everyone's so straight." It was true that the group often split
according to gender, with all the guys mysteriously going for
a cigarette at once or the girls slowly leaving their bar stools
to dance together in front of the stage.

Marcy was invited to birthday parties and fires on the
beach, she was included in all the in-jokes. She bought a pair
of black high-waisted jeans. Nothing about it felt claustrophobic until she and Linda made out against the scratchy
bricks of the UltraFar gas station on the way home one night.

It was summer and she'd been wearing sneakers with
no socks and she peed all over them. She and Linda were
crouched, their pee pooling together and spreading out to
soak the parking lot. They stood and wiggled their shorts
back up to their hips. Marcy put a hand on Linda to steady
herself and they fell into one another.

Then, they were showing each other how they behaved
in a sexy situation, their particular styles of kissing, which

parts of themselves they pressed into other people, how they moved their hands over other people's bodies, how firmly they squeezed. It was a performance they were crafting together, and each for the other. Linda bit her neck and Marcy hopped away, startled.

"Hey!" Her sneakers squelched, wet with pee. They started laughing and weren't able to stop. The laughter was an engine that kept revving Marcy's whole body, the muscles in her stomach were aching and her cheeks were stiff. Linda was braying beside her. Every time Marcy felt like she was getting control of it, Linda's laugh would set the engine rumbling again. But even as her body was lurching with hysteria, a bad feeling was settling in her stomach. The feeling: *You fucked up*.

As their laughter died down the feeling sloshed in her belly and splashed up her throat all acidic. They adjusted their clothing and started walking through the quietest and darkest part of downtown together, past Mile One Stadium, the Convention Centre, and city hall — all of them enormous and empty. Even in the daytime these buildings cast shadows that kept the sidewalks dark and cool. Linda was talking about the schedule at Destruction, everyone was trying to get time off in August. Marcy had the hiccups, every ten seconds a loud gulp erupted out of her and made Linda giggle, but Marcy wasn't finding anything funny anymore.

She was thinking of how Brit had fried two eggs for her that morning, just the way Marcy liked them, the yolk creamy but not yet stiff. It was worse than just that, she'd been complaining to Linda for weeks at work, about how Brit let water from the shower drip on the bathroom floor, how Brit didn't like any of Marcy's party outfits and never wanted to do anything fun.

Marcy and Linda walked up Queen's Road, music and hollered taunts riding the wind up from George Street. A woman in a tiny, glittering dress swayed on high heels, a phone pressed to her face. "I am, I am, there's no fucking cabs around here. It's actually fucking annoying. Like for all he knows I'm going to end up raped." Marcy and Linda looked at each other meaningfully but Marcy wasn't sure if they were sympathizing or condemning the flippancy, maybe a mix of both.

When they got to the bottom of Prescott Street they hugged goodbye like they'd been doing after their shifts for the past few months. She knew that Linda would tell all their friends about making out behind the gas station.

She continued towards the place she and Brit shared at the edge of the Battery. She fit her key in the lock, walked the creaky stairs to their bedroom. Brit woke when Marcy opened the door but she pushed her face back into the pillow.

Marcy decided this was the moment to tell. If not now then never. She slipped between the covers and wormed her way into Brittany's arms, landing on never.

The next weekend she and Linda made out in the bathroom at Destruction. Both of them in plastic ponchos speckled with drips of jellied rain that shivered in time with the soundwaves of a band tuning up. Then in the laundry room at a house party at Pleasant Street. Marcy sat on the dryer with her legs wrapped around Linda. Always when they were fucked up and out somewhere. Never in the daytime. And they never talked about it, even immediately after as they were scrambling their clothes back on. There was nothing tender in it. That made Marcy think maybe it didn't count.

Brit found out. She read Marcy's phone, or maybe she just intuited it because of something in Marcy's demeanour. She said, "Are you cheating on me?"

Marcy denied it. "She's not even gay." Which seemed true to Marcy, she couldn't picture Linda actually dating a woman. If it was just about sex that was different, in Marcy's opinion.

Brit said, "Okay."

The way she said it meant she knew Marcy was lying but she wasn't going to argue. Like Marcy had made her move and now Brit would decide how to respond in her own time. They sat at the table in silence. When Marcy swallowed it made a noise that sounded guilty.

"I was thinking I might try to make meatballs tonight," Marcy tried. "Do you want that? Spaghetti?"

"Sure," Brit said coldly and stood up.

MARCY AND LINDA were scheduled to serve tables together at brunch the next day. Normally Marcy looked forward to working brunch with Linda. Before the restaurant opened, they performed their usual ritual of divvying up the start-of-shift chores. Marcy was polishing the cutlery and Linda was folding napkins. Marcy knew she should wait for the end of the shift so Linda could leave if she wanted but she was afraid she wouldn't say it if the whole shift went by with the Motown Morning playlist on loop and the two of them falling into the comfortable rhythm of seating and watering each other's tables. It came out blunt. "We can't fool around anymore."

She had a terry cloth rag in her fist, and she was dragging a butter knife through it, trying to get the streaks off.

"Why don't you break up with her?" Linda said.

"We live together," Marcy said.

"Whatever, it's your life."

"And I love her."

"It's none of my business," Linda said. "I don't really want to hear about it."

Marcy was surprised to see tears in Linda's eyes.

"I want to be friends," Marcy said. "I mean obviously."

"Yeah, it's fine, I'm going to check on the coffee."

After that Marcy was still invited to things but it felt like people stopped hugging her as warmly at the end of the night. More and more often, she learned her co-workers had gone for fish and chips or to the movies and no one had invited her. She started going home right after her shift when the others were sticking around to drink, sensing that people would prefer to gossip without her there.

One night when Marcy was draining the water out of a tin of tuna, Brit walked into the kitchen and stood behind her. Marcy thought she might wrap her arms around Marcy's waist and hug her but she spoke to Marcy's back. "I don't want to live together anymore."

After that Marcy and Brit smoked weed together every night after dinner and talked about how to get rid of the apartment. Marcy sat with her feet on the radiator and Brit rolled a joint for them at the table. Almost every conversation turned into bickering with an increasingly icy edge until one of them stormed out of the room. They slept with their backs to each other, a thin strip of empty double mattress between them. There were times they woke up sweaty and clamped together. It would take a few foggy moments to remember all that had transpired in the past few weeks. Marcy was mostly working evenings and she started jogging along the cliffs on the Signal Hill trail early in the morning. Often the sun would be coming up as she headed back to the apartment, her sweat-drenched clothes cooling against her body.

The weed made them chatty, and it was the only way they could be in each other's company without fighting. One night, after sharing a joint, Marcy started recounting, almost line for line, a podcast she'd listened to that afternoon. It was an interview with an old man who'd had an ice pick lobotomy at a state fair as a child.

"They pulled some of his brain out through his nose," Marcy said, swishing water around in the bottom of the kettle because they had an ant infestation. In the night, ants trooped up the side of the kettle and down the spout. She swirled the kettle, splashing the water around to kill any ants that might be crawling up the sides to escape.

"That can't be real," Brit said, but it sounded like she wanted to hear more.

"It's real." Marcy dumped the water into the sink. "It happened all the time. That's what the podcast was about."

She refilled the kettle before turning it on. Brit was working on a drawing. She had run an extension cord across the floor so she could sit the gooseneck lamp on the table. The rest of the room was dim, but the white paper blared bright in a ring of lamplight. Marcy leaned over the drawing. She recognized Brittany's mother. For the past year Brit had been working on a series of paintings of the parking garage going up across the street that was gradually blocking out the view of the harbour and keeping their apartment in darkness for more and more of the morning. The portrait was a shock.

"Your mom," she said.

"You recognize her."

"It looks just like her. I recognize the expression."

"Yeah?" Brit was dreamy from the weed. "When does she make it?"

That was when Marcy first noticed the smell. A warm chemical smell. But she was trying to think, it was a really specific look she'd seen Brit's mother make.

"Like when she told the story about giving the finger to a guy who cut her off in traffic."

"Do you smell something burning?" Brit asked.

"Is it coming from outside?"

They had cracked the window to blow the weed smoke out into their muddy backyard. Brit stuck her head out the open window and sniffed. "No. It's in here."

Marcy followed the smell into the kitchen. The electric kettle was slumped on the burner, orange flames licking up the sides.

"Fuck." She picked it up by the handle and the bottom came loose. Strands of melted plastic like chewed gum stretched away from the lid. The burning part fell on the linoleum.

She couldn't stomp on the burning kettle, her feet were bare. She dropped the melted half-handle into the sink and tried whipping at the burning mess on the floor with a dishtowel. The fire stayed close to the ground, but it kept spreading out, consuming the linoleum. Brit was standing in the doorway.

"Get my sneakers," Marcy said.

Everything was happening so slowly. She didn't feel panic, just dread. About the money the floor was going to cost and about what the rest of the night would be like. Brit would be self-righteous and furious. Marcy turned away from the fire and opened the window beside the fridge to let the toxic fumes out. Wind blew in and bolstered the flames; they grew wide and high.

"Be careful!" Brit dropped the sneakers on the floor.

Marcy slid her toes in and shuffled over the flames with her heels hanging out the backs of the shoes.

"Fuck." For the first time Marcy started to feel afraid. The fire wasn't going out, it was making its way towards the wall.

Brit filled a glass of water from the tap and splashed it over the fire. She filled a second glass and tossed that on. The flames died but bright embers still glowed around the curling edges of the flooring. Marcy stomped them.

"Watch out." Brit dumped another glass of water on the floor.

The bottom of the kettle was hardening into a new shape in the centre of the blackened floor. They dropped dish-towels over the mess. By that time Marcy was bawling. Brit held her.

"I'll pay for the floor, it's my fault."

"It's fine," Brit said. "The fire's out. Everything's okay. It's just some shitty, ugly flooring."

"I'm going to leave," Marcy said.

"What?"

"I'm going to Montreal. " She hadn't even thought about it that much before she said it.

"Marcy, don't go. It's going to be okay." Brit held Marcy's head against her chest and smoothed her hair.

"I just want to," Marcy said. "Not even because of us, I just want to go."

"Okay go," Brit said, but not coldly.

That night they slept in each other's arms. In the morning Marcy looked out the window and saw freezing rain was puckering the surface of the harbour.

WHAT SHE KNEW about Montreal was mostly from a trip she'd taken in the seventh grade. When she was twelve Marcy's best friend was Taylor Lawlor. Marcy and Taylor were transitioning from spending their evenings dunking Barbie dolls in a Tupperware hot tub to three-way calling boys they'd met at the Avalon Mall. They were obsessed with a coffee-table book about the Love Parade festival in Berlin. It was a collection of glossy full-page photographs of ravers dancing in the street; there were feather boas and silver bikinis and rainbow tube socks and pacifier necklaces. The girls would take Taylor's CD player to the front step and play badminton in her gravel driveway. Taylor had a zippered circular pouch for her CDs and they would flip through the clear plastic sleeves looking for just the right one. Aqua and Prozzäk were falling out of rotation, replaced by No Doubt and Sublime and then Crass and Cock Sparrer and X-Ray Spex.

Around this time Taylor's mom invited Marcy to go on a road trip to the mainland. Taylor's mom had family in Ontario, they went every summer and came back with the type of clothes you couldn't get in Newfoundland. A pale blue silk miniskirt with an intricate pattern embroidered on it. A Buzzcocks T-shirt with "ever fallen in love with someone you shouldn't have . . ." in bright red cursive on the back. A pair of purple velvet platform sneakers. (Marcy had begged to try those on but her feet were too big. She'd tried scrunching her toes but her heel still stuck out the back. She could have walked in them like that, but she was afraid of damaging a precious artifact from the mainland.) Marcy's mom said, "You know two weeks is a long time to be away from home. Longer than you've ever been away from us before."

On the day they left for the mainland they drove across the island for an entire day before boarding the overnight ferry in Port aux Basques. Taylor's mom bought them Jello parfaits from the cooler in the cafeteria at ten o'clock at night. They wandered the ship after Taylor's mom fell asleep sitting up in a plastic chair, her mouth hanging open.

The next day they drove again, across Nova Scotia and New Brunswick. Taylor's mom played every tape they requested and stopped every time they needed to pee. Marcy crouched on the shoulder, bracing herself against the dusty door, terrified and exhilarated by wind coming off the cars speeding past. Warm pee soaked her sock. In the back seat the girls purposely burned each other with the sun-heated, shiny part of the middle seat belt and shrieked. They bickered over quizzes in magazines, they sang all the words to the Rancid self-titled album twice in a row. Marcy's mother would have been threatening to leave them on the side of the road.

On the evening of the third night, they stayed with a friend of Taylor's mom in a farmhouse in rural Quebec. That night Marcy fell asleep with her Discman on listening to Liz Phair, curled towards the wall with her spine touching Taylor's. She woke already standing up, looking out a window with her headphones covering her ears and the

Discman on the floor, tethered by the headphones. She'd been sleepwalking, dragging the Discman along behind her. The CD had ended and nothing was coming out of the headphones.

She found herself staring out the window at a damp field, yellow light starting to burn the mist. This was the farthest she'd ever been from home. There was a feeling buzzing in her chest that was hard to understand; maybe she was scared, but maybe she was just fine, maybe even good.

She slid the headphones down to her shoulders. There were spaces between the slats in the walls that let light and sounds through. She could hear the heavy breathing of everyone sleeping in the bedrooms around her.

Each step creaked beneath her weight. Cold was seeping through the floor of the kitchen. She lifted the latch on the back door and was careful to pull it closed quietly behind her. With her first footstep into the field her toes landed on a slug, it squished up between them. She wiped her foot desperately back and forth on the slick grass. There were all kinds of animals on the mainland they didn't have at home. Porcupines and raccoons and skunks and groundhogs and deer. She looked at the seam of scruffy bushes where the field met the woods and willed a strange creature to appear. Nothing. She got back in bed beside Taylor with her wet feet stained green and a little bit of iridescent slug skin between her toes.

When it was time to get up, Taylor's mom's friend served them croissants out of a brown paper bag and rose-petal jam. She'd made the jam herself, it was translucent and gelatinous. CBC radio was murmuring in the background. Taylor's mom's friend found a pair of kitchen scissors so

Taylor could chop her pink fishnet tights into arm bands before they packed everything up and hit the road. In the driveway Taylor stuck her arms straight out in front of her and Marcy carefully shimmied the fishnets up to her elbows.

Then on to Toronto. They stayed in the suburbs with Taylor's grandfather and he had a pool. Marcy had never been in a backyard pool before. Kensington Market felt like stepping into the pages of the Love Parade book. Taylor's mom gave them twenty dollars each and left them in a vintage shop. She was going to look for a special cheese she wanted to deliver to her father. Marcy bought a sixties-style, double-breasted coat that hung to her ankles. Taylor bought a red velour corset with white fluff along the bust. A Christmas-themed corset. The woman working behind the counter had both her eyebrows pierced.

"You're allowed to buy this?" she asked Taylor.

Marcy squeezed the long jacket against her chest, guilty by association.

"Yeah," Taylor said.

"Okay," the woman said. She didn't believe it but she'd done her due diligence. She clunked buttons on the register until the cash drawer flew open. Taylor accepted her change shamelessly. When they got outside the store Taylor's mom wasn't around. They sat on the pavement to wait. Marcy put on the coat even though it was hot out.

Later they went to the Chinatown Centre and got freeze-dried ice cream from a vending machine. You fed a five-dollar bill into the slot and a paper cup dropped out of the machine into your hand. There were crunching mechanical sounds and then a spew of pastel-coloured beads of ice cream shot into the cup.

On the way back to Newfoundland they stopped in Montreal and hung out in Taylor's uncle's stuffy apartment until Taylor's teenage cousin got home from Cegep. He was five years older than them. They walked along Sainte-Catherine Street and saw all the blinking strip club signs. He brought them to an alleyway to look at some graffiti that said FUCK HARPER and explained he'd stood watch a few nights ago while his friend spray-painted it. After that they went into the army surplus store and ran their hands along the used parkas. Marcy was haunted by the names Sharpied on the sleeves. Taylor's cousin pointed out the hunting knife he was planning to buy. They took the metro back home. Marcy had never been on a subway before.

Of the whole trip, Marcy loved Montreal the most. People were dressed even more outrageously than in Toronto. She liked hearing French and seeing people making out in parks.

When she finally got home, she rang the doorbell and no one answered. She remembered her key in the front pouch of her knapsack, stowed there since she left. This was the longest it had been away from the keyhole since the day the guy at Home Depot had fed it into the machine that shaved it to match her mother's.

She called out, "Hellooooo."

No one answered. She had been expecting them to be awaiting her return with bated breath. She thought maybe her dad would make a dessert like he often did for special occasions. Even semi-special ones. He pointed out how ordinary things are special by marking them with a dessert. She had assumed her homecoming would be a dessert-worthy occasion.

A cool draft was swirling through the house. She walked

up the stairs and found a hole where the bathroom window used to be. The curtain whipped back and forth, inside and then outside. She stuck her head out and looked down at the sidewalk.

Later Marcy learned her little sister had broken the window by bouncing a basketball against it, and her parents had gone to her uncle's place to look at some old windows he had in his shed. They came home with Kentucky Fried Chicken and banished her sister to her room for the night. When they asked about the trip Marcy found she didn't want to say anything, it felt too precious to share.

IN JUNE SHE and Brit found someone to take the apartment for September 1st. Marcy took every shift anyone offered during the summer to save money and to be out of the house. She covered shifts for co-workers who wanted to go swimming at the Punch Bowl, co-workers who were going on tour, co-workers who were flying home to Ontario to be with their families, and co-workers who'd accidentally double-booked themselves with shifts at another job. She worked almost every day. She shut the place down and she opened it up. People asked her if the Costco order had come in and if the tips were ready and if they were working tomorrow. She was exhausted, and when Leo, the owner, traipsed through the bar and called her a saint one afternoon, it pissed her off.

That night when she was doing off the cash from the restaurant side, she deleted a few sales that had been paid with cash. She knew how to turn so her back was to the camera and no one would be able to see her hand sliding bills from the register into her pocket. Walking home with the money she felt the first bright glint of happiness burst through the guilt that had been dampening everything since she got tangled up with Linda behind the UltraFar.

After that she took home some money every time she closed up alone. Each time she scrunched the bills up in her fist she thought about Leo's smug face. He was a middle-aged guy with a big suv and a brown leather jacket. Taking the money felt like swatting a mosquito right before it stuck its needle-straw of a proboscis in her.

If it was a slow day, she'd only take twenty dollars. Usually, she took fifty. The most she took was a hundred dollars, from a very busy day when a co-worker had called in sick. When she left with five twenties in her pocket, the happiness was smudged with nauseating anxiety. It was hot and the sun was peppering the harbour with glittery splashes of light. Marcy loved podcasts about catfishing and frauds and heists, stories where people ruined sustainable scams with a tragic cocktail of greed and cockiness.

If she were caught, nobody, especially not Linda, would get it. Linda was always saying how she couldn't imagine working anywhere else. How at other jobs she'd been asked to cover her bra straps and take her piercings out. How nice it was that Leo didn't mind jumping on bar when it was packed, and he never took tips. Probably Marcy could be charged with fraud. She went into Kaine's and bought a lime green popsicle with one of the twenties. She ate it on her front step, trying to look at the glinting harbour without squinting. She wouldn't take any more money. She was good at quitting things.

As fall approached everyone wanted their regular shifts

back, they needed to financially recover from the reverie of summer, and they were ready for routine again. Marcy started the process of moving out of the house in the Battery. First she posted her plants on Facebook Marketplace. She photographed the oldest, lushest plants first and she priced them a little below what seemed to be the average based on a quick search. She went to the supermarket and when she came back her inbox was flooded with messages. She made herself a grilled cheese and posted the next batch of plants, the ones with dry spots and limp leaves, and based on the success of the last round she upped the prices. Again, her phone lit up endlessly, people who'd asked for the first batch would love to have the second ones too. In the following weeks she went through the house photographing everything that was unambiguously hers, first clothes and knick-knacks and then bigger items. On the days when Brit was at work and she was off, she waited around the apartment for people to show up and collect her things. She sold the couch and the toaster without asking and then she slept on her mom's couch for two nights to avoid Brittany. She knew Brit would read the sales as a cold and hostile gesture, but whatever, her grandmother had given her the couch.

Marcy deposited the money from selling stuff along with her tips and the money she'd stolen. She loved feeding an envelope fat with cash into the lit-up mouth of the bank machine. She would hold the end of the deposit envelope when it was half in the slit and feel the machine tug at it a little. She went early in the morning. She worked Friday nights but she'd stop in to work and make herself a latte to take to the bank machine. The alcove where the ATM was had two big glass walls, to discourage muggings. The morning sun made it damp and warm like a greenhouse. The faint smell of pee didn't bother her. She was holding mass at the altar of actually leaving the city. People were always saying they were moving to the mainland but never actually doing it. This was a ritual to cement her faith that she'd really buy a plane ticket, performed under the blinking eye of the bank's security camera.

THEY WENT WITHOUT a couch or toaster for most of August. For a while Marcy slept on an air mattress in the living room. Then Brit started seeing someone and the first night she didn't come home Marcy decided to go sleep on the couch at her mother's. She ended up sleeping there until she left the city.

Marcy learned things about the new girlfriend from Brit's Instagram. She was a social work student. She seemed to own a car. She wore her shiny hair in a high ponytail. Marcy was shocked by how bad it felt. She cried in the bathroom at work and during aerobics class.

Marcy had promised to help move Brit's things out of their old place in the last week of August. When she got there, the apartment was a mess. Brit was emptying the hamper into a duffle bag. She just turned the hamper upside down and shook it. Then she dragged the duffle to the bathroom and stuffed damp towels into it. There were new sheets on the bed. Marcy stood in the doorway taking them in. New sheets for the new girlfriend.

"Do you want to pack up the kitchen?" Brit asked.

In the kitchen Marcy saw evidence of the girlfriend all over the place. The most glaring was dishes used to make

French toast and two plates smeared with syrup. The bread
slouched in an open bag on the counter beside a brand of
juice she'd never known Brit to buy.

"I'm not cleaning the kitchen," Marcy called out. "I'm
here to help carry stuff to the van. I thought you wanted
help lifting heavy things."

"Can you please," Brit said. "We only have the U-Haul
for the day."

"No," Marcy said.

"Then throw them out."

Marcy pushed the plates off the counter into the garbage
bucket.

When she got back to her mother's place she went online,
found a plane ticket, and finally clicked Purchase.

4

Marcy went out with the arts administrator a second time, to a dumpling place on Saint-Laurent. This time Marcy paid. The woman wore a long blue trench coat and she looked beautiful. She talked about cleaning out her mother's basement and how her sister hadn't helped.

"Still, I'm the least favourite child," the woman said.

Marcy laughed even though it wasn't a joke, but then the woman laughed too. She laughed a lot — she was relieved it had been turned into a joke.

After dinner, the woman walked Marcy halfway home. They stopped at the mouth of the damp, dark underpass at Van Horne and Saint-Laurent. Someone whizzed past on a bike with a little speaker attached to the handlebars. The chorus of "What Is Love?" bounced around inside the underpass as they swooped down the hill, full speed ahead. Marcy could feel this was the moment to kiss.

"Okay, well thank you, have a nice night!" She found herself waving in the woman's face.

She went on a date with someone named Laurence later that week. They arranged to meet on the crowded patio of a bar. They drank a few beers, got cold when the sun went down, and moved inside where they continued drinking. Marcy could hear herself rambling about Newfoundland, about the boom and bust economy, the collapse of the fishery and then the oil industry, and the environmental racism of the Muskrat Falls hydroelectric dam. She had never really understood the inter-connected nature of all these things until she'd dated Brittany.

Laurence was from rural Quebec, they'd grown up in a small town that had problems too. Marcy was trying to listen but she wanted to switch to liquor and kept being distracted by the waiter passing by.

When they were good and drunk they split the bill and walked the long way back to Laurence's apartment. They had to be quiet in the entrance because Laurence lived with their brother and his girlfriend. In the bedroom, Laurence closed the door and they both got naked. Marcy crawled to the middle of the tightly made bed and Laurence flopped down beside her. But when they started kissing, Laurence kept saying things like "I want you to know you're beauti-ful," while holding Marcy's chin. Or "I'm really appreciating being here with you right now," while looking into her eyes. Beer was crawling back up Marcy's throat and making her feel bloated. She shook her chin out of Laurence's grip, flipped over onto her belly and swished her hand around under the bed until she found her sports bra.

"I think I need to go," Marcy said, tugging the bra down over her tits.

"Okay, of course, are you going to take the bus? I can get you a cab."

"That's okay, I'm going to walk, I think." Her under-wear was still looped around one ankle, the crotch portion stretched over her heel. She hopped off the bed and pulled them up to her hips. She found her jeans and T-shirt on the floor. Laurence grabbed a bathrobe from the back of their door and followed Marcy into the hallway.

It felt like getting her sneakers on took forever. Laurence turned on the light to help but Marcy wished they'd left it off.

"Are you sure you don't want an Uber? You live in Little Italy? You can take the bus, I think the 70."

"No, I'm okay, thank you good night," Marcy said. When she got into the street she ran up the block until her chest burned.

As she walked home the sky went from black to navy and then eddies of white washed through the dark blue. She stopped at a gas station and bought a bottle of Gatorade and a bag of chips. The sun emerged between two condo towers. When she finally reached her block, she saw the intersections at either end of her building closed by strands of yellow caution tape. The cop tape was knotted around one of the construction cones that had been sitting in the intersection for the past two months.

There were small yellow tags littering the road in front of the entrance to the chandelier store, the kind that appear in the opening montage of true crime dramas. Three police cars were parked inside the tape; lights twirling, sirens off. Cops were wandering around, flipping papers on their clipboards, getting in and out of their cars. A motorcycle was on its side in the middle of the road with twisting skid marks behind it. It made her street look like the set of an action movie. She walked up to the tape and a cop approached her.

"I live here," she said. The crumpled chip bag bulged in the pocket of her tight pants. She smelled of alcohol and sweat.

"Here?" The cop looked up at the building. "Okay."

He lifted the tape. When she got inside the tape Marcy saw the man in the road. He was face down, one arm raised above his head. The blood around his head had spread out over the asphalt.

"Oh," she said.

"Sorry. They're getting the sheet ready," the cop said. "They have to finish with the photos first."

Marcy turned her back on the dead man and climbed the stairs to the front entrance on her tired legs. Inside Kathleen was layering up for her morning jog.

"You should go out the side door," Marcy told her.

"Are you just getting home?" Kathleen asked.

"There was an accident." Marcy lay on the couch with her sneakered feet hanging over the arm, too tired to undo her laces. "In that spot with all the pylons, a motorcycle accident."

"That's awful," Kathleen said. "This fucking construction."

Marcy was relieved to have dodged the question of where she'd been. It felt humiliating to admit she'd been on a date. That she wanted affection and intimacy so badly she was willing to post on the internet and meet up with strangers about it. That she was filling her free time with internet dates to stave off loneliness because she didn't want to lean too much on Hannah, the one friend she'd made since moving to the city.

Later, in the thick of her relationship with Leanne, she'd think back to this time and wonder: Of all the possible futures she could have leapt into, why did she pick this one?

Two

Getting Colder

5

Kathleen got a job with some friends who repaired pinball machines and other vintage table games all over the city. She did it in the afternoons before bartending. One of their biggest clients was the Bell Centre, where a semicircle of pinball machines had recently been installed in the entrance of the humongous stadium. Through this gig Kathleen had ended up with two tickets to see Korn. On the night of the concert Marcy, knowing she'd be alone in the apartment, invited Leanne over for a first date.

That evening, she had gone to spin class at the Econofitness around the corner and got home just as her roommates were getting ready to leave. She walked in the front door chilled but still flushed and sweaty.

The gym was open twenty-four hours a day and only cost eleven dollars a month. The outline of two muscular women with ponytails standing back to back and flexing, sculpted out of neon tubes, glowed on the side of the building. The fact that the gym never closed meant the cleaners had to maneuver between the tightly packed tread-mills with spray bottles and rags, kneeling to wipe down the machines as people were jogging on them.

Many of the bikes in the windowless room where spin took place were broken. The class was popular so you had to get there early to find one that didn't whine or sway alarmingly beneath you. Marcy's favourite instructor was a woman who wore thick-strapped ribbed tank tops and bike shorts. She had an array of mid-2000s-style tattoos. A red nautical star outlined in black capped each shoulder, and fading comic book scenes ran down both her arms. She pumped her legs so fast that they became a blur while she shouted instructions in English and French over the music. Sometimes she hopped off the bike and stomped around the room shouting encouragement in a menacing voice. She would point one finger at the ceiling like the singer of a hardcore band and scream, "C'est tout? That's all you got? No way, you got more!"

Marcy wondered if she might be a wrestler.

When she got home from the gym there was someone in the bathroom. They were wearing an ankle-length A-line leather skirt and black sports bra. They were leaning into the mirror in the bathroom, examining their makeup. When they turned and faced Marcy it took a moment for the fea-tures to make sense.

"You shaved your head," Marcy said.

"Do you like it?" Sharon asked.

"Where did that skirt come from?"

"Doesn't she look great?" Kathleen appeared in the door behind Marcy. "You should feel it."

"Can I touch it?" Marcy asked.

Sharon bent at the waist and Marcy ran her hand over the stubble. She did one slow pet from the nape of Sharon's neck to her forehead and then back the other way. It was silky smooth in one direction and stiff and prickly in the other. She rubbed quickly back and forth on the very top, feeling the changing texture.

Sharon straightened up.

"Feels amazing, right?" Kathleen asked.

Marcy nodded sheepishly. She was aware of the stink of sweat on her. And then she remembered about the date she'd arranged with Leanne. She needed to shower and find something to wear. Sharon turned back to the mirror to finish her makeup.

Marcy went to the kitchen sink and filled a pint glass with water. She drank it in three long gulps, holding the edge of the counter. She sat on the arm of the couch in her damp gym clothes while Kathleen laced her boots and gently reminded Sharon, "Gotta get going soon."

Marcy's foot was tapping the floor, leaving a jittery pattern of sweaty footprints on the cement. They finally left twenty minutes before Leanne was supposed to arrive. Marcy showered in under five minutes. She forgot to bring a towel into the bathroom so she ran across the loft naked to find one. When she started rubbing herself down with the rough beach towel she'd bought at Rossy, she realized she hadn't washed the soap out of her armpits. She turned the shower back on and scrubbed them quickly. For dates she always ended up dressing extra sloppily out of fear of being overdressed. She put on black leggings and a sweatshirt.

. . .

THERE WAS A knock on the door, she opened it, and there
was Leanne with a helmet under one arm. Marcy had sort
of forgotten what she looked like. Her profile on the dating
app had shown her working at a pizza place, an apron knotted around her waist and a thin disc of dough rotating above
her head; leaning against a bike on the side of the highway
in summer; and a broody selfie. Leanne was tall and just a
little bit chubby in a way Marcy found very sexy. That was
something she hadn't noticed in the photos. In the photos
she'd noticed her how red her hair was and how green her
eyes were.

Marcy stepped backwards to let her into the apartment.

"You can go up on your roof." Leanne stayed in the
hallway.

"I don't think so," Marcy said.

"Yeah, the door's open, I just passed by."

"Oh weird." Marcy moved farther into the apartment,
wondering if Leanne felt crowded.

"We should go up."

"I've never seen anyone go up there. I don't think we 'have
roof access.'" Marcy hoped her tone conveyed that she was
using the phrase sarcastically.

"It's open now."

"Maybe the landlord is up there."

"Come with me, I'll go up first and poke my head around,
if I see a landlord-type dude—is it a dude?"

Marcy paused. "A pair of dudes, yeah."

"So if I see someone who looks like a landlord we won't
go up."

Leanne put her helmet and bookbag down just inside the door without stepping into the apartment.

"Okay, let me put my sneakers on," Marcy said.

"It's weirdly warm right now, I'm sweating in this," Leanne pinched her windbreaker.

Leanne led the way to the stairwell, as though they were in her building. A trap door in the ceiling was open, showing a square of pink sky. A skinny metal ladder attached to the cinderblock wall, like you see on the side of a pool, led to the hatch. The first rung was level with Leanne's waist. She grabbed onto a rung above her head and hauled her body up. When she was halfway up the ladder Leanne looked down at Marcy. "How high do you think this is?"

Marcy realized she'd been watching Leanne's butt.

"You're about eight feet up there now."

Leanne turned back to the cinderblock wall and continued climbing.

"It's probably twenty feet right? Like from the floor? I'm not good at estimating."

Leanne straightened her body out and rested her folded arms on top of the opening, her head and shoulders sticking into the sky. Marcy could hear her talking but couldn't make out what she was saying. Leanne started crawling onto the roof. For a moment her sneakered feet kicked in the air above the opening and Marcy's stomach swooped. Then Leanne's head appeared in the hole and she yelled, "I said there's no one up here, come up."

Marcy looked down the hallway, afraid of disturbing the neighbours and attracting attention. But there was no one.

Marcy exhaled through her nose. She'd been focused on avoiding breaking the rules and disturbing the harmony in the building, she hadn't thought about climbing the spindly ladder. She grabbed a rung above her head and wrenched her stomach muscles to pull her feet up. The roof might not even be safe. She kept her eyes on the wall, which was less than a school ruler's length from her face. When she got to the top she looked down before looking up.

The jolt that went through her was like tipping backwards on the swings as a kid. Her legs went liquid; it was a mistake to climb this ladder after spin class. She could feel her butt and lower back beginning to dissolve into cool watery nothingness. Marcy had chronic low blood pressure, a condition the doctor thought probably came from "a slight hormone imbalance" that was also responsible for her moustache and possibly what she speculated to be an above-average level of horniness. She'd passed out from low blood pressure before and she knew that once the weightless feeling reached her shoulders, a wave of pixelated darkness would crash across her eyes. Already the rush of static that accompanied the darkness was filling her ears.

"Hey." Leanne's voice came through the blaring white noise.

Marcy tilted her chin up and then forced her eyes to follow. Leanne was on her knees at the edge of the hatch.

"Are you okay?"

Marcy breathed. Seeing the steady skyline was helping.

"Come up, you're practically here."

Marcy took hold of the ledge; wind blew over the top of her head and it helped drain the liquid out of her back.

"You need to just flop your top half onto the ground." Leanne took a handful of Marcy's sweatshirt in her fist.

"Come on, do it now," Leanne said firmly.

Marcy reached her arms out and let her chest fall against

the warm roof. The edge of the hatch dug into her stomach, just below her ribs.

"Keep going." Leanne sounded like a sports coach. "Get your legs up."

She twisted the shirt tight around Marcy's middle. Marcy scrambled her sore legs up. She ended up embarrassingly slumped on her side. Leanne let go of her sweatshirt. "Your face is all sweaty."

"I got freaked out." Marcy swung her knees around and pulled them into her chest. She tugged at the sides of her sweatshirt, loosening it. "Sorry, I just got freaked out."

Leanne had a gummy smear of tar with little rocks stuck in it on her front. Marcy looked down and saw she did too. It was just a plain sweatshirt but it had been one of her favourites. She dusted the rocks off. The navy clouds were stretching themselves across the pale sky. The dark roof held the heat from the day but the air was cold.

Looking at the horizon settled her. There was so much sky above the buildings. There was a lineup outside the Glitz, probably a metal show, based on the crowd. Her neighbour from across the hall was walking his little pug mix past the fish shop on the corner. The trees had lost almost all their leaves. She could see a crane swinging around inside the pit on the corner where they were digging out a parking garage for a new condo. It all belonged to another, shrunken dimension.

"I wish we had some beers." Leanne was looking down over the edge of the building.

"I wonder why the hatch was open, I've never seen it open," Marcy said.

. . .

THEY WENT BACK to the apartment and Marcy found some Miller High Life that belonged to Kathleen in the crisper. They drank the watery beers and made out on the couch. Leanne left around midnight.

After locking the door behind Leanne, Marcy got in bed, her stomach turning from the beers. She flipped onto her belly and rooted around under the bed for her Magic Wand. She thought about biting Leanne's neck and the feeling of Leanne's ass in her hands. She heard the deadbolt swing back the other way as Sharon and Kathleen stumbled in, giddy from the concert. She had to concentrate hard to drown out the thought of them and stay focused on the makeout.

A couple of days went by without any word from Leanne. Marcy swiped through other profiles on various apps and even set up some dates, but she found herself cancelling a couple of hours before. She spent a long time drafting a text to Leanne suggesting they take mushrooms at the Botanical Garden as a second date but then invited Hannah instead.

THE DAY OF the Botanical Garden excursion was exceptionally mild for the end of November. Marcy packed the black leather mini-backpack she'd found in the take-a-thing-leave-a-thing pile on the second floor of her building. She slid in her wallet, a water bottle from the dollar store that made everything taste of plastic, the pack of cigarettes she'd regretfully bought the day before, and her stained sweatshirt — rolled up tight — in case it got colder. She wore a silky burgundy bomber jacket Hannah had given her the last time they'd hung out. They'd agreed to meet at eleven and Marcy washed down a couple of pinches of mushrooms with the last mouthful of her coffee. She smoked a cigarette before unlocking her bike. Google Maps said it would take her forty minutes to get to the Botanical Garden — she'd arrive exactly on time.

She biked along Clark with a stream of cars cutting in front of each other to one side of her, a wall of parked cars on the other. In Newfoundland biking was considered a childish activity that some weirdo hippies indulged in. People would yell out their car windows for you to get on the sidewalk. She pumped her brakes lightly just to test them. She thought of the story Kathleen had told her about getting doored when she was a bike courier. She'd flown through the air and landed on the hood of another car, smashing the windshield.

"My bike was completely mangled."

"But you were okay?"

"No, I had a concussion and a broken arm. I had to work at a call centre for a few months. It was so hard to sit like that after the courier job. I was used to constantly moving."

Soon Marcy was able to turn onto a bike lane and coast at a leisurely pace towards the Botanical Garden. She pumped her legs to scoot around parents with children. She passed a car dealership with a drooping chain of reflective flags strung above the perimeter of the parking lot. She ground to a halt, one foot resting on the median, mesmerized by the way the light danced on the decorations as they moved with the breeze. It was like sunlight on the surface of a pond. Someone cruised around her in the bike lane and the magic of the flags wore off. She remembered she'd taken mushrooms.

When Marcy arrived, Hannah was sitting on the edge of a planter with dried stalks poking up out of it. She was wearing zebra-print pants and a fuzzy purple sweater, rolling a joint in her lap. Marcy bent over to lock her bike on, all sweaty. She was so glad to see Hannah, so glad she'd invited her instead of some Tinder date, and so glad that Hannah had accepted.

"Where'd you get that bike?"

"It's Al's, who I stayed with when I first moved here?" Marcy said. "I have to return it, actually, but they said I could use it until I find another."

"It's so you," Hannah said.

"I know." Proof that Hannah truly *got* her.

Inside the Botanical Garden, the mushrooms made Marcy feel anxious about interacting with the woman behind the front desk. She hadn't realized admission was twenty dollars. It seemed insanely expensive. She knew there were three fives and some change in her wallet. She was scooping the bottom of the little pouch, feeling for big coins, when Hannah stepped in front of her with her card extended. "I got it."

"Are you sure?" Marcy asked.

She felt relieved to still have the fives in her wallet and to be released from her conversation with the woman behind the desk. She followed Hannah past the admissions counter, through a heavy door, and into the warm damp of the greenhouse.

They followed the stone paths through neatly planted beds of tropical plants. Every few minutes a shower of mist spurted out of the ceiling. Hannah pointed out a tiny pineapple growing on top of a bush. Marcy told her about her date with Leanne.

"Did you like it?" Hannah asked.

They'd stopped by the wall of hanging orchids, mesmerized by the intricate patterns on the leaves and the way the stamens licked out of them like tongues.

"I froze up and she lifted me onto the roof by my sweater."

"Was it hot?"

"I felt like a puppy getting picked up by the scruff of the neck. How they go all dopey and docile?"

"I can't tell if you liked it."

Marcy petted a velvet petal with one finger. "The view was cool."

"You should keep dating other people. You basically just moved here," Hannah said.

"She hasn't messaged me anyway," Marcy said.

Hannah took out a Tupperware filled with date balls rolled in coconut.

"Here, have a snack," Hannah said. "I have some news."

"What?" Marcy asked.

"I got a job, working at a coding boot camp. It's a short-term contract but it's nine-to-five, steady paycheque. They say all this bullshit about being an inclusive workplace, but they don't offer any job security or benefits, you know what I mean?"

"I think so," Marcy said. "I am high, though."

"Fair," Hannah said.

"Are you still going to have time to hang out with me?"

"I hope so," Hannah said. "I don't want it to take over my life. But I am glad to be making money right now."

"Congratulations."

"Thank you."

"Sorry. I should have said that first." Marcy giggled.

They both started laughing with an intensity that far out-stretched the funniness of what had happened.

THE NEXT DAY, Leanne messaged Marcy and invited her to a surprise birthday party at NDQ. Marcy had heard of the bar but she'd never been. She'd walked by and seen the windows all steamed up, plants pressed against the glass. She'd seen the crowd gathered outside smoking. They wore ankle-length jewel-toned parkas or '90s-style leather trenches.

On the night of the date there was no one outside. Inside there was a narrow space between the bar and the wall. People were crowded around two big tables in the back near the bathrooms but no one was sitting at the bar. She scanned both groups for Leanne's red hair but didn't see her. She ordered a beer and then asked, "Is it okay if I sit here?"

The bartender stared at her bewildered for a moment and then said, "Yeah, totally, of course."

"Cool, thanks." Marcy hung her jacket on the back of the chair and fished her phone out immediately so he wouldn't think she expected him to talk to her. The bartender stood in front of her washing pint glasses with a machine on the counter that shot water up into them. There was yowling laughter from the tables at the back.

Marcy sipped the beer slowly, hoping to have at least half left when Leanne showed up. She had budgeted to buy two drinks tops and probably she should get one for Leanne.

On Instagram she saw there was a show at the Rose and

Thistle in St. John's. The floor-to-ceiling windows were open behind the drum kit and people were hopping from the street into the crowd. It had been so long since she'd stood in a crowd where she knew most of the people. Where people casually touched her shoulder and she could make small talk with anyone. The person filming panned around the inside of the bar and Marcy saw Linda nodding along to the music. She flipped the phone over the counter.

A flux of new people were suddenly in NDQ but they hadn't passed behind Marcy. It made her realize there must be another room. She craned her neck and saw an archway in the wall. She stood with her beer and walked towards the opening. If she didn't recognize anyone she could pretend she was heading for the bathroom at the back.

In the other room there was a single bowling lane and a counter where you could order pizza. A glass case with three tiers where slices were displayed. Leanne was standing on a stepladder attaching a pinata to a hook in the ceiling. It was a pale blue fish with googly eyes stuck on either side of its face. It swayed, paper scales fluttering as Leanne knotted the string to the big hook. There were four or five people gathered around the base of the ladder. Someone with a bleached mullet and leggings that showed off their very muscly legs was holding the ladder. When she finished tying the knot, Leanne looked out across the bar and saw Marcy in the doorway.

"Marcy!" she called, waving her over the threshold.

Leanne took a step down the ladder and the mulleted person at the bottom backed away to give her room. She slung an arm around Marcy's waist and introduced her to the collection of people gathered below the pinata.

Including the birthday girl, Marina, who was turning twenty-six. Marina was a trans girl with shaggy brunette curls and checkered knee socks.

Marcy took big gulps of her beer. Marina said she was learning to make violins.

"I did cabinetmaking, and now I'm apprentising with this seventy-year-old guy from Italy," she told Marcy.

"That's amazing, does every violin make a different sound? Like based on how you carve it?" Marcy asked.

"Exactly, yeah," Marina told her.

Marcy got another beer; she no longer felt obliged to get one for Leanne. She'd already seen two other people present her with drinks.

Marcy talked to someone who had just adopted a pit bull.

"It's not about the breed," he told her.

"It's how they're treated?" Marcy asked.

"This dog wasn't treated well," the guy said. "So I have to put a muzzle on him. But I've been watching YouTube videos on how to train them."

"What did you learn?"

"Stare into their eyes, don't look away until they do, even if they're growling."

Someone approached them and hugged the new pit bull owner. This person had a business photographing people's apartments so they could advertise them on Airbnb.

"I mean, that's just for money, obviously. I don't like doing it, obviously. Airbnb is evil. I like photographing my friends' bands and stuff but that doesn't make money."

The pit bull owner was nodding, familiar with the photographer's dilemma. Marcy thought about the graffiti in the pedestrian tunnel in the underpass by her house. Someone had written *don't air bnb* in jagged lower-case Sharpie on the wall, small enough to fit on a sheet of paper but right at eye level. Marcy passed it almost every day. She was tempted to ask why the person didn't just do something else to make money but she thought about her Amazon bedding and she just nodded.

Then it was time for the pinata. Leanne pulled a gauzy purple scarf out of the pocket of her denim jacket. She tied it over the eyes of the person with the blond mullet first and Marcy was surprised by the trickle of jealousy she felt in the back of her throat.

"Yeah, Jace!" people chanted as Leanne placed an upside-down broom in their hands. They spread their legs wide and made a stance like a baseball player. Leanne backed up theatrically. She sidled up to Marcy and squeezed her hip. "I'm glad you're here."

Jace swung hard and missed. A dust bunny from the broom bristles floated down and landed in their bangs.

"How many swings do I get?" Jace asked.

"Two," Leanne called loudly beside Marcy's ear.

"Did you make that?" Marcy asked.

"Yup," Leanne said. "It took a really long time. Do you want to know what it's filled with?"

"Yes," Marcy said.

"It's a surprise," Leanne said.

Jace swung hard again and hit the pinata. The broom dented the fish and it flew into the ceiling but it didn't break. Jace untied the bandana and assessed the damage they'd done.

"I wanted to give other people a chance," they told the room.

"Okay, now Marcy," Leanne announced.

"Oh, I don't have to go," Marcy said.

"Yeah you do." Leanne extended a hand and Jace placed the bandana in it. Leanne stood behind Marcy and knotted the scarf over her eyes. She could still see pretty clearly through the purple haze but she closed her eyes. She felt the buzz of the beer and the warmth of the small crowd around her. Leanne put the broomstick in her hands.

"I don't want to hit anyone."

She heard them shuffling away from her.

"You're good," Leanne said. "You've got room."

Marcy swung and smacked the fish. She felt it crinkle inwards on impact. People cheered.

"Keep going?" Marcy asked.

People cheered again. The first time she didn't care if she made contact but now she wanted it. She swung again and hit it, she felt the pinata swing away from her and heard it hit the ceiling. Something bounced off the top of her head, she opened her eyes under the scarf in time to see the disembowelled fish carcass swinging back towards her. A rough edge of papier-mâché scraped her cheek, caught the bandana and tore it off her face. People were kneeling to collect sample-size packets of makeup from Sephora off the floor.

After the pinata Leanne asked Marcy if she wanted another beer, but Marcy declined because she couldn't spend any more money.

"Are you ready to go?" Leanne asked. "I could leave."

"Are you sure?" Marcy asked.

"If you're ready."

Marcy nodded. Leanne lifted her jacket off the back of a chair and announced, "We're heading out! Have a lovely night!"

It was a big display about how they were leaving together, and Marcy loved it. They walked back to Marcy's apartment. The crowd outside the Glitz were smoking coatless in skimpy strips of pleather and mesh. Probably some kind of queer dance night. She and Leanne made out in the elevator and held hands walking down the hallway.

Sharon and Kathleen's boots weren't on the boot mat, so Marcy knew they were out.

"I don't think you saw my bedroom when you were over before, did you?" Marcy asked, the beer making her bold.

They made out for a long time, rolling over and taking turns pinning each other down. Then Marcy undid Leanne's pants. "You want this?" she asked, tugging down the fly. Leanne nodded and lifted her hips so Marcy could get her jeans off. She flutter-kicked for a moment while Marcy tugged the cuffs over one ankle at a time. Marcy bit her way up the inside of Leanne's legs, holding her hips against the mattress, and then she rubbed her face against Leanne's underwear. When she pulled the fabric aside Leanne clamped her thighs against Marcy's head, holding her there. Everything went quiet with Leanne's thighs pressed against her ears; Marcy was released from all responsibilities besides getting Leanne off. When she came, Leanne's legs pulsed even tighter against Marcy's head before flopping open.

"I want you to sit on my face," Leanne said, her voice sounded especially crisp and clear after the suction-quiet Marcy had experienced between Leanne's thighs.

When they finished having sex Leanne said, "I have to work in like three hours, I'm going to go home and shower."

Marcy nodded, suddenly finding it very hard to keep her eyes open. "I'll see you to the door."

Leanne stood and bent over to kiss her cheek. "You're fine, stay there."

So Marcy stayed.

THE NEXT MORNING Marcy composed a text standing in the bathroom with the frothy head of the toothbrush tucked in her cheek. She could hear Sharon cooking, the screech and clunk of the drawer below the oven. The fridge door slamming shut.

I had a fun time last night, I'd love to hang out again, if you're up for it

Marcy was pleased with the message, it felt warm without being overly eager. She turned the phone face down on the side of the sink, spat and rinsed. She brushed her wet hair in the mirror. She rubbed moisturizer all over her face and then slapped each cheek hard to get the blood flowing.

She looked at the screen once before leaving the bathroom, no reply. But how long had it been? Just seven minutes. Anyway, if it didn't work out, whatever. She crossed the living room in her towel. Sharon was absorbed in combing through a Tupperware of spice packets. Splashes of red sauce were hopping out of a pot onto the stovetop. Sharon often left soups and sauces simmering for the whole day. Marcy would notice the smell of it in her hair and clothes when she was out in the city.

In her room she threw the phone on the bed, face up. As she was getting dressed the screen lit up.

I'm going to Romados with my sister for supper tomorrow night, want to join?

Outside the window a pack of pigeons swooped towards

the ground and shot back up. At the top of the gecko bill-board across the street they dispersed. Marcy smelled sausage frying in the kitchen. The birds were coming together again, they did these loops outside her window every morning, diving vertiginously towards the ground and back up, before flaring apart, then gathering again. Did she have a little catch in her chest? About seeing each other so soon after the second date, about meeting Leanne's family right away? Hard to say, because she interpreted the invitation as confirmation she was good in bed and that made her overwhelmingly happy.

It rained torrentially that night. Marcy got under the covers with all her clothes on and sorted hate speech until her eyes burned. After 700 hate speech phrases she got in her pajamas, made herself some instant ramen, and sat at her desk for a while. Her goal was to reach 1,500 phrases that night, but she closed the browser at 800 after a particu-larly disturbing sentence. She finished her ramen, turned off her lamp, and climbed back into bed without brushing her teeth. The lights above the gecko billboard had come on; they illuminated the sheets of rain washing over it.

6

In the morning it was still raining. The empty ramen bowl was sitting on her desk next to her closed laptop. Brown water gurgled in the gutters, carrying bits of litter along the street. Sharon had been decluttering that week and she'd left a pile of things near the door that she intended to bring to Renaissance. Marcy had offered to post the items on Bunz and Facebook Marketplace instead. She sorted things into two piles, based how desirable she deemed them to be — one for things to be traded, the other for things to be sold. Sharon and Kathleen had been raving the night before and they'd slept most of the day. All through the quiet morning there was this pleasant humming in Marcy's chest because she was probably going to have sex later.

As she gently untangled the strands of a beaded curtain she'd found rolled up under the couch, she remembered sliding her fingers into Leanne's wet pussy. The memory sent a current through her that gathered in her nipples and groin and behind her kneecaps. She backed up and took some photos that didn't quite do the curtain justice. It was made of trails of plastic emeralds on waxy strings. She tried hanging it over the back of the bathroom door. She even made a short video of her hand brushing the strings back and forth; she wanted to show how the light sparkled in the jewels. Natural light would be best, but the sky was navy, rain was still lashing the windows. The type of vertical downpour they never got at home, where the rain was almost always accompanied by wild wind.

She'd planned to do some work in the afternoon, either hate speech sorting or workplace safety captions, but she kept cleaning. She had the kitchen chairs balanced on the table and was swiping mop water underneath when she thought of Leanne taking her by the hips and shimmying her forward until her pussy was hovering over her face. Marcy'd eased down onto Leanne's mouth, bracing herself against the wall with a palm, tilting her pelvis back and forth. She was looking up at the ceiling, seeing and not seeing the ridiculous paint job the previous tenants had left behind, dark purple trim sloppily overlapping the pale blue wall. When she'd lifted up a little, Leanne had pulled her down again, and when she'd said she was about to cum, Leanne had held her hips tighter.

SHARON AND KATHLEEN were still asleep when it was time to leave for dinner. Marcy felt both relieved and disappointed that she didn't have to tell them where she was going. It was early for a third date and especially one with family. As she locked the apartment behind her, Marcy remembered helping Brit load the moving truck. Carrying the heavy furniture had forced them to maneuver their bodies together one last time, and they were gentle with each other when they could have been hostile. Marcy hadn't cried about Brit since she'd moved to Montreal; in that moment it felt like she might but she took a deep breath and pulled it together. She didn't want to look like she'd been crying.

Just as she left the building, the bruise-coloured clouds rolled away. She glided through the bike lanes with music blasting in her earbuds. The sun shone hard at the city and turned the sky from grey to blue for the last half hour before sunset. Leanne lived on Saint-Urbain, just around the corner from Jeanne-Mance Park.

Marcy braked hard at Saint-Joseph Boulevard, making the back wheel bounce. One foot on the curb, she waited for a break that would let her pass through two double lanes of traffic heading in opposite directions. She took her phone out of her back pocket and checked the map, another six minutes to Leanne's place. Then she kicked off and sped through an opening in the traffic, cutting it a little close in the farthest lane. She coasted into an empty Clark Avenue.

A wrought-iron fence surrounded a little stretch of mud in front of the building. Leanne lived on the side of Saint-Urbain that was perpetually in shadows. When Marcy locked her bike to the inside of the fence, the mud rose up to stain the fabric of her sneakers as she fiddled the key in the lock. Finally the lock burst apart, releasing a dribble of rusty water. Marcy looped the U part of the lock through the fence and her frame, then clicked the bar in.

Inside the front porch there were six rectangular mailboxes with glowing doorbell buttons below. Marcy stuck her finger in the one with the label that read *Basement*. Leanne's voice came through the crackly intercom: "Just one minute. I'm coming up."

At first Marcy stood with her hands in her pockets but then she slid her phone out, just to look like she was a person with a life. A tall woman with a Shih Tzu in her arms entered the porch and Marcy pressed herself against the wall to let her pass. The dog was level with Marcy's face and she breathed its kibble breath.

When Marcy stopped making eye contact with the dog, there was Leanne jogging up the stairs towards her. She was wearing a white vinyl jacket with cherry red stripes down the arms. It made her look like a race-car driver.

"Sorry about that, I couldn't pick what to wear, is this too much?"

"I love it." Marcy followed Leanne out of the dark porch.

"Not too flashy?" Leanne did a little spin. Marcy saw she had no bra on under her sweater and thought about their chests pressed together, Leanne's mouth on her neck.

"I have to warn you my sister's a lot, when we're together it can be a lot. Everyone in my family has a temper, if we fight it's not a big deal." Leanne took Marcy's hand. "Do you know what I mean?"

It felt so good to lace her fingers through Leanne's. Streetlights gleamed in every wrinkle of the shiny vinyl jacket.

"Yeah," Marcy said.

Leanne tugged Marcy's hand and they took an unexpected left down an alley. The tall fences on either side were wrapped in vines, the leaves had turned yellow and burgundy. The searing sun following the rain made the air smell of damp vegetation.

"Anyway, she's fun, it'll be fun," Leanne said.

Leanne's sister was waiting for them outside the Portuguese chicken place. Marcy recognized her immediately. They were like twins. Except Claire's red hair was a neat bob while Leanne's was long and loose, full of tangles. Leanne hugged her sister and then stepped aside, presenting Marcy.

"Claire, this is Marcy." It was an unexpectedly formal introduction.

"Nice to meet you," Marcy said and extended a hand.

Claire had fake nails with pointy tips and white half-moons at her cuticles. Marcy noticed a wedding ring.

"Have you been keeping on top of paperwork for the settlement?" Claire asked.

"I'm working on it," Leanne said.

Three guys in soccer shorts and hoodies joined the line behind them.

"Don't talk to anyone on the phone, put everything in an email," Claire said.

"I know," Leanne said.

"Did you sign the form I sent you?"

"I'm going to do it," Leanne said.

"Likely, right?" Claire directed the question at Marcy like they were both familiar with Leanne's shortcomings, and then she asked, "What do you do?"

"Oh, a few things. I edit closed captions on workplace safety videos. They're automatically generated, so there's typos? I just correct them for grammar or like proper names, it often gets proper names wrong, things like that. It's nice because I can do it from home and it's contract-based. There's a lot of work and I can kind of choose how much —"

"That's a rude question, Claire," Leanne cut her off. One of the guys behind them had his friend in a headlock. The pair jostled themselves off the sidewalk and into the bike lane. A mom tugging a toddler in a cart behind her bike had to brake for them. Claire narrowed her eyes at the young man still standing on the sidewalk, her glare making his shoulders curl inwards.

"Guys," he said to his friends; he raised his eyebrows and then shifted his eyes towards Claire.

They apologized, first to Claire and then to the sweating mother, who pedalled on.

"How is that a rude question?" Claire asked, pivoting back to their conversation.

"People's worth isn't determined by what they do to make money. It doesn't sum up who they are as a person," Leanne said.

The line shuffled forward.

"Oh my god, you're such a drama queen," Claire said. "It's called making conversation."

There was a moment of cold silence.

"Should we get a full chicken?" Claire asked.

"I want poutine," Leanne said.

"Okay, we can get a large to share, the portions are huge here," Claire said. "What about you? I'm sorry, I forgot your name."

"Oh no worries, I'm Marcy."

"Full chicken and a large poutine to share?"

"That sounds great," Marcy said.

"And beer, a pitcher," Claire said.

"To start," Leanne said.

"To start," Claire echoed.

Inside the restaurant Claire told Leanne to find them a
table and got in line at the counter. Leanne took Marcy's
hand and led her through the crowded restaurant to a two-
seater in the window. It was warm and loud, people's plates
were piled high and drenched in gravy. A television on the
wall was playing a soccer game.

"Where will your sister sit?"

"I'll get another chair." Leanne left Marcy guarding the
only empty table in the restaurant. Marcy watched her
weave through the room to a couple sharing a poutine.
Leanne put a hand on the woman's shoulder and leaned in
close. She straightened up, one hand still on the woman's
shoulder, the other making a sweeping gesture that took in
the whole restaurant. The couple nodded vigorously, smiling. Leanne carried the chair back to their table. Marcy got
up and was about to head to the cash.

"What are you doing? Sit down," Leanne said. "I'm going
to pee."

"I should offer to pay," Marcy said. "For some of it at least."

"Don't worry about it, she's loaded, sit down," Leanne
said and started back across the restaurant. The couple who
had given her the chair smiled up at her as she passed. Marcy
sat. She was very hungry all of a sudden.

Claire arrived back at the table with the pitcher and three
plastic glasses stacked one inside the next. She set the jug
in the centre of the table and hung her jacket on the back
of the chair across from Marcy. Claire was wearing a silky
white blouse tucked into black dress pants. Marcy pulled
the cups apart and poured three beers, tilting the cups so
only a thin film of foam collected on top. She'd learned that
trick at Destruction.

"How long have you been in Montreal?" Claire asked her.

"Just a few months," Marcy said, sliding a beer across the table to her.

Claire put a tab with a number in the centre of the table. "They're going to call us."

"I didn't mean for you to pay for everything, I don't have any cash on me but I could e-transfer you," Marcy said.

Leanne arrived back at the table and squeezed into the aisle chair. There was only a small space between the edge of the table and her stomach.

"Your girlfriend is insulting me," Claire said.

Leanne ignored her. "Is this mine?" she said and lifted a glass. "Cheers."

All three touched cups. Marcy felt the first sip of beer loosen the blood vessels in the front of her brain.

"That's ours," Claire said. "Leanne? Can you?"

But Marcy leapt up from the table first. "I'll get it."

She swiped the paper off the table. People were crowded tight around the counter and the man behind it was yelling her number in French.

"Me, that's my order." Marcy touched a woman on the shoulder. "Excuse me, that's my order."

The woman moved aside, and Marcy laid her bit of paper on the counter as proof. Lumps of cheese were already turning liquid on top of the thick-cut fries. Beside the poutine, a whole golden-brown chicken. She walked slowly to the table, picturing the heavy load sliding off the tray and splattering on the floor.

"Okay, and we're going to need side plates and forks and knives," Claire said when she arrived back with the tray. "Leanne, why don't you."

"I'm up." Marcy headed back to the counter.

The man behind the counter was yelling order numbers and the people who owned them moved in to collect their trays. He was looking at her, but the orders kept coming and he had to keep yelling them and slapping tray after tray onto the counter.

"Uber Eats?" he asked her finally.

"No, I need side plates."

He pointed at a little station under the TV. There was a stack of clean side plates and two large metal cups holding sets of forks and knives wrapped in paper napkins.

Back at the table Leanne and Claire were finishing their beers.

"Jesus, I forgot your name again," Claire said. "I'm sorry, I'm terrible, I promise it's not you."

"Marcy," Marcy said.

"Drink up," Claire said, filling Marcy and Leanne's glasses.

Leanne unravelled her napkin, letting the cutlery clatter on the table. "This is exactly what I'm in the mood for. Thank you, Claire."

"I'm worried your girlfriend's not going to keep up," Claire said, sipping the second beer.

Leanne edged her side plate under the poutine and clawed some fries onto her plate with the fork. Marcy kept expecting her to explain to her sister that they'd just met but she didn't say anything. Marcy rubbed her knee against Leanne's under the table, gentle like maybe it was an accident. Leanne put a hand on her thigh and squeezed.

"We really need a better knife to cut up the chicken, but I guess we'll just make this work," Claire said and started sawing into the breast.

Marcy drank half of her second beer in one mouthful, with Leanne's warm hand halfway up her thigh. Leanne lifted the pitcher with one hand and swirled the yellow liquid in the bottom before dumping it into Claire's glass. The beer almost overflowed and a fat disc of foam sat on the top.

"I'll get us another." Leanne stood up with the empty pitcher and rocked the table.

"Do you want —" Marcy started.

Leanne put a hand on her shoulder, holding her down in the seat before turning on her heel. Claire lifted a piece of chicken breast across the table, it wobbled for a moment between her fork and knife and then she dropped it on Marcy's plate.

"Take some fries," she said. "So you're a student? At McGill?"

"I'm not in school."

"Oh, so you just do the videos?" Claire asked.

"Right now. I mean I have some other gigs, off and on," Marcy said. "And you?"

"I'm a lawyer," Claire said. "Divorce lawyer."

Marcy finished her beer.

"That must be interesting." All the appropriate things to say were sliding out of Marcy's head. "You must meet lots of interesting people . . . at an interesting time in their lives."

Leanne was back with the beer, she squeezed her stomach in to get in the chair.

"I'm just talking about my work."

"Any rich-people drama to share?" Leanne filled Marcy's glass.

The beer was cold and bubbly. Marcy leaned her knee against Leanne's again.

"I have a client now, she lives out in Trois-Rivieres." Claire pierced a fry that glistened with gravy. "Her husband owns this ferry business."

"You told me this." Leanne filled their glasses again.

"Well, I didn't tell —"

"Marcy," Leanne said.

"Marcy, I know, I was going to say. Anyway, I didn't tell you this part, I just found out today. He was sleeping with the ferry captain."

"A man?" Leanne asked.

"A man," Claire said.

Marcy drank what was left in her cup.

"So what?" Leanne said. Her hand was back on Marcy's knee and her grip was tightening.

"You asked about work." Claire ate a fry.

"That's not why you told it."

"I guess I thought it was funny," Claire said. "Or surprising, I don't know, noteworthy. It's a story, god. Marcy? What do you think, noteworthy?"

"Don't drag her into it," Leanne said.

Marcy was drunk.

"Let her speak, is she allowed to speak?" Claire asked.

Leanne's hand flew off Marcy's knee.

"You always have to be like this." Leanne screeched the chair out and stood up. She hauled her vinyl jacket on and zipped it up.

"Thank you for dinner," Marcy said.

Outside it had gotten bitter cold. There was still a steady stream of people cruising along the bike lane.

"I'm sorry she's such a bitch," Leanne said. "Do you want to come over?"

On the walk back Leanne held Marcy's hand tight.

"I'm not going to let it ruin our night but that really pissed me off," Leanne said.

Marcy noticed a black-and-white cat coming down the alley. Its head was bowed and its shoulders rose and fell quickly, one after the other. Places to be.

"Did you think it was fucked up?" Leanne asked.

"The story?" The cat slowed a little as it passed, it almost brushed against Marcy's ankle. If she were alone Marcy would have crouched and cooed and maybe scratched under its chin.

"The whole situation. She was rude," Leanne said.

Marcy turned her head to see where the cat was going, it'd quickened its pace again.

"It was nice that she paid for dinner," Marcy said.

"She loves stuff like that. It would be ridiculous for us to pay, she'd be insulted."

"Okay," Marcy said.

"She loves it, she loves treating people."

"Do we need anything from the dep?" Marcy asked, hoping to distract.

They were passing a garishly bright convenience store, the door was held ajar with a cinderblock. Marcy stopped.

"More beer?" Leanne asked.

"Or wine?" Marcy said, her hand moving involuntarily to her bloated stomach.

Marcy chose the cheapest bottle of white from a small fridge by the counter. When it was time to pay she tapped the machine with her debit card. She only felt a little guilty because dinner had been free.

"Merci, bonne soirée," Leanne said to the man behind

the counter. The way she said it after Marcy paid was like they were a couple. Marcy's cheeks burned, the beer in her stomach felt bubbly again instead of flat and acidic.

When they stepped outside, the light from the dep made Leanne's hair glow. Marcy held the slippery neck of the bottle of wine in one hand and linked her other arm through Leanne's.

They walked intertwined through the neighborhood. Up the concrete walk that divided the muddy yard, to Leanne's front door. Through the lobby to a steep set of stairs that led down into the basement units.

The building's dryer was thumping outside the door to Leanne's apartment, even though a piece of paper taped above the machine read *PAS DE BLANCHISSERIE APRÈS 20:00h*. Leanne slapped a button on the front of the dryer, and it cranked a few more slow turns before stopping.

"There's a sign," she said, pulling off her sneakers and arranging them neatly on the rug outside the front door. Marcy unlaced her own shoes and set them next to Leanne's. She wondered what Leanne had thought about the chaos of the shoe area at her own apartment.

Inside, Leanne hung Marcy's jacket on a hook by the door. Then she went around the room turning on lamps. She bent to plug in a tall one by the couch, then reached up into the shade of one on top of the fridge. When she was done the small apartment was lit with warm yellow light. There wasn't a lot of space, but it was carefully decorated. There was a framed black-and-white photograph of some trees growing on a cliff above the water.

"Is that B.C.?"

"Yeah, my friend took that, it's near where we grew up."

"Near the ocean."

"Yeah."

"See, that's why we get along," Marcy said.

Leanne walked over and took her by the hips.

Leanne kissed her hard and then led her to the couch. Marcy pushed Leanne down so she was sitting and straddled her. The little side table by the couch got jostled and the lamp tipped from side to side on its metal base, casting strange shadows around the room. Leanne caught the shade before it crashed to the floor. "Shit! Sorry," Marcy said.

"It's fine." Leanne wrapped a fist around Marcy's hair and pulled her back into a kiss. They squirmed against each other on the couch for a long time. Leanne worked a knee between Marcy's thighs and Marcy see-sawed back and forth across it with her ass hanging off the sofa.

Then Marcy got on top of Leanne, one knee down between the cushions and the spine of the couch, the other pressed against Leanne's crotch. Leanne was breathing hard on the side of her face. Marcy moved her knee steadily back and forth in time with Leanne's breath, the couch squeaking with them. She worked her hand up under Leanne's sports bra. Leanne went rigid and tried to get up. Marcy sat back against the armrest of the couch, her hands in the air. "I'm sorry, are you okay? Was that too much?"

"I'm okay," Leanne said.

She tried to read Leanne's face.

"Are you sure?"

"Let's get in bed," Leanne said.

"I can go home."

"I don't want you to go home." Leanne stood up.

"Okay, I mean, or we can just chill out."

"I want to keep fooling around, I just need a minute." Leanne crossed the room to the little kitchen and got a glass out of the cupboard. "You're hot."

"You're so hot," Marcy said. "Did that feel okay? Did I do something that didn't feel good?"

Leanne got a Brita jug out of the fridge. That fall, letters had gone out across Montreal warning people they'd tested the pipes and there were toxic levels of lead in the water. Kathleen had bought the same Brita jug, the cheapest one at Canadian Tire.

"Everything felt good, sometimes I need a minute," Leanne said.

"I shouldn't have put my hand under your shirt. I should have asked."

"No, it's fine."

"Is it because I was on top?"

"I like that, I like it both ways. "

"Okay, just checking, because I only want to do stuff that feels good for both of us." Marcy remembered her date with Laurence and worried she was sounding too earnest, like she'd ripped off an Instagram infographic on consent.

"Do you want to smoke a joint?" Leanne sat on the couch with a glass of water in each hand. Her thighs fanned wide but she didn't press her leg up against Marcy's.

"Yes," Marcy said, more because she wanted Leanne to be at ease than because she wanted to be high.

Leanne opened a drawer in the table next to the couch and pulled out a baggy of weed, papers, and a grinder. "I don't really want the wine right now. Do you?"

"Weed will be nice," Marcy said.

The water felt good. Marcy finished it and got up to pour herself a second glass. She noticed the dish rack was empty aside from one shallow bowl and a lonely spoon in the utensil holder. The neatness put Marcy on edge. She was someone who let things pile up and sprawl.

"Do you want to smoke this in bed? We could watch something."

"Sure," Marcy said. "I could also go home, if you want alone time."

"If you want to go you should go but I'm having a nice time."

"Okay." Marcy followed her into the bedroom. The sheets and bedspread were black and most of the surfaces were bare.

Leanne lay down and balanced an ashtray from the bedside table on her stomach. Marcy lay on her side, propped up on an elbow, careful not to lean against Leanne. She was acutely aware of how little they knew each other.

"Want to pass me the lighter? It's in that drawer."

Marcy found a small Bic and handed it to Leanne. After exhaling three times Leanne passed Marcy the joint.

Being stoned made it easier between them. Marcy curled into Leanne, her face resting on Leanne's chest, one leg over her hips.

"Is this okay? Do you feel okay?"

"I feel good." Leanne put a hand on Marcy's thigh and squeezed.

Leanne's hand was warm and strong and Marcy felt like she could fall asleep. But when her eyes closed, her brain started calculating the money she'd spent that day: she'd taken the metro, and she'd nearly bought a Gatorade she'd thought was on sale but at the counter it turned out to be almost five dollars, so she'd stalled before returning it to the cooler. Leanne's hand moved towards the inside of her thigh, Marcy tilted her face up and Leanne kissed her hard. Suddenly everything went liquid inside her, all the money thoughts dripped out her ear and her mind was calm and blank. Leanne rubbed Marcy's crotch through her pants.

"You like that?" Leanne asked.

"Yeah." Marcy's voice was raspy, and she couldn't tell how much she was putting it on.

"Are you a bad girl?" Leanne asked.

Marcy shook her head no.

"No?"

"I like —" Marcy started. "Well, it doesn't matter."

"What?"

"Nothing."

"I want to know what you want." Leanne took her hand away from Marcy's crotch.

"I like being a good girl."

"You're an obedient little slut?" Leanne asked, her hand pressed firm against Marcy's crotch again.

Marcy nodded, making puppy-dog eyes.

"Okay, undo these pants for me if you're such a good little slut."

Marcy unbuttoned her pants and tugged them down to her knees.

Leanne was stern, like on the roof. "Are you going to let me finger you?"

Marcy splayed her thighs open.

"Wow, I'm lucky to have found such an obedient little slut. What a good girl."

When Leanne wasn't talking she kissed Marcy's mouth.

Every muscle tightened when Marcy came and Leanne kept fingering her until she came again.

"Do you want anything?" Marcy asked.

Leanne shook her head. "I'm good right now."

Marcy fell asleep with her pants around her ankles and a wet spot under her butt.

She knew it was early when she woke up even though there weren't any windows in the bedroom. Leanne was fully clothed beside her, sleeping on her stomach. Marcy pulled her pants to her hips, leaving the fly open, and sat up slowly. She was grateful that the futon mattress was quiet beneath her. She went to the bathroom, stopping on the way to get her phone from her coat pocket. It was 5:45 a.m., what time had they fallen asleep? Definitely before midnight. The small rectangular window in the bathroom was eye-level for Marcy and showed a slice of sidewalk. The front and then back wheel of a bicycle flew by the window. Marcy knew she couldn't go back to sleep. The small, tidy bedroom seemed claustrophobic to her now.

She went back to the bed and lay a hand on Leanne's shoulder. "Sorry, it's early."

"What time?" Leanne was gentle when she first woke up. It had to do with the limpness of her body and a soft tone in her voice, how easily she expressed affection. Later, Marcy would convince herself that sweet sleepy Leanne was the real, uninhibited Leanne. When she was cold and distant, it was just a front for this more genuine version of herself.

"Really early. But I'm going to go."

"Okay. Is everything okay?" Leanne raised herself up on one elbow, blinking at some crust in the corner of her eye.

"I just have a lot to do today," Marcy lied.

Leanne sat up. "Can I kiss you goodbye?"

Marcy leaned in and kissed her.

Outside it was too cold for the jacket she'd worn the night before. The jacket was made to look warm but it was really just a useless shell. She'd got it at the Sally Ann and the tag sewn inside the collar said *Forever21*. It would be worse biking. She could still be curled up beside Leanne's warm body. The little den seemed cozy instead of claustrophobic now that she was out in the cold morning, alone. She felt her phone vibrate in the back pocket of her jeans. A text from Linda.

I think I'm gonna be in Montreal sometime this winter for my sister's bb shower

Maybe we can hang?

Marcy put the phone away without responding. She wasn't even mad at Linda, she just didn't want to think about her or Destruction or about anything that had happened before she left. She certainly didn't want any of it intruding on this new life. She biked home in the cold and got into her own bed with all her clothes on.

THAT EVENING SHE was at the PA supermarket on Parc, marvelling for the hundredth time at how cheap the produce was compared to in Newfoundland, how lush and vibrant and unwilted it seemed, when she felt a buzzing in her pocket. Leanne's name flashed up on the screen. She slid a finger across the smudged glass to accept the call.

"Hi, are you busy?"

Marcy could hear wind on Leanne's end. She turned sideways to let someone pass in front of her with a cart. She tripped towards the produce display and damp fennel fronds brushed her belly. It was a type of supermarket experience she'd never had at home — people darted in front of you or kept pushing their carts right at you, trying to scare you out of their way.

"No."

"Where are you?"

"The supermarket."

"I'm just calling to say hi," Leanne said. "Do you like talking on the phone? We don't have to."

"I guess I haven't done it much recently. I mean except for logistical kind of things," Marcy said. "I used to like it when I was a kid. Or a teenager. I talked on the phone a lot as a teenager."

"What are you getting at the supermarket?"

Marcy realized she needed a basket. "I don't know yet. Where are you? What are you doing?" She walked to the front of the store. An employee was waving people into different checkout lines like a traffic cop.

"I'm walking on the mountain. I just got off work. When I do the early shift I try to go for fresh air and to catch the sunset. But the sun is setting so early now."

Marcy walked beside the line of people waiting to be checked out with the phone to her ear. She crouched at the front of the line — "Sorry, just grabbing this." She swooped a basket out of a stack at the end of a conveyor belt. She was assimilating, getting in everyone's personal space at the supermarket.

"I had a really nice time last night," Marcy said. "Did you?"

She walked towards the back corner of the store, where the breakfast cereals and dried noodles were, mostly because it was a low-traffic area.

"Yeah, it was fun. You know, I don't think we talked about relationship styles? Like are you seeing other people?"

Marcy had anticipated this conversation. Even after having spent only a few months in the city she realized that barely anyone was in a monogamous relationship. Hannah was seeing someone with two partners, and she went on dates all the time. Kathleen met a couple in Verdun for dinner parties where all the guests hooked up.

"Not right now." Marcy tried to keep her voice even. "I've been going on dates but none that really turned into anything."

She felt pleased with this answer. She waited for Leanne to say something, and when she didn't, Marcy said, "You?"

"Not right now but I might want to in the future."

"That's cool," Marcy said.

"Have you been in a non-monogamous relationship before?"

A man came down the narrow aisle holding a pile of groceries against his chest, a bag of frozen peas flopping over his arm. He gestured with his head that he wanted something behind Marcy. She set her empty basket down on the floor and headed for the exit.

"Not really, I've dated a couple people at once but not like full-on polyamory," she said as she passed through the front doors. It felt sort of like a lie and she'd been trying so hard not to lie. Outside it was dark and cold again. She needed to get a real coat.

"How do you feel about it?" Leanne asked.

"I'm open to it."

"Hmmm," said Leanne.

"I just want to have a nice time together," Marcy said.

"Right," Leanne said.

Marcy was walking away from the supermarket, towards the apartment. She could feel a tightness rising in her chest. She said, "Like just being honest and respectful with each other."

"Yeah, me too," Leanne said. "I made it to the top."

"Congratulations." Marcy regretted the little bit of nastiness she heard in her voice.

"Maybe I'll let you go. I'm just going to chill out up here for a bit and collect my thoughts."

"Okay," Marcy said.

"It was nice to hear your voice." That sleepy tone again just before the line went dead.

Now Marcy was closer to home than to the supermarket. She decided to stop at McDonald's and get nuggets instead of groceries. She'd do groceries tomorrow.

7

Falling in love with Leanne was like running into the icy ocean at Beachy Cove at Chris Avery's birthday bonfire. At first, it had been about proving something to the people on shore and to herself. She'd had to immerse herself right away because otherwise she wouldn't do it. She had to run in, let the waves slap her thighs, feel the pain shoot up through her groin. The power of the water slowed her when it reached her hips but there was just a little farther to go before she could dunk her head. She'd come this far. When she was under, she held her breath and made a couple wide strokes with her arms, she kicked her legs, shooting herself out into the bay, eyes squinted against the water. Then up for air, a jolt of pain in her forehead above each eyebrow.

Her friends were huddled around the bonfire and they waved to her. She treaded water and waved back like *Hi, all good out here*. When they called out their voices carried to her, but she wasn't ready to get out. She floated on her back and the salt made her feel more weightless than she ever had before. The waves rocked her and she could feel how massive the ocean was, she could feel the tug of it. She knew she might get carried too far out but she thought fuck it. She'd heard drowning was peaceful. Maybe her friends were calling but her ears were under the water. More and more of her was going numb and it felt good to give in and be carried.

The reason she got out was that she got water in her mouth and started coughing. She tried to stand but there was nothing beneath her. She kicked into the bottomlessness and it was colder. She could feel in her gut that the ocean floor was miles down and there was a kind of darkness down there she'd never experienced.

She started kicking as hard as she could towards her friends. They were tiny and no one was looking at her. Clara White had just arrived with more beer and everyone was cheering for Clara. Marcy's body felt stiff from the cold. Her chest was tight, and her breaths were short but she kept moving. She was shivering so hard she couldn't get her clothes on. Linda had crossed the rocky beach with a towel for her. She let Marcy rest a hand on her shoulder as Marcy struggled to drag her underwear up her wet thighs.

MARCY WOKE UP to a grey sky, hail bouncing off the windows. It took her a moment to remember where she was, that this was her bedroom, that she was in Montreal. She checked the forecast and saw that the temperature would continue to drop all week. She still needed a winter coat. Soon snow would stay on the ground and she would have to give up biking. Hannah was encouraging her to put thick tires on her bike and ride through the winter, but she'd only just begun feeling comfortable weaving through the traffic. She wasn't ready to add the challenge of ice. She ate a bowl of instant oatmeal and waited for a break in the hail. Outside the building she crouched and jimmied the key inside her bike lock for a long time. It refused to come loose. She ran back up the stairs and boiled a small pot of water on the stove, her sneakers and bomber jacket still on.

"Going out?" Kathleen asked.

"My lock's frozen," Marcy told her. "I'm going to pour hot water on it."

"Oh, hang on." Kathleen found her knapsack over by the coats and fished a small bottle out of the front pouch. "Take this, you can have it for the day, I'm not leaving the house."

Marcy turned the white bottle over in her hands: lock de-icer.

"Oh, thank you so much," Marcy said.

She jogged down the stairs with Kathleen's elixir in her fist. A couple of drips greased the insides of the lock enough that it clinked open when she tried the key.

Marcy had been spending pretty much every second night at Leanne's. Leanne never wanted to come to Marcy's because of the soundproofing issue. If they had sex, even quietly, Sharon and Kathleen could hear it through the walls.

It felt like the friendship she'd been building with Kathleen and Sharon was losing momentum because she wasn't there as much to share the minutiae of their days. The last few times they'd invited her out she'd told them she was going to sleep at Leanne's, and now she worried they'd stop inviting her. But she loved waking up with Leanne's arm draped over her. Leanne's arms were big and heavy from kneading pizza dough and her body got hot in the night. Marcy loved wiggling her butt into Leanne's warm lap, feeling Leanne's belly squish against her back. Even though they hadn't been seeing each other that long, it was starting to feel hard to fall asleep without Leanne's body clamped around her.

It was almost the end of November. This would be the last rent payment she could cover with the money from St. John's. The coat would have to be cheap. She had been keeping an eye on the types of winter coats people were wearing. There were some flashy '80s-style coats with geometric shapes and coloured fur on the hood, but there were also a lot of plain black puffer coats. She glided all the way downhill to Complexe Desjardins Mall, hoping for a sale. The bike ride was bitter, cold wind stung her hands and neck. Big flakes of wet snow melted against her face and dripped down inside her shirt.

As she locked her bike on outside the mall, she felt her phone buzzing against her butt. Her mom was calling, the third time this week. She was afraid talking to her mother would dissolve all her determination to stay on the mainland. It would be so easy to go home, sleep on her parents' couch until she found a place. But who could she live with? The only one-bedroom apartments in St. John's were chopped-up townhouses, renovated for oil executives in the early aughts. The oil people left after the crash and the rent on those spots remained exorbitantly high. And where would she work? Who would she hang out with? What if she ran into Brit and her new girlfriend?

"Marcy? You're there?" her mother was yelling into the phone.

"I'm here, I can hear you."

"Where have you been?"

"Just busy, working." Marcy clunked the lock together. "Is everything okay?"

"You got a job?"

"I got some work," Marcy said.

"Excellent, Marcy, that's excellent. Where are you working?"

"It's short-term contract stuff for the university."

"Oh wow, does it pay well?"

"I mean, sort of I guess, but I have to keep looking, it's just short-term."

"Marcy, are you coming home for Christmas? Your father wants to know."

"I don't think so," Marcy said. "I'm just getting settled."

"You know, I've never been away from Newfoundland for Christmas in my whole life," her mother said. "You might be lonely up there, you might think you're fine, but when Christmas Day comes you'll be missing us."

Marcy did feel afraid of that.

"I want to come back in the summer when it's nice," she told her mother. "When I'm a little more settled. I've got to go, I'm at the mall, looking for a winter coat."

"Make sure you get a good one, it gets cold up there. Colder than here."

"I know," Marcy told her. "I love you."

"I love you too, call your mother sometimes."

"I will," Marcy said.

. . .

INSIDE THE MALL she followed a hallway that smelled of donuts to a wide-open plaza. She immediately recognized the fountain Al had told her about. There was purple light shining up through the dimpled surface of the fountain and five jets of water shot twelve feet into the air. Slowly the light beneath the surface changed from purple to blue, the power of the jets gradually subsiding so the streams of water burbled at ten and then nine feet and so on, until they were barely breaking the surface. The lights turned green and jets suddenly spewed water at the ceiling full-force.

Marcy rode the elevator to Winners on the second floor. She stood backwards on the escalator to watch the fountain until the last possible moment. There were lots of people looking for winter coats. Marcy checked the tags of a few puffy black coats and all of them were more than a hundred dollars.

She decided to try the army surplus store. When she googled, she saw it was in the same location as the one she'd been to as a kid. Only a nine-minute bike ride.

The store smelled just as she remembered it. The man working behind the counter asked in French if she was looking for anything in particular. She shook her head no. She saw knives were still displayed in the case at the front where Taylor's cousin had pointed out the one he'd coveted years ago. In the back of the store she found a light blue parka with yellow fur around the hood. The tag said it was good for up to minus forty. The salesman had followed her back there and pointed to a skinny mirror hung between some waffled undershirts and camo raincoats. She took her jacket off and draped it over the coats on the rack. The parka was bulky on her and the sleeves were a bit too long but she liked the fat aluminum zipper. The coat was as thick as a sleeping bag and the lining was clumped in places. She liked the bright orange on the inside. She flipped the hood up and admired the fur against her dark hair.

"Coyote," the salesman told her in English.

At the cash she stuffed her bomber jacket into her book-bag and put on her new coat. She shrugged the cuffs over her knuckles for the bike ride home. When she got to the apartment, she lugged her bike up the stairs to store it at the foot of her bed for winter. After she'd wrestled the bike between the bedframe and the wall, she climbed under the covers and balanced her laptop on her stomach. She looked up flights home next month. They were even more expensive than she'd thought. She slammed the lid of the computer closed.

She picked up her phone and replied to Linda's text.

Would love to see you if you come :)

Right after she sent the message, she slid her thumb back-wards over it and tapped the red garbage can that appeared in its place, deleting the entire thread. She shoved her phone under the pillow. She felt the same sloshing, con-fused guilt as the night she had kissed Linda behind the gas station. Even though this time, technically, she hadn't done anything wrong. When her and Leanne had talked about non-monogamy, Leanne had wanted to leave things open. And Marcy and Linda hadn't spoken much after they stopped sleeping together, but on record, she and Linda were friends. Officially they'd only ever been friends.

Marcy kicked the blankets off, she was suddenly too hot in her fleece pajama bottoms. She stood on the mattress to knot the long curtain and open the window. As soon as she slid the squeaky pane open, the whooshing of cars in the street below, mixed with the shrieks and belly laughs of people standing outside the Glitz, flooded into her bedroom along with light pollution and gusts of wind full of construction dust. She stretched out, coverless, on the bed, welcoming the loud, dirty city into her sanctuary. She didn't have any big feelings for Linda. Linda was easy to be around and she liked having fun, but the things that Linda liked, aside from partying, Marcy didn't get. She liked indoor rock climbing and tabletop role-playing games and French bulldogs. Marcy hadn't even been attracted to Linda before they'd kissed. She could see Linda had a pretty face and she looked good in her clothes but it hadn't stirred anything up in Marcy until they made out that first time. Kissing Linda had made her feel like she wasn't in her own body anymore and sometimes that was a relief.

THAT WEEK MARCY found a gig through the Facebook group Montreal Weirdos Work. She texted a number and arranged to meet someone at an address near Charlevoix metro. The ad offered: *60$ cash to be recorded reading 200 phrases aloud (approx 2 hours)*. It would be her first non-virtual job since the weed cutting.

Marcy took the metro to Charlevoix and used Google Maps to find her way to the address. She watched her pulsing blue avatar travel along the street as she walked. She heard a crack and looked up in time to see an enormous icicle let go and shatter into glittering cubes on the sidewalk across the street. A woman pushing a baby stroller towards the exploded ice stopped and put a flat hand on her chest before carrying on, grinding the stroller's clunky wheels through the glimmering shards. Marcy zoomed in on her moving dot again; there was a turn coming up soon.

She had been expecting an office or some kind of co-working space with a recording booth, but the address matched a house. It was one of a long stretch of identical houses, all of them narrow and short, covered in beige siding, each with a set of steep concrete steps leading to a front door. She couldn't tell if they were expensive, she didn't know anything about the neighbourhood. Thick icicles attached to an overhang above the door were dripping onto the welcome mat.

There was a square of paper plastered above the knob of the front door with overlapping strips of packing tape. *If you're here for recording, please come in and sit on the couch, do not ring the bell, thank you.*

Marcy took her boots off in the porch and sat on a leather couch. She set one foot on top of the other, trying to hide her mismatched socks. Somewhere in the house she could hear the murmur of constant talking. She looked around the room for clues about what she'd been recruited to do. There was a home office with a desktop computer that was at least five years old. There were some books and papers gathered around it, she could only read one spine, *Coding for Dummies*. There was an enlarged photograph of a family gathered in a backyard. Smaller framed photos were clustered around it: a little girl rollerblading at the park, then in a rhinestoned dress and ombre hair, then wearing one of those graduation hats with a tassel on top.

Eventually a woman entered the room from a door behind the couch. She was dressed in jeans and a long grey sweater. Marcy guessed she was in her early forties.

"Hi," the woman said quietly, almost whispering, "So I actually have someone still recording upstairs. But he just has thirty phrases to go."

Marcy nodded.

"So, that'll probably take a little under ten minutes," the woman said.

"I was early, I'm sorry."

"Why don't you take off your coat. Your recording will take about two and a half hours, so you're welcome to use the bathroom over there before you get started. Can you remind me of your name?"

Marcy unzipped her coat and pulled her arms out of it as she introduced herself.

"Okay, great. Hi, I'm Veronica. I just have so many people coming through I can't keep track of all the names. When he's done upstairs I'll take you up and we can do a few run-throughs together okay?"

Marcy nodded. "That's the bathroom, there?"

She didn't really have to pee but she was curious.

It was a small bathroom. A shelf above the toilet was cluttered with makeup and face cream, but also home repair supplies. An open package of deck screws, some Krazy Glue. Marcy picked up a small cardboard box — cat laxatives. She put it back on top of the haphazard pile. She flushed the toilet and washed her hands with scented soap that foamed out of the bottle.

When she left the bathroom Veronica was ready for her. Marcy followed her up a set of carpeted stairs to another home office. There were what looked like a junior high student's school assignments thumbtacked to the wall above a small desk. An iPhone was face up on a stack of three, thick hardcover books, and a recording device was duct-taped to a microphone stand.

"You can have a seat," Veronica said, pulling out a padded office chair for her. "This is a backup mic on the stand here."

She asked Marcy to write her name and sex and home city and phone number with a pencil in a spiral-bound notebook. The pages had puffed from lines and lines of personal information recorded with a pencil.

Marcy sat in the seat and Veronica adjusted the mic for her, then delicately tapped the phone's screen and the words *pool was small and dirty — very disappointing* showed up on the screen.

"You just read what appears on the screen and then click Next. If you read it too loudly or too quietly or too quickly this red light will come on. Then you hit Back, and re-record. So, go ahead." Veronica was warm and encouraging.

"Pool was small and dirty — very disappointing." Marcy felt unexpectedly nervous, she was afraid of tripping over her words.

Veronica hit the Back button. "Too quiet, try again."

"Pool was small and dirty — very disappointing." A green dot appeared on the screen and the next phrase appeared. Marcy found herself looking up at Veronica, craving some approval.

"Go ahead, again." Veronica's demeanour hadn't changed.

"Beds were comfortable, staff was friendly, would recommend." The green light appeared on the screen.

"Great, so you just keep going like that. Are you okay on your own now?"

"Yeah, I think so, thank you."

"Just come down when you're done."

After a hundred phrases the words began to lose meaning. Most of the phrases seemed to be from online reviews of hotels but occasionally there was dialogue from movies or TV shows. Some sentences were political and sounded like they had been lifted from news articles or transcripts of a government meeting. Marcy read the words *Mr. Speaker* several times. Mostly it was about staff and towels and business centres and continental breakfast. There were typos and occasionally there was profanity. Marcy paused before saying "The maid was a bitch." The red dot appeared when she spoke it and she hit Back and read the phrase more clearly.

When she was done Veronica came back in and played a couple of the phrases back. Marcy's voice sounded unfamiliar and unmistakably her own at the same time. Veronica paused the playback mid-sentence.

"Great, do you want to make another sixty bucks?" Veronica peeled three twenties off a folded wad of bills from her pocket and held them out to Marcy.

"I think so."

"I have another, shorter job, just forty minutes."

Veronica explained they would go down to the garage for this one. Marcy would sit in a Mercedes, turn the car on, and speak as clearly as possible over the motor.

"This one is just fifty phrases. Mostly commands like, 'turn on the radio.' You're okay with that?"

"Yeah, sure."

She followed Veronica down the stairs past the living room and then down a second set of stairs. They walked through a basement bedroom, maybe it was Veronica's or maybe it was a guest room. There was a bed covered with a floral bedspread and a matching lamp on a small table and a couple of suitcases pushed up against the wall.

Veronica opened a door that looked like the type of door that sometimes connects two apartments, but it opened onto the garage: a narrow room with a cement floor that smelled of gas. Walking into the garage felt like riding a bike with bad brakes on a busy street; she could get off and walk but she was sailing along, braced for impact. Veronica left the door to the apartment open behind them.

Marcy didn't think she knew what a Mercedes looked like, but she recognized the brand when she saw it. Sleek yet robust with a big, fat grille.

"You can just get in the driver's seat, should be unlocked."

Marcy got in and pulled the door shut, careful not to slam it. It smelled like new sneakers inside. She put her hands on the steering wheel, the cover was made of stiff brown leather.

Veronica tapped the window.

"You see the phone there? Same deal as upstairs, just hit Start."

The phone was mounted to the dash with a hot pink tripod on bending legs. Marcy leaned forward, touched the screen and read, "Start engine."

ON HER WAY back to the metro station Marcy saw Laura, from weed trimming, on the opposite side of the street and waved to her.

They met on the corner under a pack of icicles.

"Are you going to do the voice thing?" Laura said.

"I just did it."

"What did you read?" There were lazy clouds drifting across the lenses of Laura's sunglasses.

"Mostly hotel reviews, like online comments, sometimes it was just parts of sentences," Marcy said.

"Makes sense, it's called the Hotel Project. My friend said 'text Veronica and say you want to be part of the Hotel Project.'"

"There's no waiver or anything. At first I thought maybe it was some kind of university study, like linguistics or sociology."

"No, I think it's AI." Laura said. "Training AI."

"I hope we're not like training drones or some kind of military thing." A drip of icicle water landed on Marcy's forehead and slid down into her eyebrow. She wiped the cold water off her face. It felt refreshing, but it was probably full of pigeon-shit diseases.

"I don't know, that crossed my mind," Laura answered.

Marcy walked back to the station with the bills clenched in a fist in her pocket.

MARCY SPENT SOME of the money from the Charlevoix gig on ingredients for a lemon meringue pie for Leanne. She bought a block of nice butter to use in the crust and filling, and that alone cost almost ten dollars. You could buy a pie from a bakery for less than half of what Marcy had spent on ingredients. What were the chances she'd use ultra-fine sugar again? But she enjoyed squeezing and zesting the lemons, pouring dried black beans onto a piece of tinfoil to weight the crust, setting timers for ten, twelve, fifteen minutes, whisking the filling, beating the egg whites, counting heaping tablespoons of the ultra-fine sugar, watching with the oven light on as the fluffed peaks of meringue browned in the oven.

Marcy had never been the hottest or the most fashionable, she wasn't good at dancing or cooking, she didn't have any particular talent, she couldn't drive. But she felt pretty confident about making people feel loved. She was dependable. She answered her phone, she never cancelled at the last minute. She loved going down on people and she came easily. Usually when people fell in love with her they stayed in love with her.

She walked along Saint-Laurent with the pie balanced on her forearm, toothpicks keeping a sheath of saran wrap from stifling the curved peaks of meringue. She was swinging by Leanne's and then they were getting the metro downtown to watch the *Black Christmas* remake at the Cineplex with Leanne's sister and her husband.

Kathleen's glass pie dish was heavy, Marcy had to keep switching arms. Men in orange safety vests were working in pairs, attaching giant wire snowflakes to the lampposts. Tinny speakers at the top of the lampposts were playing an instrumental version of "Frosty the Snowman." It occurred to her that the annual staff party at Destruction would be happening soon, and she thought about crowding together for a photo with her friends the year before, everyone dressed to the nines and sloppy drunk. The snowflakes ignited all along Saint-Laurent. Marcy hadn't noticed the wire frames were wrapped in twirled strings of white lights. It felt special to witness their illumination. Before long it would be a brand spanking new year.

As Marcy walked down the stairs to Leanne's apartment she could feel snowflakes melting on top of her head, down into her scalp. She kicked her shoes off as she twisted the knob, the pie held high on a flat palm.

"I made you this," she said as she entered the apartment.

Leanne was on the couch bent over her phone. Marcy placed the pie on the table in front of her.

"Wow, you made this?"

"Yeah." Marcy shut the door. "For you."

"For me?"

"Yeah."

Leanne lifted the plastic off the top and balled it in her fist. "Can we eat some now?"

"Of course," Marcy said.

Leanne got a big knife and two small plates from the kitchen area. She kneeled on the floor. "This is very girly of you," she said. "Making a pie."

"I'm girly sometimes." Marcy felt like the comment was meant as an insult but she acted like she hadn't noticed.

Leanne stuck the tip of the knife into the centre of the pie and brought the blade down.

"What did I do to deserve this?"

"I like you," Marcy said. "A lot."

Leanne didn't reciprocate, instead she lifted a slice out of the dish. Marcy saw it had set perfectly. The meringue was tall and the filling was holding its shape.

When they were both reclined on the couch with their plates in their laps Leanne said, "How come you're not going home for Christmas?" The pie's filling was just the right mix of tart and sweet and the crust was flaky. Marcy wanted to ask Leanne what she thought but she restrained herself. The compliment would feel better if it came organically.

"Plane tickets are too expensive," Marcy told her. She nearly said about Linda and about the money, it was in the back of her throat like vomit, when Leanne asked, "Is your family okay with it? Are you close with them?"

"I'm close with them. They're not happy about it. Especially my mom," Marcy said. "Do you like the pie?"

"It's really good. Do they know you're gay?"

"Yeah," Marcy said. "Are you close with your parents?"

"I haven't spoken to them in six years."

"I'm sorry."

"You didn't do anything." Leanne swiped a finger over the plate. "It's nice your parents don't care that you're gay. Like not even a little bit?"

"I guess my mom really wants me to have kids."

Leanne stood up. "We should get going. Do you want to put that in the fridge?"

"It can sit out." Marcy smoothed out the ball of saran wrap that Leanne had left on the table, and she draped the wrinkled plastic over the toothpicks that still protruded from the pie.

SOMETIMES THE STEEP escalator into the metro station, the lack of windows, the dank underground air made Marcy claustrophobic. Other times it filled her with the thrill of the big city; she was a ninja turtle heading to his lair or the no-nonsense career-lady protagonist of an '80s rom-com about to be struck silly with love.

They were meeting Claire and her husband at the theatre. Leanne hadn't said anything about making up with her
sister after the incident at the Portuguese chicken place and
Marcy hadn't asked. Leanne often flared into a rage about
things that didn't seem worthy of it to Marcy. The other day
she'd stormed out of a liquor store after someone cut her
in the line, and she'd smashed a dish when her boss sent a
snotty note saying people shouldn't be giving their friends
free slices. If Leanne's anger wasn't directed at her, Marcy
just let it flutter past.

When Marcy and Leanne arrived, the lobby of the theatre
was crowded with Christmas shoppers. There were posters
for Christmas movies behind glass on the wall.

Marcy spotted Claire across the crowded lobby and they
began shouldering their way through the throngs of people,
many of them holding paper shopping bags that crumpled
against her as she passed.

"Here you are!" Claire held a ticket out to each of them
with a flourish. Claire's husband, Graham, looked a lot
older than her. Somehow Marcy ended up sitting beside
him during the movie. She had to pull her T-shirt up over
her eyes several times to shield herself from the gore on
the big screen. At one point he leaned over and asked if she
wanted to leave.

"I'm okay, thanks," Marcy answered.

"You could walk around the lobby for a bit," he suggested.

It was tempting but Marcy didn't want Claire and
Leanne to wonder where she'd gone. She just nodded
stoically at Graham.

After the film, Graham and Claire drove them home. It'd
been weeks since Marcy had been in a car, and it felt warm

and cozy. She reached across the seats and took Leanne's hand.

"I'm going to tell you what your Christmas present is because actually it involves Marcy too," Claire said.

"Okay," Leanne said.

Claire was looking at them in the rear-view. "I'd like to pay for you two to rent a chalet sometime this winter. Graham and I rented this place in the Laurentians last winter and it was so romantic. I could try to find the link. Or you can find something, there's lots available in the off-season."

"That's too much," Marcy blurted out.

Leanne squeezed her hand hard, making her knuckles scrunch together uncomfortably.

"Let us decide what's too much," Graham said.

Marcy felt like a scolded teenager in the back seat of Graham's car.

"That's such a nice present," Leanne said.

"You like that?" Claire said. "You can borrow my car."

"If Marcy doesn't want to go, maybe I'll bring a friend," Leanne said.

"Bring whoever you want," Claire said. "I'm so glad you're into it."

"It's not that I don't want to go," Marcy said. "It is such a nice gift."

"I bet Heather would go with me," Leanne said.

One of her co-workers at the pizza place. A thin girl with short spiky hair who wore baggy rave clothes.

"You're going to Jean-Talon, Marcy?" Graham asked.

She and Leanne hadn't talked about their plans for the evening yet. Marcy looked at Leanne to see if she was invited over but Leanne was looking out the window.

"Jean-Talon and Clark?" Graham asked again.

"Yeah, thank you," Marcy said.

There was a fresh layer of snow on the ground and Marcy's boots left the only footprints on the building's steps.

WHEN SHE ENTERED the apartment she could tell it was empty just from the atmosphere. Then she remembered Kathleen was working at the bar. Sharon was probably at her studio working on the bassinet she'd been commissioned to make. Without taking her coat off Marcy turned and left the apartment again. She went for a long walk down Saint-Laurent, trying to convince herself she wasn't hoping to run into Leanne. She hated feeling like she'd ruined the evening.

Down by Barfly, where she'd once had a drink with Kathleen, she noticed a sandwich board advertising pay-what-you-can life drawing classes in a second-floor gallery on the following evening. The need to meet people and fill up her life was ripping around in her chest. She missed Hannah. Hannah was working all the time at her new job, and when she wasn't working she was tired from working, or she needed to go to bed early to get up for work. Marcy didn't take it personally, but she still missed her.

Leanne didn't text her at all the next day. Marcy bought a sketchbook and pencils at the dollar store and walked to the gallery, grateful for the long walk because it ate up more of her time.

At the gallery a girl was sitting door with a grey cash box. Her hair was dyed yellow and crinkled into waves with a curling iron or crimper. She was wearing a tight black shirt and baggy black jeans. She had a sharp chin and high cheekbones and big, wet brown eyes. It felt like the girl's beauty was hanging in the air between them, embarrassing them both.

"Five dollars?" Marcy asked, holding the bill out to her.

"Have a seat anywhere." She opened the cash box a crack and crammed Marcy's money into a mess of bills sitting on top of the coin shelf.

Moody French music was playing in the narrow room. There were already a handful of people sitting in twenty or so fold-out chairs set up in a semicircle. A square table in the centre of the room was covered with a white sheet. On top of the sheet there was a dirty cushion with the bottom half of a mannequin laid across it. Marcy sat in a chair facing the mannequin's severed waist. A Black guy next to her was sketching the legs starting from the toe-end. Two girls sitting together in front of her were also drawing the legs — one in a hyper-realistic style, the other was more impressionistic.

Marcy eased her sketchbook out of her knapsack. She flipped it open quickly, ashamed of how bright and brand-new the cover looked. She got out the pencils.

She was trying not to stare at the girl doing door, but she heard someone climbing the stairs to the studio, turned that way on impulse, and was mesmerized by her again.

A white guy came in with a cardboard container of fries, a fork sticking out of the top. He nodded at the girl and walked in without paying. She was sitting sideways with her back against the wall, legs crossed, foot tapping. Would the door girl be the model? Marcy felt guilty for hoping she would be the model. The guy with the fries sat on the windowsill with his coat on. She smelled gravy.

Suddenly a flood of new people poured in and filled the remaining chairs. The girl at the door locked her cash box. She crossed the room, lifted a sheet thumbtacked to the wall and stepped into an expansive space on the other side. It was dark in there. The girl reappeared from behind the sheet seconds later.

"Your model will be out in five minutes," the door girl announced. She settled back into her chair and opened a coil notebook. She arranged a row of pencils beside the cash box. A black cat slinked underneath the chairs, buffing its shoulders against people's dirty boots. Marcy dropped a hand and rubbed her fingers together. When the cat got close she could see specks of white dander in its short hair. It stuck its head into her bookbag and then its two front paws. People smiled. Marcy tried to scratch its back but it hopped out of her bag and made its way towards the guy with the fries.

A woman stepped out from behind the sheet. She was topless and wearing some kind of pinstripe, steampunk-style skirt with a ruffled split in the front. She was plump with curly hair down to her butt and she was smoking a wizened little roach. She looped around the back of the semicircle of chairs, flicking a sputtery lighter and taking quick inhales off the joint.

"This is okay, right?" She raised the roach at the door girl who nodded.

Then the door girl stood, holding a blank pad against her thighs, a sharp pencil between her fingers. She spoke to the room.

"This is our model, Leora —" The door girl paused for applause but there was none, so she continued. "We'll start with some two-minute poses, then a few five-minute poses, then two twenty-minute poses. Is it warm enough in here?"

"It's pretty warm," the model answered. She put the joint out with the bottom of her lighter and hefted the mannequin legs onto the floor.

"Too warm?" the door girl asked.

"Any warmer and I'd be sweating," the model said over the heads of the people seated between them. "It gets hot up here, holding the poses."

"I'll open a window then." The door girl set her pad on the table. She passed behind Marcy's chair and Marcy didn't turn her head. There was the creak of the window opening and then a cool breeze that smelled of wet pavement.

The model stood on the table. She turned her back on the people gathered around her, pressed her fingers into the ceiling and turned her hips. Marcy started with the fingers and they came out as spikes, too narrow at the top and too wide at the bottom. She glanced at the pad of the man next to her. He already had a streaky sketch of the model's whole body and was shading in the ripples of fat on her twisted waist. Marcy tried to emulate the loose strokes he was making and the forearms came easier. The door girl had an alarm on her phone and it shrieked through the room as Marcy was adding a U-shaped dent to an elbow. The man next to her had a whole drawing that captured the pose. Marcy was aware that everyone behind her could see her unfinished torso with its cone fingers, and she curled her body around the pad.

"Two-minute pose beginning," the door girl called across the room.

The model undid her skirt and dropped it on the floor before quickly rearranging herself on the table. Her legs were folded under her and she was bracing herself with a hand against the wall. This time her face was turned to Marcy's side of the semicircle. Marcy was staring at the model's slack face. She looked into her eyes and smiled the kind of smile you give a stranger who's holding a door for you. The model surprised her by smiling back and Marcy realized the model was nervous. There was sweat on her forehead, rising out of the crevice of a wrinkle, ready to drip into her eyes. All the swagger with the joint was to cover up her nerves. The guy next to Marcy held his pencil in front of his face and moved his thumb along it, measuring proportions.

The class was an hour and a half with a fifteen-minute break in the middle. During the break people collected their coats from a rack in the back of the room and left. The model disappeared behind the curtain again. There was a swell of chatter in French and English as people trooped down the steep stairs and out into the night. Marcy stayed in her seat with her closed notebook on her knees, her boots resting in the pool of melted slush they'd left on the hardwood floor.

The door girl was working on a drawing, her head bent close to the page, her pencil flicking quickly. The music seemed louder in the almost empty room. Eventually people trickled back in smelling of cigarette smoke and holding cans of beer from the depanneur across the street. They hung their coats up, found their seats, and fell silent.

The model weaved her way through the chairs to the front of the room where she unzipped her skirt and took it off over her head. She was wearing a pair of black cotton high-waisted underwear.

She balled the skirt up and laid it on a broken chair. Then she climbed up on the table and sat with her legs twisted to one side, back against the wall, hands clasped in her lap. The soles of her feet were dirty from crossing the room barefoot. The guy next to Marcy cracked a beer and foam burbled down the silver side of the can. He tilted his head, put his mouth on the tin and sucked it up.

"Ten-minute pose beginning," the door girl said and pressed a button on her phone.

The tip of Marcy's pencil had worn down and the model's body came out in thick, easy lines. Big swoops for the curves of her belly and butt. For her hair Marcy did a bunch of loose scribbles and this time she put a crease in the corner of her eye that gave the face a little bit of depth. When the timer went off Marcy saw the model glance at her book before rearranging herself on the table. There was something of her there. Marcy's other drawings looked less like her, but sliding her sketchbook into her bag at the end of class she felt satisfied by that one drawing that kind of worked.

People mingled and flipped through their sketches. Beneath the music and voices she could hear sounds from the street coming in through the open window. She got her coat on.

There was a frostbite warning that night and she had an hour-long walk ahead of her, but she didn't mind. She stopped in front of Cinema L'Amour and stepped backwards into the street to take a picture of the neon sign and the garish collage of nude women plastered on the doors below it. A little farther down the street a woman was sitting on a milk crate with a ripped Tim Hortons cup and a cardboard sign on the ground in front of her. Her face was almost completely covered with scarves. Marcy felt the sting of the wind through her jeans as she walked past her with her gloved hands deep in the pockets of her new coat. She passed a hair salon where an old man was sitting alone in a barber chair watching the news on a big-screen TV anchored to the wall. In a restaurant window, chickens were stacked on top of each other on turning spits, their skins glowing golden-brown.

In bed after her long walk home from life drawing, Marcy decided to call Leanne. They hadn't spoken since the car ride after the movies. First she made her bed and dripped CBD oil down the back of her throat. She closed one curtain so she wouldn't have to look at the smug gecko, but left the other open so she could watch the planes descending as they approached the airport. Sometimes Leanne didn't pick up when she was annoyed, but this time she picked up on the second ring.

"Are you busy?" Marcy asked. "I'm just calling to say hi mostly."

"I'm just getting some laundry together, the washer is broken so I have to go to the laundromat." Leanne sounded happy to hear from her. Marcy had thought there was an argument on the horizon, but now it didn't feel that way at all. She'd fabricated all this tension and loneliness on her own. That was the problem with big swaths of time to yourself.

"I went to a life drawing class," Marcy said. "It was really great."

"Cool," Leanne said.

"I sort of wanted to ask you something," Marcy said. "About non-monogamy."

"Okay."

"I guess, are you seeing anyone?"

"No, not at the moment."

"But you want to?"

"Not at the moment, no."

"Okay, me neither," Marcy said.

"We should look for a chalet with a hot tub," Leanne said.

Marcy felt relieved that she was still included in the trip. She scrolled through chalet listings on her laptop and read the descriptions to Leanne. She had planned to explain about Linda maybe coming to visit; that even though they'd had a thing, it was over and this visit would be totally platonic. But a pleasant sleepiness was slowing Leanne's speech and Marcy didn't want to spoil it.

FOR CHRISTMAS MARCY decided she'd make the lemon meringue pie again, this time for her and Hannah. Sharon and Kathleen had gone home to Saskatchewan for the holidays and she had the apartment to herself. Leanne had driven an hour and a half outside the city with her sister to have Christmas with Graham's family.

In the morning Marcy called her family. All the cousins were at her parents' house and there was a chaos of shrieking interspersed by a new toy fire truck's siren. When she got off the phone she did feel a bit sad and lonely but she didn't cry. She poured a bath and sprinkled some of Sharon's lavender Epsom salts in the water. As she was soaking, her phone dinged on the floor. She reached a wet hand over the side of the bath and picked it up. A text from Linda.

Hi happy xmas, hope you're doing good up there I'm booking a ticket to MTL to see my sister in Feb, looking forward to seeing you :)

Marcy dropped her phone onto the bathmat. She stood and unhooked her scratchy beach towel from the back of the door. She resented Linda messaging her on Christmas Day, when she was feeling all lonely and vulnerable. She wished she'd never responded to her message about a visit in the first place.

She left her phone face down on the bathroom floor and went to look through the linen trunk for a tablecloth. She found one with yellow daisies embroidered along the hem.

Then she got to work on the pie. As the crust browned and the filling set she put Linda out of her mind and started to feel excited about spending the evening with Hannah, who was bringing roast duck.

Marcy put two candlesticks and a bottle of wine on the table. Hannah arrived with the duck in a deep pan covered with tinfoil and they heated it in the oven. There were six chairs at the table and Marcy set two spots next to each other. Hannah made the gravy. Marcy liked the way Hannah opened the cupboards and took the things she needed as though it was her own kitchen.

8

The chalet they decided on was a cabin three hours outside of Montreal; they would go for a weekend with two of Leanne's friends from work at the pizza place, Heather and Alice. In Quebec everyone called cabins *chalets* — Marcy liked how extravagant it sounded but she couldn't bring herself to say it yet. She had found the listing, she'd picked it because of the hot tub and the pictures of people lighting a fire in a snowy pit beside the cabin. There was a photo of a group of deer standing on the frozen lake. Marcy had never seen a deer in real life; they looked like a sleeker version of moose.

Leanne was driving and Marcy sat up front with her. They'd meant to leave in the early afternoon but they'd spent a long time at the supermarket picking up wine and beer and ingredients for a shakshuka. Leanne had packed a cast-iron frying pan, a stovetop espresso maker, and a couple small glass bottles of spices. It made Marcy feel so in love when she opened the trunk and saw those things neatly packed in there.

It was four o'clock by the time they got on the road.

They crawled along Saint-Laurent Boulevard towards the highway. Marcy didn't know this part of the city. They passed a used sporting goods store with at least a hundred mismatched skis attached to the outside like weather stripping. A woman was leaving with a pair hoisted over her shoulder. The conversation in the car had turned to job-hunting. Heather had emailed a carefully composed cover letter for a job where you got paid by the hour to sext, as a side gig to supplement her income from Pizza Dream.

"Are you yourself?" Alice asked her.

"No, they pick a random photo of some skinny model from a gallery on the website."

"And you say like, 'I'm touching myself'? Is there a script?"

Heather sighed. "I guess I'll find all that out, if I get it."

"Sounds like a sweet gig," Alice said.

"If I get it," Heather said.

They passed a business that did lighting and special effects for movies. The building had a gabled roof, and a hand-painted sign hung on chains from an elaborately carved wooden balcony above the front door. It looked like a haunted house from *Scooby-Doo*. Multicoloured lights splashed all over the house and strobes pulsed in the windows.

"A lot of Anglo queers do landscaping," Leanne said.

"Yeah, my ex did that," Heather said. "It's a sweet gig if you're strong. It was nice 'cause they worked mostly with friends but it is physically demanding."

"What about the thing where the government pays you to learn French, is that real?" Heather asked.

"Not really," Leanne answered.

"Yes it is, I know someone who did it," Alice said.

"I mean it exists, but they don't actually pay you enough to live, considering how much rent is going up. It's like forty hours a week and you're only allowed to work a certain number of hours outside of that anyway," Leanne said. "Unless it changed."

Marcy nearly backed Leanne up about the French program by saying Hannah had told her the same thing when she'd asked about it, but Leanne seemed annoyed whenever Marcy mentioned Hannah so she kept it to herself.

They stopped at a McDonald's drive-thru in a suburb outside the city and ate in the parking lot. Leanne passed the tray of drinks to Marcy so she could distribute them to everyone in the back seat. Marcy loved moments like that, where she got to be the girlfriend in front of Leanne's friends. The car filled with the smell of warm grease. Marcy had ordered a large milky coffee that she slipped into the cupholder.

The cabin was deep in the woods and the GPS stopped working as they were driving along a narrow, snow-covered road in the bulky minivan.

"Does this have snow tires?" Marcy asked.

"Stop talking," Leanne snapped. "This is dangerous."

Everyone was silent until they arrived at a mailbox on a numbered post.

"This is it." Leanne put the car in park and leaned over for a kiss. Marcy resisted the urge to pull away. It was the first time Leanne had used that sharp, condescending tone with her in front of other people. She used it when Marcy did stupid things like leaving her bike unlocked in front of the dep or forgetting to put detergent in with the laundry. Leanne's aunt had died of lung cancer and when Marcy

accepted a cigarette someone offered her outside NDQ
Leanne had lectured her the whole icy walk home from
the bar in that exact voice. Marcy didn't mind it that much
when it burst out of Leanne in private, but in front of other
people it felt like a betrayal. She kept her distance from
Leanne as they crunched through the snow to the cabin. She
didn't want Leanne wrapping an affectionate arm around
her waist or trying to hold her hand.

The cabin was better than the pictures. The vaulted ceiling with exposed, lacquered beams was higher than she'd
expected. It smelled of sawdust. There was a cast-iron stove
with a pile of junked wood stacked neatly beside it. In the
kitchen a wall of windows faced a stretch of lawn that slid
down into a snow-covered pond. Each of the three beds
was covered with a homemade quilt. Marcy didn't want to
be mad at Leanne anymore.

"This will be so beautiful in the morning," she said to
everyone. "I'm going to check out the hot tub."

"Right now?" Leanne said.

"Yeah, then we can get in and drink a beer."

"It's dark," Leanne said. "I think Alice wants to play
cards."

"I'll just make sure it's filled up and ready for tomorrow." Marcy was getting in the tub that night, whether other
people wanted to or not.

When the tub was filled, she went back into the house
and took two beers from the fridge. Everyone was gathered
around the table playing cards. She skulked back out to the
garden with her cans, grateful that no one had noticed her.

She turned on the jets and the surface of the water burbled. It reminded her of the Desjardins fountain.

Halfway through her second beer, her eyelids got heavy. She recognized the feeling. Usually, falling asleep took a special kind of concentration; if she thought about how much she wanted to be asleep she couldn't get there. Now sleep dragged her down like an undertow.

For some reason, looking out at the frozen pond — here they'd call it a lake — she was thinking about her grandfather. Later in life he'd become a real estate agent but she knew that when her dad was small her grandfather had been a land surveyor. That was why he could draw precise plans with bits of neat math all around them on sheets of graph paper. Plans for the cabinets her grandmother wanted and a dog house her cousin wanted and the deck her aunt wanted. Plans that led to sturdy structures that continued to store or house or support for years after he'd passed away.

The eyelid thing was happening and also a pleasurable weightlessness in her body, maybe she was floating. She knew it was wrong to indulge it, just like when Leanne had wanted her to stay awake until the end of *Midnight Cowboy* but she'd let herself slide into unconsciousness.

The *Midnight Cowboy* night had been a rare night, when the two of them stayed at Marcy's. That afternoon, before Leanne came over, Marcy had borrowed Kathleen's hockey skates and spent a few hours looping around the duck pond at Jarry Park. When she'd arrived the pond was packed with children and teenage couples holding mittened hands. A bunch of men in jerseys were shooting a puck through the crowd, sending up sprays of ice when they ground to a stop just before crashing into someone.

For the first fifteen minutes on the ice, Marcy had been very aware of how stiff her body felt. She thought about her centre of gravity and clenched her stomach muscles to steady herself. Every time she tripped on a fissure or hump in the ice her stomach swooped. But after a half hour, she was weaving between people in a hypnotic trance. She never wanted to go back to shoes, to the awkward business of lifting and lowering her feet. It was one of the times when being on her own made her feel insanely lucky instead of lonely. The sun set behind the dried willows that ringed the pond, and families started plunking themselves down on the lip of the rink, parents leaning over to loosen the children's skates. Marcy was making a deal with herself, one more trip around the pond and she'd go home; the tips of her ears were stinging and her phone had died from the cold. But then she noticed a young guy who must have come down the ramp installed at the north end of the pond. He was wearing a lime green puffy vest over a fuchsia waffle-weave long-sleeve shirt, and a bedazzled trucker cap. He was skating backwards down the centre of the pond and he was going hard. Marcy noticed that his bright yellow headphones were plugged into a Walkman clipped to the back of his pants. He leapt into the air and twirled like a ballet dancer. When he landed he raced backwards and then spun himself into a blur in the centre of the pond. The hockey players gathered their things and left. Soon it was just Marcy and the figure skater in the dark. She kept circling the edge of the pond, slow and steady, completely transfixed by the glamorous skater. Every so often a plane flew overhead, close enough she could hear the engines.

When she got home her fingers were stiff from the cold and it was hard to unbutton her pants to pee. Her cheeks were burned bright pink by the wind. Sharon and Kathleen were getting ready for an early show at Casa and she had to wait for them to finish with the bathroom (Sharon lining her eyes and Kathleen gelling her hair) before she could take a hot shower. The water made the skin on her thighs prickle back to itchy life. She heard her phone vibrating on the counter in the kitchen where she'd plugged it in when she got home. She read the text in her towel, hair dripping on the kitchen floor. Leanne was coming by for a movie. Marcy's legs were aching and she felt exhausted.

When Leanne arrived she rolled them a joint while Marcy set up the projector and found the adaptor for her computer.

"Rhinestone Cowboy?" Marcy asked, typing.

"*Midnight Cowboy*. 'Rhinestone Cowboy' is a song." Then Leanne sang, "Like a rhinestone cowboy."

"Right," Marcy said, scanning for the file with the most seeders. "Got it!"

Leanne lit the joint and a curl of smoke caught in the projector light. Marcy hopped over the back of the couch, yelping from the flare of pain in her legs and lower back, and landed close to Leanne who lifted the blanket draped across her lap, inviting Marcy to share. Marcy fell asleep almost immediately. Leanne kept shaking her shoulder and asking, "Are you asleep?"

"Not really," Marcy would mumble.

"I came over to watch this movie with you, I've seen it before."

"I know, I'm watching," Marcy said. "He's living with the guy from the bar?"

"I'm not answering that. Move over."

Marcy sat up and straightened her legs out in front of her, exhaling slowly from the pain. She tried to focus on the movie — it was some kind of psychedelic party scene.

"Is that supposed to be Andy Warhol?" she asked.

"Yeah."

Marcy's eyes closed all on their own again. When she startled awake the credits were rolling, and when she asked what had happened in the movie Leanne refused to tell her.

"I'm going home."

"Don't go home," Marcy said.

"You just slept through our time together. It was rude."

"I'm sorry, I just overdid it skating."

"Whatever." Leanne slammed the door when she left.

Leanne always got the last word.

Marcy pressed her spine into the bubbling jet of the hot tub. The walk back across the lawn would be cold. She would have to tell everyone she'd got in without them. She realized she wasn't looking at the stars or the pond anymore but at the lip of the hot tub.

When Marcy's grandfather was a land surveyor, he was supposed to get on a small plane with three or four other men to survey a remote place in central Newfoundland. For some reason he didn't get on the plane. He'd messed up the date or the time, which was not like him. He was punctual and organized. He wrote the grocery list in capital letters on grid paper, each letter occupying a single box. The plane had crashed and it wasn't found for thirty years.

The hot tub liner was made from thick beige plastic speckled with blue dots. She concentrated on it. She reached for the railing and held on. She wanted to pull herself up but her limbs were full of pins and needles, the cold air stung her skin. She was facing the pond — she tried to hold the rocky shoreline on the opposite side of the pond in place. In Total Sculpt Toning class the instructor told them focusing on one spot helped you maintain your balance. There was a line of rocks and a second line of transparent rocks that hovered around it. A pixelated wave of darkness unrolled in front of her eyes and she held the metal rail, surrounded by nothing.

Her uncle had told her that as soon as he heard they'd found the plane, he knew he had to go see it. He'd just met Kate, who he later married. He and Kate drove out to see the plane on one of their first dates. Kate worked at the Dominion by his house and he came to pick her up after her shift. He drove up to the back door of the supermarket on his snowmobile. They drove out to the charred plane skeleton in puffy snowsuits, the sun setting behind the metal carcass.

The first thing she felt when she came back to the world was the cold air against her exposed skin. Then a sting on her cheek. Someone was slapping her face. She was standing in the hot tub. Leanne was standing in the hot tub in her pants and boots holding Marcy up. Leanne took her chin.

"Can you hear me? Marcy?"

Marcy could hear the fear in Leanne's voice and it felt so good to know she cared about her. Leanne said her name one more time before Marcy managed to nod.

"We have to get inside, okay?" Leanne said. "Just lean on me, your boots are there, you can step into them."

She knew Leanne wasn't strong enough to carry her.

"I'm okay, I got it."

That night they made a bonfire in the snow and cooked sausages with liquid cheese injected into them. Marcy drank three tall cans and then she and Leanne had sex in the bottom bunk. They took turns holding an open palm over the other's mouth, sternly whispering "Shut up." Afterwards Marcy rubbed her cum-covered face in the sheet and they both giggled, high from their respective orgasms. When they held each other, naked under the heavy quilt, Marcy thought again about telling Leanne about Linda, and the bar, and the whole mess in St. John's. She could start by just telling some parts of it. She didn't want to ruin things by not being able to tell the truth. Leanne's head was on her chest, between her collarbone and her breast. Marcy smoothed her hair.

"A friend of mine is coming to visit," she said.

Leanne made a small, sleepy noise that lifted like a question.

"Oh, nothing," Marcy said, trying to give into the calm. Maybe she didn't even need to mention the visit, it was just a friend passing through town.

MARCY FOUND THE entrance to Hannah's work between a Frank and Oak store and a vegan restaurant with a sandwich board out front advertising 23 types of smoothie. The lobby had a small coffee shop, and a television above the counter was playing CBC News. The text at the bottom of the screen said *Six arrested at Wet'suwet'en anti-pipeline camp*. There was a still image on the screen of two huge white men in bulletproof vests with POLICE in bold on their chests and weapons strapped to both sides of their hips, holding an Indigenous woman dressed in a parka. Then footage of a white newscaster, with the text *Coronavirus in Wuhan, China* scrolling beneath her. There was a family trying to come back to Canada. There was glitchy footage of the mother on webcam. The closed-captioning was full of strange typos but Marcy understood that roads into and out of the town were being shut down. It was still a few more minutes before Hannah could take her lunch break so she stood and watched the silent news. A medical expert was saying people didn't need to be alarmed yet but that the possibility of the virus spreading within Canada couldn't be ruled out.

When it was time to go upstairs Marcy crossed the marble lobby and saw her reflection in the shiny elevator doors. She rode four floors up. The office was open concept and separated from the hallway by a floor-to-ceiling glass wall. She saw Hannah at her desk, typing furiously. Marcy pulled open the door and a young guy with a clipboard turned to her.

"I'm just here to see Hannah." Marcy hoped she wasn't getting Hannah in trouble. Maybe she should have waited in the hall.

"Oh cool, no problem, right over here."

Marcy followed him across the room until they were both standing behind Hannah. Her screen was full of strings of letters and symbols, random punctuation spliced in all over the place.

"Hannah," the guy said gently. "There's someone here to see you."

Hannah stiffened and twirled around her chair.

"Oh, this is my friend Marcy. We're just going to take lunch." Hannah looked at the screen again, checking the time. "If that's okay."

"Totally," the guy said. "Nice to meet you, Marcy."

Marcy shook his cold, clammy hand and smiled wide on Hannah's behalf. She stayed quiet as they crossed the office to get Hannah's coat from amongst the Gortex jackets and pea coats hung on the wall.

In the elevator Marcy asked, "Is that guy your boss?"

"Sort of, he's like a supervisor but they don't use that word. It's supposed to be very chill and woke and everyone's-a-family type of vibe. Which is so stupid, I have a family thank you."

"He looks like fifteen."

"Everyone's younger than me. Do you mind if we eat at that place downstairs, I just don't have that much time."

"I'm not really hungry, I'll just sit with you. Is it okay that I came in to your work?"

"I think it's fine."

At the restaurant Hannah got lentil soup and a side of thick brown bread. Marcy was planning to make a tuna melt when she got home. If she was going to eat out it wouldn't be this bougie-hippie lentil soup.

"Did you see about this respiratory thing in China?"

Hannah shook her head no while she blew on her soup.

"I saw it on the news in the lobby. There's a couple who's stuck there because they like shut down the roads and stuff. They're quarantining the village or town."

"Oh yeah. I saw some headlines about it."

"It sounds like *28 Days Later*," Marcy said.

"I didn't read the article. Oh hey, I'm going dancing with some friends next weekend, for Valentine's Day. Want to come?"

Hannah hadn't introduced Marcy to any of her other friends yet. It felt like a debut.

"Yes! I'd love to," Marcy said. "Can Leanne come?"

"Oh, I get to meet Leanne. Sure, of course. And you

can meet Shawna and Miriam — two of the people I'm dating."

"It won't be weird, if they're both there?"

"No, we're at the same things all the time. It's nice," Hannah said. "It's the Sunday of Valentine's weekend."

"You could really go out every night here if you wanted to," Marcy said.

"Well especially Valentine's weekend. But yeah, in general you're right, it's dangerous."

"I'm surprised you like Valentine's Day," Marcy said.

"Why?" Hannah asked.

"I thought you'd be all like 'it's a made-up capitalist holiday.'"

"I mean sure, but capitalism infiltrates literally everything. I love seeing people walking around with heart-shaped balloons and flowers. All these earnest declarations of love."

"I like it too," Marcy said. "And you don't have to spend money."

"Exactly, you can go dancing," Hannah said. "Okay, I think I better go back to work."

"Going dancing does cost money, usually."

"True." They both stood and Hannah hugged her. "Like I said, it infiltrates everything."

Marcy rode the elevator up to the fourth floor so she could spend another few moments with Hannah.

THAT NIGHT MARCY met Leanne at the pizza shop at the end of her shift. Leanne stepped outside when she saw Marcy coming up the block through the restaurant window. Alice waved at her from the cash. There was white flour in Leanne's red hair. When they kissed Marcy's cold nose pressed into Leanne's warm cheek. They had planned to walk to Leanne's, get straight in bed, and stream episodes of the new *L Word*. Leanne's co-worker Heather was hosting screenings of the remake at NDQ every Thursday, where people yelled at the screen. Neither of them had seen any of it yet and Leanne wanted to catch up before the next screening.

Marcy took Leanne's mittened hand into her own as they rounded the corner onto Saint-Laurent. "Hannah invited us dancing on Valentine's weekend, would you want to do that?"

"Where? What kind of dancing?"

"I don't know. Her friend is DJing and there's like three other DJs, I think."

Leanne shook her hand out of Marcy's and slid it into her pocket. "You don't know what kind of music?"

"Dance music, electronic music I guess."

"There's a lot of kinds of dance music, Marcy — is it techno? Is it a queer party? Is it a Queb party?"

"I think she said the bar is in the Plateau."

"I didn't know you like dancing."

"Want to take a side street? This wind is brutal." Marcy veered towards an alley but Leanne kept walking into the wind, so Marcy dashed back to her. "I just thought it'd be fun to go with Hannah and her friends. For you to finally meet Hannah. And it's the Sunday, so we could have our own, like private date on Valentine's. We could make dinner or we could go out, if you want."

"I don't care about Valentine's Day," Leanne said. "I definitely don't want to go out for Valentine's dinner. That's so weird and boring and straight."

"Okay, but would you want to do the dancing thing?" Marcy knew she was pushing her luck.

"You should do whatever you want," Leanne said. "It was rammed at work tonight, I think I'm going to be too tired to watch the show."

"Yeah, I'm tired too," Marcy said.

When they got inside Leanne unzipped her coat and dropped it on the floor. Marcy picked it up and tucked the hood onto the hook on the back of the door. She draped her own over the back of a chair. In bed Leanne didn't hold her.

Marcy couldn't sleep so she got up and quietly rolled herself a joint, sitting on the edge of the couch. Leanne's weed was strong and she woke up at five in the morning, curled on the couch, feeling foggy. She thought about putting on her boots and leaving without saying anything. Make Leanne wait around for her to call for once. But then Leanne spoke from the bed, her voice sweet with sleep, "Did you sleep over there?"

Marcy was standing between the couch and the door in her underwear and a T-shirt, looking at her boots. "I couldn't sleep so I smoked some of your weed, I hope that's okay, I'll get you back."

Leanne lifted the covers. "Come here."

Marcy climbed into the warm bed and Leanne wrapped an arm around her and pressed a flat palm against Marcy's chest just above her breasts. Marcy shut her tired eyes and squirmed backwards into Leanne.

. . .

MARCY AND LEANNE took the metro downtown for a demo in support of Wet'suwet'en hereditary chiefs fighting the pipeline Justin Trudeau was trying to push through unceded Wet'suwet'en territory. Hannah had told her about the demo but wasn't able to go because of her job.

They arrived late and had missed the speeches. The crowd was already moving slowly south. People held hand-painted signs that said LAND BACK, WET'SUWET'EN SOLIDARITÉ and SHUT DOWN KKKANADA. Cop cars were parked along every street, blocks of cops in riot gear marched along the side-walks on either side of the crowd. A brigade of cop cars brought up the rear and two rolled slowly in front of the crowd, boxing in people walking with a banner that read NO PIPELINES STOP RCMP INVASION ON INDIGENOUS LANDS. As they got deeper into downtown, people began dispersing into smaller groups.

Word spread through the crowd around Marcy and Leanne that cops were spraying tear gas two intersections over. A truck with a loudspeaker on the roof crawled up a side street, a robotic voice repeating in French and then English, "This is now an illegal protest, disperse or you will be arrested." The people around them glanced at each other.

Two cops stepped off the sidewalk and grabbed a young guy with long dark hair who was walking a little ahead of Marcy and Leanne. They pulled his arms behind his back and started dragging him backwards towards a cop car. There was yelling. Some people recoiled and others surged towards the cops. The cops were shouting in French and blowing loud whistles. People begged them to let the young man go, they were hurting him. Marcy and Leanne moved to the edge of the crowd and Leanne asked, "What do you want to do? You want to leave?"

"Maybe," Marcy said. "Do you?"

"Yeah, let's go."

On the metro Marcy rested her head against Leanne's shoulder. They'd been allowed to just walk away from the demo. Regular life was rolling onwards for them while the guy who'd been dragged off ahead of them had been hauled into a nightmare legal situation that would at minimum last months and probably cost tons of money, not to mention the horror of whatever was happening to him right now.

"I've never really been to a protest like that," Marcy said.

"Like what?"

"The cops don't use tear gas in Newfoundland. I mean not at any protest I've been at."

"Quebec cops have an enormous budget. That's the kind of shit they spend it on. They're some of the most violent police in the country. And there's all kinds of evidence about like, systemic racism in the force and stuff."

"There's lots of corruption in the RNC, the cops in Newfoundland. Like, just before I left there were a bunch of cases in the news of them trying to cover up police violence. They murdered an elderly disabled man in his own home because of an incoherent tweet that could have been interpreted as 'threatening a politician' but it was really, like I said, incoherent. They shot and killed him. Then they moved stuff around at the scene to try and cover it up. An on-duty cop raped a girl who asked him for a ride home because she was too drunk to walk and the cops showed up in droves to the courtroom to defend him. There's tons of that kind of thing. But people don't really get arrested for protesting there. In Labrador, where there's a much bigger Indigenous population, it's a different story."

"Did you hear them chanting 'get a real job' at the cops?" Leanne asked her. "I love it when they do that one."

WHEN THEY GOT back to Leanne's she heated up canned soup for them. Marcy's feet were cold, and she tucked them between the couch cushions.

"Can I show you something?" Leanne flipped her laptop open. She pulled up a Kijiji ad for a '70s-style van. "I'm trying to buy this." Leanne started clicking through the photos. "Look, I love the curtains."

"Are you really buying that?" Marcy had seen the headline at the top of the ad, which included the price: $6,000.

"I didn't tell you about my settlement?"

"No."

"I got hit by a car on a crosswalk and the guy kept going."

"Holy shit. When?"

"Like seven years ago. My sister's been helping me with it. But the money is supposed to come through soon. Maybe next month. I hope it does because I really want this van, it's exactly how I've been picturing it."

"Were you hurt?"

"He broke both my legs."

"Fuck."

"Yeah, it was really shitty, but now I'm getting this van."

"Where will you park it?"

"I'm going to leave."

"What do you mean?"

"That's the point of the van. I'm just going to drive around for a while. Do you know iOverlander? Here, look."

Leanne swung the computer screen towards her. There was a map of Quebec covered in numbered circles glowing yellow and green. "These are informal campsites. You can pick from all these different options depending on what kind of amenities you need. It'll show you places you can park overnight and sleep without getting a ticket, Walmart parking lots and stuff."

Leanne clicked an icon of a camera and a window popped up with the heading *Tourist Attraction: Abandoned Mining Town*. She clicked again and opened a photo of a plaque on the side of a dusty road.

"That's actually a cool spot. See, I need to start writing this stuff down," Leanne said.

"How long are you going for?" Marcy asked.

"I don't know, my lease will be up, I might not come back."

Marcy felt like her lungs had been shrink-wrapped. "When?"

"The lease? July first."

"What about your stuff?"

The two of them looked around the apartment.

"This sofa is nice," Marcy said, compensating for the wobble in her voice with forced practicality. "Maybe you could sell it."

. . .

THE NIGHT OF the Valentine's dance party Marcy stopped by
Leanne's work. When it wasn't busy Leanne would sometimes come outside, so they could stand near the dumpsters
and recycling bins in the alley behind the restaurant, to chat
and kiss in private for a few minutes with the smell of fresh
pizza blasting out of a vent above their heads.

But it was very busy at Leanne's restaurant on Valentine's
weekend Sunday. Marcy edged her way around the people
trying to get to the counter so she could wave to Leanne,
who was dropping translucent slices of soppressata onto
a pizza. One of Leanne's co-workers tapped her on the
shoulder and pointed to Marcy. People were glaring at
her, thinking she was trying to cut the line. Marcy's coat
was damp and the fur smelled like wet dog. When Leanne
looked her way Marcy blew a kiss and Leanne nodded
before turning her attention back to the pizza. Marcy shuffled across the greasy floor and back out into the cold. She'd
wanted to remind Leanne she was going dancing but now
she wouldn't have a chance.

Marcy had scrounged change for the bus from the bottom
of a jar filled with thumbtacks and guitar picks and bits of
beach glass that had been in her room since she'd moved
in. She kept the change inside her mitten as she waited for
the bus.

Hannah was smoking outside the bar in a black puffer
jacket with a glossy, iridescent sheen that created oil-slick
rainbows every place it wrinkled. She was standing with
two girls in high-heeled boots and plainer black puffers.
Shawna and Miriam, Hannah's lovers. Hannah introduced

Marcy and they all hugged each other. Marcy had been noticing that everyone in Montreal hugged anyone present when they showed up somewhere and hugged every single person again before they left. She liked it.

"Ready to go in?" Hannah asked. "I'm done with this cigarette. I was waiting for my friend Isha but she just texted, she couldn't get a ticket."

Marcy felt her cheeks broil with embarrassment. "Oh, I don't have a ticket." Mostly she didn't want Hannah to feel bad for her.

"I got you a ticket." Hannah smiled. "You can pay me back or not, I'm a fancy tech bro now."

Marcy followed Hannah up a set of narrow stairs to a big room where lasers shot through smoke-machine haze. The music was loud and the beat was fast. There were a few swaying cones of bright white light shining from heavy rigs attached to the low ceiling. It made the dancers look like they were about to be abducted by aliens. There was someone in each of the cones, all of them making a collection of jerky movements flow together faster than seemed humanly possible.

A middle-aged woman with stiff ringlets and a tight white T-shirt leaned out of a window in the wall near the stairs. Hannah held out her phone with a QR code on the screen and the woman held her phone above it, checking their tickets. The two of them spoke in French, leaning in close and whisper-yelling over the music. Hannah unzipped her coat and passed it to the woman through the small window. For a minute Hannah's iridescent puffer filled the opening in the wall and the woman disappeared behind it before reappearing with the jacket wrangled onto a hanger. Hannah dropped a toonie in a ribbed plastic cup on the window's ledge. She had on a neon-yellow tube top and wide-legged light denim cargo pants.

"Coat check." Hannah nudged Marcy.

Marcy took off her wet coat. She'd worn her high-waisted black skinny jeans and a faded black T-shirt — it wasn't the right outfit at all. When they got to the dance floor Hannah was immediately swept into a flurry of hugs. She kept introducing Marcy to people but the music was too loud to hear anything. After the hugging everyone turned back to the DJ. Marcy saw that Hannah could make her body move with that same combination of liquid and jolt as the dancers under the UFO lights. It looked like a stop-motion animation of Hannah.

Marcy went to the bathroom and closed herself in a stall, wanting to check if Leanne had messaged her on her break. Then she remembered her phone was in the pocket of her coyote jacket, locked away in the coat check behind the ringleted woman. She pressed her palms into her eye sockets. Hannah had the ticket in her pocket and she was out in the middle of the dance floor. Marcy didn't feel up to negotiating with the woman about seeing her coat without the ticket and she didn't want to interrupt Hannah, but she was afraid that if Leanne had texted and she didn't respond it would seem intentionally hurtful. When she re-emerged from the stall, Miriam and Shawna were on their way into the stall next to hers. One of them caught her arm — "Hannah's friend!"

"Come, come, we want to know you." Shawna tugged Marcy into their stall.

One of them locked the door behind them and when

she turned back around Marcy saw she had her eyebrows shaved off. She was wearing a baggy neon-orange hoodie. The other, shorter and smaller, girl was wearing a spaghetti-strap tank top and clingy miniskirt, both highlighter pink. She pulled a little baggy of white powder out of her bra. "We're doing K, want a bump?"

She'd never done ketamine but she'd heard Sharon talk about how it made you experience the music in this super-embodied way. Maybe this would help her dance without spending money on drinks.

Marcy nodded. "Yeah, thank you."

The butchier girl pulled a key from her pocket and scooped some dust from the baggy for Marcy. A moment after she snorted, a sour chemical taste hit the back of her throat. The other two each took a bump. Shawna put a hand on Marcy's back. "Okay, let's dance."

They shuffled past a group of people waiting to get into the occupied stalls, through the swinging bathroom door, onto the dance floor.

Marcy felt the drugs quickly and it was easier to move with the music. She was lost in lifting her feet in time to the beat when Hannah appeared beside her, sweaty and smiling.

"Are you having fun?"

"Yeah, are you?"

"Yeah," Hannah answered. "What do you think of Miriam and Shawna?"

"Yeah! I mean I didn't really talk to them that much," Marcy said. "They gave me K though."

"Oh sweet."

Hannah went to speak to the girls and the four of them went to the bathroom together.

When the music ended Marcy was shocked. She couldn't believe she'd been inside the bar for five hours. She hugged all of Hannah's friends outside, even the ones she hadn't been introduced to yet. She felt like she knew them because they'd been dancing around her all night. She really meant it when she hugged them.

As Marcy made her way up Saint-Denis, she tried to think about what there was to eat at home. She thought there might be a bag of freezer-burned dumplings.

She took her phone out of her pocket and saw she had three missed calls from Leanne. There were a string of text messages, some of them in all caps. She scrolled through the texts quickly as she walked, only taking in a word or two at a time. The final message said, *WHERE ARE YOU?? My sister made me feel really shitty*

Marcy called as she walked to her apartment. The phone rang through to voicemail and she called again. Still no answer. She texted, *Sorry my phone was in my coat, tried to call but I couldn't get through, are you up? Call me back*

She read through the texts.

Hey, are you at that party?

Call me on your way home, I miss you

I'm having a bad night, can you please call me

Marcy are you still at the bar?

WHERE ARE YOU?? My sister made me feel really shitty

She felt her heart pounding in her chest. She called once more, a third time, and then sent another text, *I'm sorry you had a bad night*

She turned her ringer on and pumped the volume up all the way. As she walked home, she kept pulling her phone out of her pocket to see if she had missed a call or a text.

Probably Leanne had fallen asleep.

In the morning she tried calling at 10:30, which she knew
was when Leanne usually woke up after a night at work.
But she didn't pick up the phone. Marcy was tempted to text
again but couldn't think of anything to add to the messages
she'd already sent.

That afternoon, as she was adding captions to a safety
video about draining a deep fryer, her phone dinged with
a message from Leanne. The noise startled her. Normally
she never turned the volume on.

*Sorry, I know I overreacted, I think I should probably take some
space*

Marcy tried calling immediately but Leanne didn't pick up.
She knew she should wait and think more before responding
but she sent a message immediately.

Okay, call me when you're ready

9

Linda arrived the next afternoon and Marcy still hadn't heard from Leanne. Even though she showed up exactly when she said she would, Marcy felt startled to see Linda standing in the dingy hallway beneath the caged fluorescents. It was like Marcy was in a time travel movie and someone from the past had plunked themselves down in the present. Marcy wondered what Linda noticed about her, if anything. Often she felt shrunken in Montreal, because she didn't have a consistent job or as many friends as she'd like, and because she couldn't help hanging off Leanne's every word. But with Linda taking in the high ceilings and exposed pipes of the loft, she felt suddenly proud of her life in Montreal.

She made her back tall and her shoulders wide. "Welcome to the big city."

Marcy suddenly remembered Linda sitting on top of the dryer in a musty laundry room, legs wrapped around Marcy's back. The bass thudding through the floor. Marcy on tiptoe with the edge of the dryer digging into her stomach, a handful of Linda's ass in her hand, face planted in her cleavage.

"Mercy buckets," Linda said.

"Let me give you a tour of the apartment and then I thought we could get some supper? Unless you have plans?"

"That sounds great," Linda said.

Marcy and Linda walked to the bus stop on Clark. It was the kind of cold that turned nose hairs stiff. Marcy pulled the strings of her hood so that the coyote fur rubbed her cheeks. They got seats together on the bench in the back and when the bus swayed their shoulders bumped together.

"Okay, so I have to tell you something," Linda said.

"Yeah?" As the bus got closer to Leanne's place, Marcy found herself scanning the sidewalk for Leanne's bright red jacket.

"I'm sleeping with Leo."

"Leo? Not the manager from Destruction?" Marcy felt like she'd lost all control of what her face was doing.

"He's sexy."

"How old is he?"

"Fifty-four." Linda was enjoying Marcy's shock. "It's hot."

"Whatever floats your boat," Marcy said.

"I seduced him."

"You seduced him?"

"I made the first move."

"Okay."

"I'm just saying it isn't creepy."

Marcy nodded, squishing her lips together and raising her eyebrows, like whatever you say. They didn't speak until they reached the restaurant Marcy had chosen for them. She led Linda to a booth in the back.

"You're happy here," Linda said when they'd taken off their jackets. "Your place is so nice."

They ordered cheeseburgers and a pint of beer each.

Resentment made Marcy's chest tight. They were sitting in a booth, looking right at each other's faces. She had been excited to show Linda the restaurant. She knew Linda would appreciate the taxidermied fox on display in the back corner, the long list of imported beers and cocktails, the mirrored tiles behind the bar. She'd planned to surprise Linda by covering the bill, because she'd just received an e-transfer from the hate speech people and it was more than she'd expected. She also thought it would be a nice, friendly gesture, especially if she had to gently turn down Linda's advances. Now she was only going to be paying for her own meal, so she ordered a second beer.

"I was surprised you wanted to see me," Marcy said. "That whole situation between us was really fucked up."

She had imagined they'd have this conversation towards the end of the meal but it was coming out of her now.

"I wasn't mad or anything. It's not a big deal," Linda said.

"I took money from the bar before I left."

"What do you mean?"

"I stole money, when I did the cash-out."

"How much money?"

"Kind of a lot, over time. But I spent it all."

"Marcy, that's fucked up. That's not cool."

"Why? Leo's got lots of money right? Doesn't he own like three houses?"

She'd expected to feel cathartic relief after saying it. Instead the inside of her chest turned into sludgy cement. If Linda didn't say the right thing soon it would be concrete forever.

The server placed a beer next to each of their elbows and both women thanked her, which suddenly felt like making small talk at a funeral.

"St. John's is so small," Linda said when the waitress left.

"What does that mean?" Marcy's voice came out loud and there weren't many people in the restaurant. It was too late anyway, her insides were solid, a slab pebbled with small blue stones.

"Like imagine if you got caught," Linda said. "That's all."

It sounded like a threat, but Linda's face looked like she was trying to make amends. Marcy's phone lit up and her eyes automatically darted to the screen. It wasn't Leanne.

Marcy said, "Charlie Tobin is messaging me."

"Do you talk to him?" Linda said. "I forgot he lived here."

Charlie Tobin was from Newfoundland. Marcy knew him from when she was young; they'd both gone to all-ages punk shows in church halls and sport centre basements in St. John's. But he'd moved away long before Marcy left the city. She'd bumped into him only once since she'd moved to Montreal.

"No, not really." She looked back down at her phone. "He's giving away a portable washer." Marcy clicked to reveal the whole, long message.

"Oh, and you're looking for one?"

When Marcy didn't answer Linda bit into her burger. Her fingers cracked the shiny domed top of the bun.

A Kijiji exchange had fallen through and Charlie needed the washer gone that night, he was leaving in the morning. Marcy was already imagining how Sharon and Kathleen would respond to her wheeling the washer through the front door. She could finally contribute something significant to the apartment, make herself useful.

"I think I have to get it tonight, is that okay? It shouldn't take long. You can wait at my place if you want." Marcy was formulating a response to Charlie, typing and backspacing. "I'm going to taxi it back, he said it could fit in a minivan."

"I'll come with you, that'd be fun. I'd say hi to Charlie."

Marcy ignored how quickly Linda was jumping on this. She suggested a time and Charlie replied with a big blue thumbs up. Marcy flipped the phone screen-down on the table.

She took a sip of beer, it was cool and creamy. Linda was stuffing a forkful of lettuce that glimmered with dressing into her mouth. Anger splashed against the wall in Marcy's chest and then it washed out of her. The universe had presented her with a free washing machine.

"We can walk over after this, he lives in Parc-Ex," Marcy said. "That's not far from me."

"You don't hang out, like at shows?"

"I don't see him out, we haven't spoken in ages," Marcy said. "But my roommate and I were just talking about a washer. This is a good brand too, I've been researching."

Marcy didn't say that in the fall, when she'd just moved in above the chandeliers, she and Charlie Tobin had ended up alone together at a mutual acquaintance's apartment during an afternoon thunderstorm. Jessica, the acquaintance, had been moving to Halifax to be with her girlfriend just as Marcy arrived in the city. Marcy and Charlie Tobin had both responded to a Facebook post where Jessica listed all the furniture and small appliances she didn't need anymore because her girlfriend had a fully stocked apartment. She was giving Marcy a stack of novels and Charlie was getting a food processor.

"I've been wanting one for hummus," he said as the three of them stood in the breeze blowing in from Jessica's open balcony door. It had been 27 degrees with the humidex earlier in the day. But by then the smell of barbeque was starting to be overwhelmed by the smell of wet pavement and the temperature was dropping vertiginously.

"I have a blender too, good for smoothies." Jessica held up a little blender, the body was a clouded plastic cup. "Dianne has a Vitamix."

Charlie raised his eyebrows at Marcy and she shook her head like go for it.

"I'll take it," Charlie said. "Thank you."

"Do you want anything else? Toaster oven? I'm not taking that with me."

Marcy had untied the flannel around her waist and put it on. There was a sound like whispering and all three looked to see beads of rain bouncing in the alley. A group of kids who'd been practising a TikTok dance in front of a slab of broken mirror leaning against the fence squealed as they gathered their things.

Jessica looked from the open door to the time on the stove. "Fuck, I have to be at work in like twenty minutes, I'm going to have to bike in this."

"I'm biking too and my brakes are broken," Marcy said.

Jessica invited them to wait the storm out in her apartment.

"You shouldn't bike in this with bad brakes," she said, pulling on a raincoat with a hood. Jessica was so delirious with love and the prospect of getting out of the city that her spirits couldn't even be dampened by riding to work in a downpour.

Charlie and Marcy ended up watching Werner Herzog's *Into the Abyss*. They chose it from a bunch of films Jessica had saved on a hard drive. They picked it because they didn't know anything about the other films but they knew this one was Werner Herzog. They'd both loved *Grizzly Man*. They googled *Into the Abyss* and there was time to turn back and choose something less bleak from the huge collection of anime on the disc, but instead, even though they'd never had a real conversation before, they ended up watching a movie about death row together. The thunder rumbled longer and louder as the film went on. There might have been some sexual tension between them but it was hard to tell because the air was so thick with thunderstorm energy and the movie was so devastatingly sad.

Every now and then a skinny strike of lightning just outside the window made the room bright. Herzog interviewed a minister who described sitting with people during their execution, asking permission to hold their ankles while they were murdered by the state. The pastor didn't use the word murdered. When the movie ended, Marcy and Charlie Tobin gave up on waiting out the storm. They put the projector away, stamped into their sneakers, Charlie wrestled the food processor into his knapsack and Marcy wrapped the novels in a plastic bag. They dropped Jessica's keys in the mailbox and stepped into the deluge. When they got to the end of the block Marcy's plaid was plastered to her shoulders and little air bubbles puckered beneath it. It was actually raining so hard that it was difficult to see. She and Charlie Tobin parted ways at the corner and hadn't spoken again until this message about the washer.

But when Linda asked again, something like, "Is it weird

he messaged you?" Marcy said, "He probably just needs to get rid of the washer." Because she wouldn't be parsing strange intimacies with Linda anymore.

When they finally found his place they saw it was a basement apartment with its own entrance. Charlie opened the door in a grey cardigan with a dress shirt buttoned to the neck beneath it.

Charlie and Linda carried the washer up the concrete steps to the sidewalk while Marcy ordered a taxi. Charlie and Linda were hunched, swinging the bottom of the washer up to rest on each icy step ahead of them. Marcy was sure they weren't lifting properly.

The three of them stood on the sidewalk surrounding the washer, waiting for the taxi. Linda explained she was in town for her sister's baby shower, staying in a hotel downtown with her mom.

When the taxi finally arrived, the driver made the back of the minivan rise on its own with a hydraulic sigh. He offered to help load the washer but they insisted on doing it themselves. On its side the washer just fit in the dip of grey-carpeted space behind the back seat. Marcy hugged Charlie Tobin before climbing into the back seat. She could tell he wasn't expecting it. Maybe he'd messaged tons of people about the washer and she was the first or only one to reply, but she felt in the hug that he was thinking about the thunderstorm afternoon too.

Back at the building Linda helped her carry the washer up the front steps of the building. They used that same method of swinging the machine up to the step above them, and Marcy could feel something in her lower back straining as the guts of the washer swirled with the motion. When they got in the elevator with the machine between them, Marcy felt a pang of appreciation for Linda that turned the cement sludgy again for a moment.

At home Linda sat on Marcy's bed while she started a pile of dirty clothes for the small washer, prioritizing underwear and socks as well as her favourite T-shirts. Charlie had said she should only put one big absorbent thing in at a time. A towel or a pair of jeans, a sweatshirt or a sheet. Charlie had warned that otherwise the washer would be thrown off balance and rock aggressively from side to side until sudsy water came out the bottom. Then you had to open the lid and rearrange things to make them swirl smoothly again.

"Are you coming home in the summer?" Linda asked.

"I don't know," Marcy said.

"You have this great place," Linda said. "And work?"

"Sort of," Marcy said. "Some work."

"And friends?"

"One friend, and my roommates are kind of friends," Marcy said. "I'm seeing someone too."

"Oh."

"I guess I do feel lonely a lot, though." Marcy hadn't said this out loud to anyone since she'd moved. "And I miss things, the drama of the landscape and the clean air and just the feeling of knowing a place inside out."

Linda asked, "Do you feel like you had to move here because of me?"

"That's not why I'm here. I've wanted to come here since I was a kid. You're right that I could have got in trouble about the money though."

"Yeah, that's all I was saying." Linda seemed relieved Marcy had brought up the money again. "Was it a lot?"

"I don't know. No? I mean not really."

"You don't know how much? Like even vaguely?"

"I know how much, I don't know if it's a lot. Like in the grand scheme of things? No. But I could definitely get in trouble. I mean, I could still get in trouble. I haven't told anyone else."

"I'm not going to tell anyone," Linda said.

"Okay, I would really appreciate that," Marcy said.

"I wish you hadn't told me. I can tell you blame me for what happened between us. And I felt bad about it but you're the one who keeps —"

"I really don't, I don't blame you." As Marcy was saying it, she realized she did blame Linda. The first kiss at least was definitely Linda's fault. "I know it's a lot to ask but if Leo finds out, he could really fuck me over I think. And then I couldn't go home."

"I said I wouldn't say anything." Linda was angry, Marcy had never seen her angry before. "And I'm not the one who had a girlfriend."

"You kissed me!" It flew out of Marcy.

"You kissed me lots of times after that. Even that first night, you were into it."

Marcy heard someone in the hall and suddenly worried about her roommates coming home. She had to de-escalate somehow. "Okay, I know. I'm sorry. None of it is your fault, I shouldn't have said that."

Linda stood up and covered her face with her hands. "I'm leaving."

"Are you crying?" Marcy asked. "Don't go. Do you want a hug?"

Linda stepped into Marcy's arms. Her tears made Marcy's T-shirt wet and Marcy felt afraid Linda would try to kiss her.

"Do you want a beer?" Marcy asked, stepping away from Linda's shuddering body. "They're in the crisper, I'm just going to pee, okay?"

In the bathroom she saw Leanne's name lit up on the screen of her phone, a missed call. She pressed the notification impulsively. It rang through to voicemail, which was a blessing in disguise. She texted sitting on the toilet, *I'm sorry I missed you*

Can you come over? Leanne wrote.

I have a friend visiting right now but I could come in an hour or two, I would love to see you, I miss you

Never mind, goodnight, sorry just in a weird mood

Linda and Marcy drank the beers at opposite ends of the kitchen table and Marcy was grateful for the distance between them.

"I'd really like to be your friend," Marcy said. "I need a friend."

That at least was true.

"Okay," Linda said.

"Yeah?"

"Yeah, I mean me too. I have friends but they aren't queer. I have no queer friends. That's why I kissed you. I thought about it a lot since you left and I think that's why."

"I understand that. Actually, maybe that's how I ended up with Brit." Marcy was feeling the beer. "Because it's confusing when you're gay and you don't know anyone else who is and then you meet someone else who is and you just want to be around them because you feel understood in this new way."

"Exactly."

"It's hard to know exactly what you want from them," Marcy said.

"Yeah."

"Especially if they're hot," Marcy smirked.

WHEN LINDA LEFT to meet her mom back at the hotel, Marcy tried calling Leanne again but there was no answer. She slept fitfully. She dreamed about biking through downtown looking for Leanne. There were no cars on de Maisonneuve and no people on the sidewalks. She cruised down the centre of the wide, empty street squinting into alleys.

MARCY AND LINDA had spent the morning before the baby shower wandering around Mile End, looking for a present for the baby. They got gnocchi with tomato sauce in little takeout containers with white plastic forks. She wanted to impress Linda with the big-cityness of a restaurant that served only one dish, and Linda was impressed.

Marcy had to take her mitts off to hold the plastic fork and her fingers stung from the cold. The hot pasta felt good.

"Can I say something? I really don't mean this in a mean way, I'm not trying to attack you, I just didn't think you were gay, or queer," Marcy said.

"What do you mean?"

"When we were hooking up, I thought it was just fooling around."

"Is that not gay?"

"It totally can be! I just think sometimes it's not."

"I am," Linda said.

"Okay."

"Or I mean like, bi."

"For some people, just fooling around doesn't mean you necessarily think of yourself as gay."

"I do, though," Linda said.

"I'm not talking about you specifically, just anyone."

"Okay, why?" Linda asked.

"Why what?"

"Why are you talking about just anyone who's not actually gay right now?"

"Oh my god, I don't know. You don't have to get pissy." Marcy tried to recalibrate, remembering that it was important not to be on bad terms with Linda. "I thought we were entering a new phase of our relationship where we talk about gay stuff."

She'd made Linda smile.

"Maybe you should move here," Marcy said. "Make more gay friends, get more gay."

"I don't know, it's so dirty."

"You think?" They were approaching a hole in the sidewalk where an A&W wrapper floated in a puddle of brown slush.

"And noisy," Linda said.

Marcy was surprised at the little burst of defensiveness she felt welling up. "You kind of stop noticing it."

"And racist, right? Like what about that Bill 21," Linda added, pointing at the button clipped to Marcy's lapel that read *Loi 21* with a thick red line through it. Kathleen had given Marcy the button shortly after she'd moved in and she saw them all over the city, on people's jackets and bookbags.

"It's true," Marcy said. "I mean Newfoundland is racist in its own ways. But yes, Quebec is supremely fucked."

They circled back to the bookstore and Linda got a stack of cardboard books in English and French for her sister's baby. Marcy walked her to the metro and hugged her good-bye. The curved corner of a book dug into Marcy's ribs when they hugged, just under her boob.

"I'll be back when the baby's born, maybe I'll stay longer."

"In April?"

"Yeah. Me and my mom will be up."

Marcy rubbed her rib on the walk home, even though it didn't hurt that much.

SHARON SHOWED HER the crushed bug when she got back to the apartment. It was in the corner of an enormous freezer bag. It was the right burgundy colour with two fine antennae, about the size of an earwig.

"I googled it," Sharon said.

"I thought they had a more leathery shell," Marcy said, smoothing the plastic of the bag around its body.

"There's different types," Sharon said. "The leathery ones are American cockroaches, apparently this is a German cockroach."

Sharon held the phone out to her, a zoomed-in photo of the bug that was unmistakably the same species as was preserved in the Ziploc.

"How did you kill it?"

"I stepped on it," Sharon said. "With my flip-flop."

"Disgusting," Marcy said. "Should I throw it out?"

"Yeah."

Marcy dropped the bag in the garbage.

"Maybe we should keep it, though, in case we need to show an exterminator?" Sharon said as the swinging lid of the garbage rotated closed.

Marcy flicked the lid open and lifted the bag off some damp coffee grounds.

"Where will we keep it?"

In the end Marcy rolled the Ziploc into a tight cylinder and stuck it in the bathroom cabinet between the eco-friendly Windex and the eco-friendly floor cleaner.

In the days that followed they spotted two more cockroaches. One was on a wet sweater Sharon pulled out of the washing machine — it seemed drunk from its time in there but was still very much alive. Sharon killed it with an empty beer bottle that had been sitting by the sink. The second was on the back of the washing machine.

"We should just throw the washer out, they're coming from the washer," Marcy said, trying to keep the self-pity out of her voice. "I'm sorry."

"It's not your fault, it's like STIs, it's no one's fault, you just have to deal with it."

KNOWING LINDA HAD left the city made Marcy feel lonely, especially since Leanne wasn't speaking to her. She texted Hannah.

Hey, wondering if you might want to come by for supper tonight, I'm making roast chicken

She was thrilled when Hannah responded immediately.

Omg yes thank youuuuu, I have zero groceries at home, I'm done at six

Marcy broke the raw chicken's back with the biggest knife in the apartment. She doused the butterflied chicken in olive oil and lemon juice and stuck it in the oven.

When she took it out an hour later, a thick layer of meat

had separated to show the spine, fluted with a flared layer of cartilage. She pulled some of the lemons out of the carcass and laid them on the cutting board beside it. The potatoes were crispy on the outside and mushy inside. The asparagus had turned a brighter green. She knew it was an unimaginative dinner but it had turned out well, everything was the colour and texture it was supposed to be.

Hannah was talking about getting her nails done. She had long black acrylic nails that tapered into a sharp point.

"This is an extension on my real nail," she explained.

"Those are your real nails?" Marcy was sawing the thighs off.

"Mostly my real nails."

Marcy pulled a thick strip off the breast and ate it.

"Mmmm." She caught herself praising her own cooking and blushed. "I'm just really not much of a cook. So I'm very relieved when things work out. Don't get excited or anything."

"I'm sure it's great," Hannah said.

"Does that seem properly carved? I've literally never done it. Come over here and get some chicken. Or I can serve you."

Hannah filled her plate. At first the conversation was stiff. Marcy knew it was because she was brimming with anxiety but she didn't want to admit it. She found she didn't want to explain about Linda's visit or how strained things had become between her and Leanne. But the trade-off for concealing the mess she'd made was that she couldn't ask for guidance about navigating the surges of emotion she was feeling.

"It's good," Hannah said after several mouthfuls. "Moist. You can use the leftovers for sandwiches."

"I'm going to make soup with the bones. Chicken noodle."

"Did you have fun the other night? Dancing?" Hannah asked.

Marcy nodded, her mouth full of meat. She swallowed and said, "Oh! Did you start the mental health project?" She was thrilled to have thought of a new direction for the conversation.

"No, but I've done that one before, or maybe it's not the same one, something similar. But I've been meaning to tell you, have you done clinical trials before?"

"Is that AI too?"

"No, it's like medical trials." Hannah swirled a piece of chicken in ketchup. "It's like testing drugs."

Marcy shook her head no.

"You can make good money that way. I have a friend who's been doing the same study for two years. Something for recreational drug users with clinical depression. Anyway this one's for a birth control pill, starting next month and they're still looking for people."

"Are you doing it?" Marcy asked.

"No, 'cause of my job. But I've done a bunch of them."

Marcy didn't want to seem like a coward. She poured more wine into each of their glasses.

"Usually it's just something that already exists, like there's a name-brand version and you're testing the knock-off. "

Marcy took up their plates and brought them to the sink.

"I can send you the info if you want, if you're interested."

"Sure." Marcy blasted cold water over the plates. "I'm interested."

Out of the corner of her eye she saw something crawl

over the lip of the counter. A thick burgundy body on tall skinny legs. It was so much bigger than the others she'd seen. Marcy froze. It crawled onto the cutting board, heading straight for the hollowed-out carcass still covered in torn-apart flesh.

"Fuck! Fuck!"

"What?" Hannah stood and scanned the room for danger. "Are you hurt?"

Marcy whined. The cockroach was inside the carcass. She'd let it crawl in there, slow and steady on its spindly legs.

"What is going on?" Hannah said sternly.

"There's a cockroach, we have cockroaches I guess. We weren't sure."

"Where?"

"It went inside the chicken."

Marcy bent down and looked inside the hollowed-out bird. The cockroach was standing on a lemon, tickling the inside of the rib cage with its antennae.

"I'm just going to throw it out."

"You have to kill it." Hannah walked over and looked inside the chicken. She straightened up. "Okay, shake it out on the floor and I'll stomp on it."

"I can't." Marcy felt her face scrunching up like a child's.

"It'll crawl out of the garbage. You have to kill it."

"Okay," Marcy said.

"Would you rather stomp it?" Hannah asked gently.

"No."

Marcy picked up the chicken rib cage, the thighs and wings she'd severed still on the cutting board. Hannah was wearing sandals — wide, black elastic straps swooped around her ankle and just behind her toes. Her toes were painted aquamarine, like a chlorinated pool, with a chunky glitter coat on top.

"Come on, do it," Hannah told her.

Marcy shook the chicken, and the quartered lemons she'd stuffed inside fell out and landed on the concrete floor. Marcy dropped the carcass back on the cutting board. The cockroach was down there in the grease. Hannah stepped right on it and swivelled her ankle, grinding it out of existence. She lifted her shoe and looked at the insect's creamy insides smeared into the grooves of the sole, antennae and legs still twitching.

"Ugh." Hannah scuffed her shoe on the floor instinctively, like a horse pawing the ground before a kick.

"You can wash it in the sink," Marcy said.

"Sorry about the mess."

"No — thank you," Marcy said, feeling tipsy all of a sudden. "You want to wash your shoe? Or I could do it."

"No, it's fine." Hannah carried her sandals over to the mat by the door.

Marcy put a plastic shopping bag over her hand and started collecting the lemons.

"Do you have Lysol wipes?" Hannah asked, now barefoot beside Marcy.

"Yeah, but I'll get this, sit down, sit down." Marcy had never thought about putting a toe in her mouth before. But kneeling beside Hannah's slender feet, she caught herself imagining how the flecks of glitter would feel grazing the roof of her mouth. Hannah found the Lysol wipes and started cleaning the shiny smear of chicken grease and mashed cockroach.

"What do you think about the chicken?" Marcy asked.

"What about it?"

"Should I throw it out?"

"No," Hannah said.

"No?"

"No, it's fine. It didn't even touch the part you eat. And you're going to boil the rest of it for broth."

Marcy urged Hannah to drink more while she continued cleaning. She didn't want any more bugs to be called out of the cracks by the smell of food on the floor, so she got the mop bucket ready.

"I guess a question I have," Marcy said, wiping the counter with a soapy sponge. It was dark out now, the moon was huge, she was drunk. "About the trials."

"Yeah?" Hannah asked.

"Well, you know this, but I don't really have that kind of sex."

"What?"

"Like the kind of sex you get pregnant from."

"Oh — no," Hannah said.

"Or do they like, inject it into you?"

"No, no. It's not anything like that, they already know about how effective it is and the side effects and everything with these trials, they're just testing how long it stays in your blood."

Marcy could feel her cheeks getting hot. "Oh, okay. That makes sense."

The sparkles on Hannah's toes winked at her from under the table. She made one more swipe across the counter with the sponge and threw it in the sink.

"That's pretty much always how it is," Hannah said.

"Okay."

"And you could just be taking a placebo. A third of the people there are on a placebo."

Marcy heard the scratch of Sharon's key in the door.

"Smells good in here," Sharon said, dropping her bookbag on the floor.

"Have some wine," Marcy said. "There was another cockroach."

Sharon took off her shoes and joined them at the table.

10

Marcy woke up to a text from Leanne.

Could we talk today?

Leanne was going to Saint-Henri to trade some rooted plant clippings for a set of handlebars, so they planned to meet for lunch at Greenspot. Leanne was always talking wistfully about when she had lived in Saint-Henri, around the time of the student strike. When people were throwing Molotov cocktails through the windows of new bougie cafes that were just starting gentrify in the neighbourhood. She talked about getting dollar hotdogs at AAA, and queer dance parties under damp streamers in the musty base-ment of a punk house around the corner, and spending countless afternoons sprawled on the banks of the canal with tall cans of Max Ice. Marcy googled Greenspot and saw it would take her about forty-five minutes to get there on the metro.

She arrived first and the waitress sat her at a booth in the back. Leanne showed up with a shiny set of chrome handlebars poking out of her bookbag. She looked beautiful and not angry. The waitress brought them laminated menus.

"I've been wanting to come here with you for a while," Leanne said. "Isn't it great?"

Marcy took in the tin ceilings, the squat silver jukeboxes on each table, the display case that kept shelves of sliced pies chilled.

"There's this deal where you can split a club and it comes with a soup, a dessert each, and coffee." Leanne was dragging her finger down the menu. "Here!"

She turned it for Marcy to see.

"Okay," Marcy said. She hadn't anticipated this brightness, she had been prepared for storminess, she had been anticipating having to grovel — now she was trying to reroute. When Leanne was giddy like this, beaming energy through her bright green eyes right at Marcy, it felt like there was a circuit between them. Marcy wanted to match and maintain Leanne's energy, to keep her from inevitably either going dark and distant or bursting into a rage.

"You want that?" Leanne asked, shrugging out of her winter coat. "I know you love a chicken club."

"Are those the desserts in that case? For the deal?" She wasn't going to be the one to bring up the angry texts and the long silence since they'd last talked.

"Yeah." Leanne fished the handlebars out of her bookbag and held them over the table like she was cruising on her bike, arms fully extended. "I'm so happy with these, remember I told you I wanted a set like this?"

Marcy's eye caught on the TV above the bar. "Did you know there was a case of coronavirus in Montreal?"

"Yeah."

"Freaky."

"Are you scared of it?" Leanne asked her.

"Hannah says they'd never shut things down here. Because of capitalism."

"Yeah."

The server returned with coffee, she gave them creamers out of her apron pocket. Leanne dropped the handlebars beside her on the booth seat and ordered in French. The restaurant was filling up.

"Okay," Leanne said. "What I wanted to say is that I love you."

"I love you too," Marcy said immediately, and it felt true but not joyous.

"I'm sorry, I was upset with my sister and I don't know why I got so worked up. I shouldn't have sent you those messages. I was just missing you."

"It's okay, it's not that big a deal." Really the messages weren't that bad, it was more the silence that had upset Marcy. "Did you fight with your sister?"

"It was just something stupid. It's her attitude about my life, which is never going to change." Leanne sank back into the booth.

Marcy nodded like she understood.

"And I'm sorry I didn't call you back. I can be prideful, to my own detriment."

"I missed your call, I wanted to talk, I wanted you to come over," Marcy said.

"I know, I need to get a handle on my emotions sometimes before I can talk."

Marcy nodded again. If Leanne was going to ask about

Linda's visit this would be the moment. She decided that if Leanne asked, she would tell the whole truth — the affair, the lying, and the money. But Leanne didn't ask.

The waitress brought them two bowls of pea soup with chunks of bright pink ham in it. Marcy shook pepper over hers. The soup was salty and delicious. Leanne put a hand out on the table and Marcy held it. It felt so good to hold her hand.

"I missed cuddling you," she told Leanne.

"I missed that too," Leanne said. "You know what I was thinking? We should go to New York for a weekend, take the overnight bus. We can stay with my friend Laurel."

"Okay." Marcy felt a spray of happiness burbling in her chest, it was like a jet from the Desjardins fountain about to shoot up to the ceiling. She wondered how much the bus cost. "Oh, guess what? Hannah gave me info about this clinical trial. I can make like a thousand dollars in a weekend."

"Medical testing? Don't do that, Marcy."

"Why?"

"Because it's dangerous, it's not worth it. You're being stupid."

"Hannah said the drugs are already safe, it's just to find out about how long it stays in your blood." Marcy was scraping thick ribbons of soup off the sides of her bowl.

"Is Hannah a doctor?" Leanne pushed her empty bowl to the side of the table. "You shouldn't do that. Why are you so obsessed with Hannah?"

Marcy was silent.

"What kind of drug is it?"

"Birth control."

"I really wouldn't fuck around with that."

Marcy said nothing.

"Can you please promise me you won't do that?"

"I don't know. I guess I'll think about it." Marcy saw the waitress approaching with their sandwich.

Three
The Trial

11

Marcy had to do an intake interview to make sure she was eligible for the trial. She had decided she wouldn't tell Leanne she was going through with it until she got the confirmation she'd been accepted.

When she arrived she said her name to a young man sitting at a desk behind a Plexiglas window. He scanned a clipboard, made a tick, and gestured to the waiting area. Marcy listened to the conservations around her and learned that the other people in the waiting area were trying for a number of different studies, but the birth control one had the best pay.

The application form had specified people aged 25–45, and you had to click a box confirming your age range. Hannah told her most study participants were usually new immigrants, students, or both. Marcy looked around the room wondering who else was there for the first time.

Hannah had told her, "Usually you have to eat pork, like

that's one of the requirements on the intake form, so that rules a lot of people out."

"Why?" Marcy asked.

"I don't know, it's basically always a requirement. I've wondered about it."

She wished Hannah was there to pass time in the waiting area with her.

Someone finally called Marcy's name. She followed a woman in a white lab coat into a small room where another woman in a lab coat sat behind a computer. She started in French, paused and asked the familiar question, "English or French?"

"English," Marcy said apologetically, as she always did.

Then came all the questions Hannah had told her they would ask: Was she pregnant? Did she take medication? Did she do drugs? When was the last time she'd been hospitalized? Was she ready to take this container down the hall and pee in it?

The bathroom had a toilet and a urinal. Hannah had told her it was fine to lie about drugs as long as there was nothing in your system. The mirror was the type they sometimes had in park bathrooms or gas stations on the highway, a sheet of scratched-up metal that threw a distorted version of yourself back at you. Marcy leaned into the mirror and watched her forehead balloon outwards. She stepped backwards and tilted her head back so her chin looked inflated. Someone twisted the knob.

"Occupé?" a voice asked.

"One second, um, un moment," she called through the door.

She untwisted the cap and laid it on her thigh, holding

the receptacle between her legs. She didn't mind peeing into the little bottle. She'd purposely drunk a lot of water before she left the house so her pee was pretty clear and it didn't really smell. When she opened the door a guy about her age was standing across the hall leaning against the wall. She saw the bright cap of an empty pee jar between his splayed fingers.

"Hi," she said, holding her own bottle down by her thigh. She wasn't embarrassed by it, but he might be.

She wanted to ask if he had done this before, and was trying to think how to say it in French.

"You are finished?" he asked.

She was blocking the door.

"Sorry." She moved out of the way. When he closed the door behind him she was disoriented. She couldn't remember which way she'd come. The walls were bare and windowless. Both directions ended in a set of grey double doors. She could hear the young man peeing into the toilet through the door. Then she heard the taps. It would be weird if she was still there when he finished.

She quickly picked a direction. When she pushed through the double doors at the end of the hall, she found herself at an elevator she hadn't encountered before. She had to turn around and walk down the long corridor again with her pee, now less warm.

She waited outside the intake nurse's office. There was a piece of paper in a plastic Duo-Tang sheath reminding all the medical professionals that they had to keep wearing their lab coats at all times.

The nurse asked if she was ready and Marcy stepped inside. She held up her jar of pee. The nurse took it and gestured at a chair close to her desk — Marcy sat. The nurse put on a pair of blue latex gloves. Blood work.

Marcy turned her head away but at the last moment she looked and saw the metal tip sink into her vein. She felt it tugging the blood up out of her. She looked at a fan spinning on top of a filing cabinet in the corner, willing herself not to faint.

"Done," the nurse said. "You can go."

"That's it?"

"We'll contact you in three days."

When she pushed open the heavy door to the outside world Marcy took a deep breath. The air was still thick with morning exhaust. No backing out now. She had given all the information they'd asked for plus a splash of her insides. That part she'd done for free. Just to see if she was eligible.

She walked to the edge of the parking lot and sat with her legs in the road. She took a receipt from the supermarket out of her pocket and found a pen in the front pouch of her bookbag. She started doing the math on how much money she had and how much she owed and how much she would have if she did this gig.

She wrote on her thigh and the scratchy tip of the pen tore through the paper in places. She felt pretty certain she would get the job, unless she had some weird medical condition she didn't know about. When she saw the number at the bottom of her calculations she felt fine about handing out a splash of her insides.

There was an early thaw and she walked home through the mild night with her coat unzipped. She decided to do an hour of hate speech sorting after supper. She found she was beginning to look forward to finally starting the mental health project — at least it would be some different content.

Getting ready for bed that night she noticed a pattern of staccato pen marks tattooing her leg with fragments of her budgeting calculations. The pen had bled through the receipt. She peeled the Band-Aid out of the crook of her arm. There was an almost imperceptible hole where the needle had gone in and come out again. She thought about the vial of her blood chilling in a small cooler in the depths of that building. Or maybe they'd already analyzed it and learned all they wanted to about her.

THERE WAS A big sale on at Home Depot and Leanne had picked out the best portable toilet on their website to go in the van she hoped to buy.

"You don't want to wait until you have the van?" Marcy asked as they zipped their boots up. "Where are you going to store it?"

"I'll put it in the closet, under my summer clothes. They never go on sale like this," Leanne said.

The box had a supersaturated photograph of a waterfall on the front. Basically a plastic toilet seat on top of a plastic tank. There was a product called Liquid Gold that you poured in after using the toilet to mask the smell and break down the shit. When it was full it had to be dumped down one of those pipes poking out of the gravel at campgrounds and trailer parks. The Liquid Gold had the same glaring waterfall on the bottle as the toilet did.

"This can't be good for the environment," Marcy said, reading the back as they headed down the narrow aisles to the alternative toilets section.

"It's too late for the environment," Leanne said. "And plus

what are you saying? Purchasing power is going to change the world? Like paper straws and —"

"I know, I know, I'm just saying."

When they found the toilets there were two sizes.

"It's this one," Marcy said, slapping the top of the box.

"Wait. I didn't know there was a bigger one. Do you think I should get the bigger one?"

Marcy saw a woman coming down the aisle and moved to the side to let her pass but the woman stopped beside them. A middle-aged woman in a forest green L.L.Bean vest. Her short grey hair fluffed around her face.

"Are you buying that?" the woman said.

"Yeah," Leanne said and slid the box off the shelf. It was almost too big for her to carry in her arms.

"For a trailer?"

"For a van," Leanne said.

"I'm just asking because I bought one for the bathroom in my trailer but it's the wrong size."

Marcy was ready to walk away from the small talk but Leanne was patient. She was always getting caught up in interactions like this. People who were desperate to talk to someone would find her and she indulged them. Actually, a lot of the time she seemed to genuinely enjoy it. The woman put an arm out and leaned on the shelf, settling in for a long chat.

The aisle opened onto the paint section, where an attendant was helping a young straight couple. Marcy watched as he took a colour swatch from the girl and keyed a code into the computer.

"This is a popular shade now, you probably know that," he said in English with a Quebecois accent. "Is it for the kitchen? A lot of people are putting it in the kitchen."

Marcy wandered over to the lit-up paint swatch display, the bottle of Liquid Gold tapping her thigh with each step. She slid a strip of dark purple out of its slot and a stack of identical strips rushed forward to fill the void.

She glanced down the aisle and saw Leanne had her foot up on the toilet box now and her folded arms were resting on her raised knee.

"Oh yeah, I'm planning to build a little platform sort of thing for it to sit in," she was saying. "With like a lip to hold it in place."

There were two choices in a situation like this — stand close to Leanne and try to beam impatience at her, or wander away and wait to be found when the conversation eventually wound down of its own accord.

The girl pointed her phone at the machine dripping liquid fuchsia into the primer. Concentric pink circles wobbled across the white paint towards the rim of the tin.

"Beau, n'est-ce pas?" the attendant said as he took the paint out from beneath the udder of the tinting machine. He held the bottom of the open tin and tilted it towards her. The fuchsia rings on the surface slid into each other. The girl said something that Marcy didn't understand and the three of them laughed. The attendant slapped the lid on the tin and lifted it into the machine that shook the paint.

"Trois minutes," he said over the noise, jerking a thumb at the shaker machine, and the couple wandered farther down the aisle. Marcy put the strip of dark purples in her jeans pocket and walked back to Leanne.

"I tried to return it but they wouldn't let me," the woman was saying.

Leanne nodded. "Fuckers."

She put an arm around Marcy's hips and pulled her in. Marcy hadn't noticed before but then she understood, this woman with the toilet problem was a lesbian. Leanne was better at picking up on that than her.

"It's still in the box, I've got the receipt, I bought it yesterday."

"I'm sure you could sell it online," Leanne said.

"I just wouldn't know how."

"Kijiji?" Marcy suggested.

"It's this model?" Leanne said.

"The four litre, yeah."

"Or Facebook Marketplace, that's what I use," Marcy tried again.

"It's out in the parking lot?" Leanne straightened up. "What if I just bought it from you?"

"I mean if you're buying the same one anyway, it's brand new," the woman said.

Leanne bent to pick up the toilet and hefted it back onto the shelf. The three of them started towards the gliding doors in the front of the store. When they passed the paint counter the couple was back and the attendant was smearing a dab of pale pink on the lid for them to approve.

Marcy walked through the doors with the handle of the Liquid Gold in her fist. She held her breath a moment waiting for the alarm. When they stepped off the curb, she lifted the bottle like cheers at Leanne.

"Nice." Leanne smiled at Marcy.

"Are you going to get cash?" Marcy asked Leanne quietly as they walked sideways between two suvs. A small dog in the passenger seat yapped at Marcy through a cracked window. It made her jump and she whacked her shoulder on the side mirror of the other vehicle.

"Can I e-transfer you?" Leanne called to the woman.

"My nephew got that all set up for me." The woman opened the trunk and lifted the toilet box out onto the ground. One corner of the stiff cardboard was crumpled. Marcy rubbed her shoulder, there would be a bruise.

"You want to look it over?" the woman asked.

"No," Leanne smiled. "What's your email?"

Marcy could hear the dog howling a few feet away.

When they got back to Leanne's, they opened the toilet box on the kitchen table. A ripped clear plastic bag was shoved down the side of the box.

Leanne lifted the toilet out and put it on the floor. "Try it out."

Marcy flipped the lid.

"Oh what the fuck." Marcy stepped backwards.

There was a long piece of shit in the toilet; half of it had fallen into the open tank and the other half was hardening inside the bowl. Marcy walked around the back of the toilet and kicked the lid shut. She felt a laugh filling her chest and pursed her lips to trap it until she could read the look on Leanne's face. After a long pause Leanne began laughing too.

And then Marcy was imagining how good it would feel to be drifting down the highway with the windows down and her bare feet on the dash of a van, Leanne driving. It would feel so good to be going somewhere, leaving something behind again.

. . .

THE DAY MARCY received the email telling her she'd been
accepted for the study, she and Leanne had made plans to
watch *Desert Hearts*. Marcy was walking along Saint-Urbain
towards Leanne's when she encountered a Shar-Pei. She
didn't know that's what it was until later, she'd never seen
an animal like it before. It was white with the wrinkled
body of a bulldog and a long snout. To Marcy it looked like
a creature that would greet you at the gates of hell. The
dog was running towards Marcy but it kept stepping off the
curb — oncoming cars would slow and swerve and it would
hop back onto the sidewalk. It was a freezing cold night,
Marcy had her hood knotted beneath her chin and thick
mittens on. When the dog finally reached her she kneeled
with two hands out in front of her for it to sniff. The dog
sat, she inspected its neck and there was no collar. She'd
been bitten by a dog before and she was leery of them but
she lifted this dog into her arms. She made a basket out of
her arms and the dog leaned against her chest, placed its
chin on her shoulder, its body spilling over her arms. She
tried not to think about the teeth so close to her neck. The
dog was heavy and she didn't know how far they would
make it together.

She walked to the nearest house and rang the bell. She
tried to ask if the person inside knew where the dog lived.
The exchange took a long time because of the language
barrier and when the man who'd answered shut the door
Marcy wasn't sure they'd understood each other. She tried
the next door and the person spoke English but didn't know
the dog. She ended up carrying it all the way to Leanne's.

It rested its snout on her shoulder for the entire journey. Her arms were aching but she couldn't let it down because it might run into the traffic.

"A Shar-Pei!" Leanne said when she answered the door.

"It kept running into the road."

Leanne rubbed her face against the dog's forehead. She rubbed its sides, speaking to it in a baby voice. Marcy had never seen her like this before.

"We should post it in a lost pet group," Marcy said.

"Just let me meet him first," Leanne whined, inviting the dog up onto the couch.

Marcy folded her tired arms.

The moment they posted a picture Marcy's inbox was flooded with messages.

"People are saying this is a three-thousand-dollar dog," Marcy said.

"If he's purebred and has his papers, yeah," Leanne said.

People warned Marcy not to give the dog to any stranger who came along. Other people offered to take the dog off her hands immediately.

"We have to be careful because people might try to steal him for a puppy mill," Leanne said.

"I don't really find it cute." Marcy was shocked by the volume of messages in her inbox.

Leanne clamped her hands over the dog's ears — "Shhh."

"People are saying take him to the vet and get him scanned for a chip," Marcy said.

"We could do that in the morning, they're all closed now."

"We can't keep it overnight," Marcy said.

But the dog slept in the bed, Marcy held Leanne, and Leanne held the dog. In the morning Leanne took it to pee and Marcy scrolled through her messages. There were several from someone with photos of the dog.

"I found the owner," Marcy said.

Leanne cried. It was the first-ever time Marcy had seen her cry. The owner arrived in a Mercedes-Benz. Marcy was waiting in the yard with the dog sitting by her feet. The owner was a woman around Marcy's age in a Canada Goose coat and big sparkly earrings. She gave Marcy a fifty-dollar bill.

When she got back inside she felt a bit guilty about how happy the money made her because Leanne was curled up in a ball crying.

"Hey," Marcy said. "It's okay, it's nice that we got to meet him. And now he gets to go home, that's nice for him. I could tell she really loves him."

Leanne pulled Marcy into the bed and wrapped her legs tight around her. "I just really liked the dog."

Marcy wiped tears off Leanne's face and kissed her. "I have to tell you something."

"Okay." Leanne sat up and wiped her eyes and then her nose in her sleeve.

"I'm doing the clinical trial."

"Marcy, what the fuck." Leanne stiffened. "Why would you tell me that right now?"

"I just didn't want to keep it from you."

"You knew I was upset. You're so selfish."

"Sorry. You're right — that was stupid."

"You're just trying to upset me, I don't get it."

"I'm sorry, I just wanted you to know."

"You do everything Hannah tells you, it's fucked up."

Marcy didn't say anything.

"I think you should go," Leanne said.

Marcy collected her things from around the apartment in silence. When she had her coat and boots on Leanne said, "Don't call me. I need space."

ON THE MORNING of the trial she set her alarm for six a.m. and got up to go for a run. She pulled the strings of her hoodie taut around her neck and tied them in a tight bow. As she started jogging she realized the dongle that connected her earbuds to her phone had broken again. Just the vocals were coming through, with intermittent half-second bursts of static and bass.

She twisted the cord, sometimes finding a position that restored all the audio for a moment. She was so absorbed in the task of trying to find the least annoying angle for the cord that she ran in front of a truck with a long ladder strapped to the roof. The driver leaned out the window and yelled at her but she couldn't hear him over the static in her ears. She just kept running and hauled the earbuds out. Even though there was still snow down and the ground was icy, the Home Depot trail was busy with clean-cut people jogging before work. Someone was armpit-deep in the recycling bin by the swinging benches, collecting cans. It'd been a long time since she'd run without music and she was surprised to find it didn't bother her so much. She passed the muddy dog park. Now, whenever Marcy passed a dog park she was on the lookout for the Shar-Pei; she wasn't sure why but part of her hoped to see the lost dog in his regular life. Inside the fence people with travel mugs made a loose semicircle, watching some puppies chase each other in a rambunctious tornado while an older dog took a solitary stroll round the perimeter of the park, squatted, and shit. The warm, wet smell hit Marcy just as she saw it happening.

Running didn't feel like too much work that morning — she was fuelled by anxiety about the clinic. She took big gulps of fresh air. She'd been sharing cigarettes with Leanne pretty much daily when they were on good terms and she'd noticed she was developing a shallow cough. But the cough wasn't slowing her down this morning. She'd been instructed not to eat or drink anything before the trial. Even without coffee, the cold made her feel fully awake.

She ran through the cool, dark underpass and into the exercise park where people were working their muscles against the stainless-steel equipment, their breath hanging in icy bursts in front of them. Just as she was reaching the Rosemont end of the trail, where she usually turned around, she saw a small, impossibly bright green creature quiver in a tree on the left side of the path. For a second she thought she'd imagined it or that she might be dreaming. It was the blue-green of a tropical lagoon and twitchy like a wild animal. When she looked again the creature sailed down from the tree and joined a flock of sparrows hopping in a bed of pine needles on the edge of the path. It was some kind of tropical bird people keep as a pet, a parakeet or a budgie. Marcy waved over a man who was jogging past.

"Look at that bird," she said.

"Someone's pet, I think," the man said.

"It's going to die from the cold."

"Sure." The man nodded. "But look, it's free."

He jogged away smiling.

When she got home she showered and got dressed for

the clinic. She chose leggings and a hoodie over her T-shirt and sports bra. Hannah had said to dress comfortably and warmly. "It gets cold in the bunks, you just have this one thin blanket. Even the cafeteria area is a bit cold."

Marcy packed three books and her laptop.

She checked Google Maps and saw it was a forty-three-minute walk to the clinic. She bundled herself in winter gear. On her way out the door she remembered her sketch-book and went back for it.

As she passed the McDonald's on the corner of Parc and Jean-Talon a lightning flash of coffee withdrawal made her head sting. She thought about cheating and drinking a small milky coffee on her way there, but there wasn't time anyway. She weaved through the people gathered on the corner. It was a spot where people cascading out of the metro station collided with the people on their way out of the McDonald's eating breakfast sandwiches in wax paper sheaths. Her stomach growled.

She reached the parking lot at 8:26 and saw a handful of women approaching the front door on foot. She arrived behind a woman who was wearing a pink sari under her winter coat and the same purple JanSport bookbag as Marcy. There was a nurse waiting inside the door with a clipboard. When she finished with the woman ahead of her the nurse waved at Marcy through the door. She asked Marcy's name in French and began flipping through the pages on the clipboard. Then she asked something Marcy couldn't understand. She turned to a table behind her and took a glossy folder from a stack with the company's logo on it. There was a sticker with Marcy's name printed on it stuck to the front.

"Anglais?" the nurse said. "Arm, I need your arm."

Marcy held out her hand. The nurse pushed back Marcy's sleeve, then took a strip of plastic from inside the folder and looped it around Marcy's wrist. She pulled it tight.

"You sign these, there's a pen inside. Then through those doors to the cafeteria."

The bracelet said MARCY PIKE and the number 7856. It looked like it had been generated by a dot matrix printer.

Marcy saw the woman who'd been ahead of her had a folder on her lap and was signing sheets of paper on top of it. Her bookbag was at her feet resting against her shins. Marcy took the seat next to her and did the same with her bag. She ticked boxes confirming that she was a citizen of Canada, that she wasn't pregnant, that she hadn't done drugs or consumed caffeine in the past twenty-four hours, that she didn't have diabetes or a pre-existing heart condition. That she hadn't eaten yet that day. She signed her name again and again and again.

Inside the cafeteria she lined up against the wall, shoulder to shoulder with the other participants. Everyone was holding their forms in their hands. A big clock on the back wall read 9:15.

Three nurses approached the end of the line closest to the door. One was carrying a flat tray with small paper cups on it, the kind you pump ketchup into at fast-food places. The second, a man, was holding a cardboard flat of plastic water bottles. A third nurse stepped forward and addressed the group. She spoke for a long time in French and then switched to English.

"So I'm going to repeat myself. Everything I'm about to tell you is in the forms in the folder you signed. You know this already but I'm going to say it anyway, now for the second time. This is a trial for Halozia. Half of you will get the Halozia and half of you will get a placebo, okay? If you need the bathroom in the next seven hours you'll be accompanied by a nurse who will take notes about your stool and/or urine, okay? If you vomit you will be disqualified and you won't receive full payment, okay? So try to keep it down. Once you take your pill you can have a seat and wait to be called up by the number on your bracelet. Any questions? As I've said it's all on the forms you already read and signed. Okay, excellent, I'm handing it over to my colleagues."

Everyone turned to watch as the nurses had a murmured conversation with the first woman in line. The shape of the line changed as the participants of the study shifted to get a better view. The woman accepted a paper cup and brought it to her lips.

Marcy felt her phone buzz in her back pocket. Leanne. This was a time Leanne sometimes called, when things were good. It was around the time Leanne got up and made herself a coffee. They hadn't spoken in three days, it was possible Leanne had forgotten she was at the clinic. Marcy looked at the big clock. The phone stopped vibrating in her pocket. They hadn't said anything about not looking at your phone but it seemed important to pay attention. Soon it would be her turn. The nurses were talking to someone four people away in the line. Marcy could see their tray. It could be her mother calling or telemarketers. Marcy could see that all the pills looked the same, the size of a Tylenol and bright blue.

The nurse asked her name and date of birth and then for her to hold out her wrist. Once he'd read her bracelet, he gestured to the tray. Marcy took a cup from the back corner and swallowed the pill in it. She'd never had trouble swallowing pills without water but she felt this one travelling down her throat. She accepted a water bottle from the muscly nurse.

Marcy took a seat in the middle of a long cafeteria table in the centre of the room. She took out her phone and saw there was a missed call from Leanne. Her empty stomach wrenched. There was no text message, just the missed call. She put the phone face down on the table.

Most people were wearing sweatpants and hoodies. There was one woman in a two-piece red satin pajama set with a pattern of polar bears sliding down snowy mountains. Marcy sat at the long cafeteria table and played with the tail of her plastic wristband. There were nurses at two smaller tables at the end of the room, they had stacks of paper on their tables and a cooler for blood samples on the floor between them.

Everyone had to give their blood once an hour for the first seven hours. Then they would move into a room filled with metal bunk beds and sleep until morning. Sometime before that there would be supper.

When the nurses called the number on your wristband you walked to the front of the room. For the first hour Marcy tried hard to read *The Mushroom at the End of the World*, which she'd taken out of the library after Hannah recommended it. The shouted numbers were distracting her; there was almost a rhythm to it but not quite. She was listening for her own number, 7856. Sometimes they would call the same number two or three times before the person stood up from the table, disoriented, and rushed up to the front.

A woman facing her one cafeteria table away had set up a chessboard and was playing herself. Every so often she'd pick up a book that was open in her lap and consult it before making a move. It was a paperback, the cover was a photograph of a chessboard floating against a glossy black background.

Another woman was studying for her driver's test: Marcy recognized the illustration of different methods of backing into a 90-degree-angle spot. She'd renewed her learner's permit three times and failed the road test twice before giving up on getting her license.

Down the bench from her in the opposite direction a young woman was playing Candy Crush. When her number got called, she continued tapping the phone screen as she walked to the front of the room. Marcy watched as the woman slid the phone into her pocket and took a seat. The nurse dug the needle in; Marcy could see the blood travel up the syringe. The nurse peeled open a bright blue Band-Aid and stuck it on the woman's arm. When she stood the nurse called, "7854."

Marcy reached into her bookbag and took out her sketch-book. She felt around the bottom of her bag for the case she kept her pencils in. She felt crumbs and bits of dirt getting under her nails. There was the case, between her laptop and *Paul Takes the Form of a Mortal Girl*, another of Hannah's recommendations.

She held the sketchbook in her lap and started drawing the chess woman, beginning with her ear. Glancing from the pad to her ear, trying to get the distance between each of the folds right. The ear turned out pretty good so she started her jawline.

After supper, bedtime was announced. It was manda-
tory that everyone move into the sleeping area; the lights
would be shut off, and no one was allowed to look at their
phones. People began gathering their things and joining
a slow procession towards the bunk beds. The woman in
front of Marcy stopped at the first empty bed. She turned
and explained that she didn't want to climb the ladder, there
was something with her knee.

Marcy was relieved to get a top bunk — it felt more private and safer than being at ground level. She kicked her
bookbag to the bottom of the bed and stretched out. The
mattress was the type where you could feel the zigzagging
outline of all the springs beneath you but it wasn't as bad as
her bed at home, which had a deep valley in the centre. She
wondered how likely it was that there were bedbugs waking
up inside the mattress. She put her hood up and tucked her
leggings into her socks. The mattress crunched each time
she moved and made her cringe, thinking of the woman
beneath her being disturbed. The pillow crinkled in her ear.
She put her hand under the pillowcase and found the pillow
was made out of a thick, waxy paper. Soon people were
snoring; Marcy could hear four distinct snores. She tried to
imagine who each snore might belong to. She moved along
the cafeteria tables in her mind's eye. She thought of those
strangers' chests rising and falling around her.

MARCY FELT HER whole body stiffen. She wanted to scream
but she couldn't even get a breath. There was a hand on
her ankle. A loud alarm was ringing through a speaker.
She looked down into the face of the person holding her

ankle, a white woman in her forties with a rust-coloured pixie cut and a white lab coat. Marcy's vantage point was so strange. She understood that she'd been asleep, that she was looking down from a tall bed, and then finally the surroundings came together and made sense.

"Critical breakfast," the woman said.

When she'd caught her breath, Marcy kicked the covers off. She kneeled in the bunk and tried to smooth out the blankets, though even as she was doing it she realized the beds would be stripped before anyone else slept in them. She dragged her bookbag close to her by the strap and climbed down the ladder.

Everyone had to go to the front of the room to collect a tray with the critical breakfast. You had to eat the whole thing in thirty minutes. Not finishing the breakfast within the allotted timeframe would mean not completing the trial and therefore not receiving full payment. Vomiting at any time during your stay, including after the breakfast, also meant disqualification from the study and reduced pay. Yesterday Marcy had been confident she would be able to finish the breakfast in time but this morning she felt queasy. She desperately wanted a coffee but coffee wasn't allowed.

There was a window in the wall with a ledge, beyond which Marcy saw a sterile kitchen. There was a regular stove and fridge in there, some counter space with an electric kettle plugged into the wall. When she reached the window, she was handed a yellow cafeteria tray by a young man in a hairnet and white lab coat. There were two slices of buttered toast cut on the diagonal, two fried eggs, two grey sausages, and a small carton of milk.

"You have to drink the milk?" Marcy said.

"You have to eat everything," the nurse in the hairnet said. "You have to drink the milk."

Marcy ate the entire breakfast. The inside of her mouth was coated in grease and her stomach sloshed. She burped and acidic liquid splashed up her throat. She breathed deep and put her head on the table. She repeated a quiet mantra to herself: *dontpukedontpukedontpuke*. She gave up on reading or drawing and found herself staring at the cinderblock wall. Many hours passed while she was lost in an exhausted trance, getting up to give blood every hour.

WHEN SHE WAS released, the cold air outside was like water splashed on her face. She wandered over to the Plexiglas bus shelter to see when the next bus was coming, but the thought of going inside anywhere was awful to her. She thought it might be better to walk in spite of how woozy she felt. She ripped the plastic bracelet off her wrist and dropped it in a sewer grate.

There was an elderly white woman sitting inside the bus stop, her legs splayed wide, a silver cane resting against one knee. She was holding a white paper bag from the pharmacy against one of her breasts, the top was rolled tight in her gloved fist. She waved to Marcy with her free hand. Marcy plucked out her earbuds one at a time and tucked them into the neck of her shirt. She stuck her head in the bus stop. She thought the woman might scold her for littering.

"Can you call me a cab?" the woman asked in English.

"Sure." Marcy unplugged the headphones and jammed

them in her pocket, thin loops of cord sticking out. "Do you have a number?"

"Yes." The woman lifted a purse off the bench beside her and slowly unzipped it, breathing heavy. She lifted out a roll of breath mints and dropped them back into the purse, then a small package of tissues, a glasses case. "Sorry, just a minute I have a book here somewhere."

Marcy should have just looked up a cab number, it was the beginning of the month, she had data. She could have figured it out, if she'd been a little more generous. She tried not to feel annoyed with the woman but her stomach was churning. She tried to put the cylinders of pork she'd eaten out of her mind. Eventually the woman found a small book with a laminated cover. She dragged a finger down a lined page in the middle and recited a number to Marcy.

"I'm sorry, again?" Marcy asked.

She repeated the number and Marcy dialled and waited as the hold music played. There had been no call or text from Leanne waiting on her phone. She pressed 2 for English. A middle-aged couple arrived at the bus stop and stood outside the booth. Marcy took a step away from them.

"Did you want to get in here?" She gestured to the shelter. The woman shook her head no.

Finally the taxi line connected but the woman on the other end said they couldn't send a cab to the bus stop. They needed another location somewhere nearby.

"Do you think you could walk to IGA over there?" Marcy pointed at a supermarket on the other end of the L-shaped strip mall.

"I can't walk, my foot's asleep, I've got no feeling in this foot that's why I'm calling the cab."

"I'm calling for a woman, I don't know her, she's in pain and she needs a cab because she can't walk," Marcy told the operator.

"Just give me a nearby address to put in the system."

Marcy tried to convey the problem to the woman but the elderly woman was becoming indignant and flustered, saying, "Tell them send it here, I need it here. Why can't they send it here?"

There were some houses down the block but Marcy couldn't make out the numbers on the front. The bus arrived and opened its doors to the warm interior. The couple climbed in and Marcy looked at the woman, checking if she might reconsider. She could tell the woman knew what she was thinking; she looked back at Marcy with a disappointed little headshake. It wasn't just that she needed Marcy's help, it was that Marcy owed it to her by virtue of being young and able-bodied and not doing anything important at that moment anyway. All of which was true. In a flash of inspiration, Marcy gave the taxi dispatcher the name of the strip mall behind them. She would flag the cab down when it got close.

"It's on the way," Marcy said with a warm smile, good deed completed.

"Wait with me, dear," the woman said.

Marcy tried to smooth out the frown she felt on her face.

"Yeah, wait with me, I'll need your help," the woman repeated.

"Of course."

Marcy watched the road — how long would it take? Aside from the minivan she'd got to move the washer, the last time she'd taken a taxi had been to move her things from her sublet with Al in Mile End to Little Italy. She remembered hefting her large suitcase into the trunk, sitting in the back seat surrounded by knotted plastic bags. She hadn't twisted the cap of her laundry detergent on tight enough and syrupy, windshield-washer-blue liquid had spilled all over the packets of spices and bottles of sauce she'd packed in the reusable shopping bag.

The sun was trying to shine through a swirl of snow. Marcy thought of all the blood they'd taken and it made her nauseous again and dizzy. She slurped warm water out of her dollar-store water bottle and thought of the microplastics sticking to her insides. The lights of the intersection changed three times and then the cab appeared. Marcy read the phone number on the plastic hat that sat on top of the vehicle.

"It's coming, there it is," Marcy said gleefully, but when she turned, the woman just looked tired.

The taxi driver was a brown man in his thirties, he was wearing a tight pink polo shirt with baby blue stripes. Marcy held out her pricked arm to the woman, who wrapped both hands around it. The taxi driver nodded at them both encouragingly. The woman tried to stand and fell back into the bench.

"I can't." She wiped beads of sweat off her forehead.

"Come on," Marcy said, she wrapped her arms around the woman's middle and pulled her up. The woman slid an arm over her shoulders and they started taking slow steps towards the open cab door. The taxi driver was on the other side, guiding the woman.

A woman with scrubs under her winter coat approached them. She spoke in French and Marcy shook her head. The woman said it again.

"English," Marcy said.

"She needs an ambulance," the woman in scrubs said.

"No!" the older woman said loudly.

Marcy and the taxi driver looked at each other, continuing their hobbling parade to the taxi.

"What will she do at home? She could lose consciousness," the woman in scrubs said.

"Are you a nurse or something?" Marcy asked.

"No, I don't want an ambulance, I'll have to pay. I'm fine. It's just my back, I know what it is."

"She needs the ambulance."

"No!" the older woman screeched into Marcy's ear.

They'd arrived at the open car door and the woman had fallen into the seat. Her legs were still out in the road. The taxi driver waved to Marcy, like I've got it from here. She turned around and started the long walk home. She tried calling Leanne but there was no answer and she hadn't really expected one.

MARCY DID LITTLE except sleep for two days. She worked her way through a bag of frozen dumplings, eating at strange hours in the same big T-shirt and bike shorts she'd been wearing since she got home. Looking at screens made her head hurt, and when she tried to read the words moved on the page like ants. Leanne hadn't been in touch since Marcy missed her call at the clinic, but Marcy's body couldn't summon the anxiety she usually felt when Leanne cut off communication. Instead she felt a vague sense of relief. She couldn't handle Leanne's intensity, whichever direction it happened to be flowing at the moment.

In the evening of the second day of recovery, her phone buzzed in the covers beside her. She flipped it over feeling dread about talking to Leanne but it was Hannah.

"Did you hear?" Hannah asked.

"About what?" Marcy asked.

"They're shutting things down."

"What do you mean?"

"The city, because of coronavirus."

"What things?" Everything felt hazy to Marcy, like she might be dreaming or hallucinating.

"What are you doing tonight? Can I come over?"

"I'm all fucked up from the study. I slept all day. I can't believe it's six o'clock. Yes, come over."

"Oh, the study! How was it? Was it okay?"

"When are you coming?"

"I could come now," Hannah said.

"Yeah, come over now. Can you pick up some takeout? I'll pay you back." Marcy crawled to the edge of her bed and lifted up her winter coat. She found her wallet and double-checked she still had twenty dollars in it.

"Sure, what do you want?"

"Anything that's on the way."

Hannah arrived an hour later with Styrofoam containers of Indian food and six cans of beer. When she heard Kathleen answering Hannah's knock, Marcy came out of her bedroom in her stale clothes. She left her phone in the bed. It felt good to be released from concern about missing Leanne's call.

Kathleen put on a Black Sabbath album and the sisters joined Marcy and Hannah at the table.

"Can you believe they've closed schools for two weeks?"

Sharon said. "Can you imagine being a kid? They're basically getting a second Christmas vacation."

Marcy felt like the world had been moving without her, she'd been completely tuned out.

"Would anyone like a beer?" Hannah pushed a can at Marcy, the sisters each accepted one. "My work said everyone should work from home. They sent a link to a video chat app we're supposed to download for a meeting in the morning."

Marcy cracked her beer. In this state a beer might kill her or it might set her straight.

"Do you two need some plates?" Kathleen stood up and gathered dishes and cutlery for Marcy and Hannah.

"I'm sorry, I'm so out of it," Marcy said.

"Food will help," Hannah told her.

"My friend Devon works at a *casse croute* and they closed for a week yesterday, as a precaution," Sharon said.

"It's so freaky." Marcy felt like the beer was helping.

"What about Leanne? What's happening with the pizza place?" Hannah asked.

"I bet they'll stay open for takeout," Kathleen answered before Marcy had to. "They're keeping the supermarkets open though, and pharmacies."

"Transit?" Sharon asked.

"Transit's open, they can't close that," Kathleen said.

"What if it's more than two weeks? Like in China," Hannah said.

"No, I can't imagine that," Kathleen said. "Everything's about money for Legault, he won't let it happen."

After the beer the sisters got a bottle of gin down from the top of the fridge. Hannah went to the gas station for mix and Marcy rolled a joint. She'd just been starting to feel connected to reality again but weed seemed like a better choice than liquor for the fragile equilibrium in her body. For the rest of the night she let the conversation about the shutdown swirl around her, enjoying the sensation of being in the centre of it without having to contribute anything.

When she got in bed that night there was a missed call from Leanne but she didn't bother returning it or even texting. Hannah had decided to sleep on the couch. It felt so good to be in her own bed, with Hannah, Sharon, and Kathleen sleeping all around her. The city outside her window seemed quieter than usual. She thought of the woman from the bus stop, who was probably sleeping alone.

Four

Spring 2020

12

When Marcy woke up the next day Hannah had already left. She showered and walked to Leanne's house, uninvited. She hadn't totally admitted to herself that she was walking to Leanne's. She'd told her roommates she needed fresh air. Then she was in Leanne's small, muddy yard thinking about whether to ring the buzzer, and when she entered the cool porch and pressed hard on the button, she was still full of doubt.

"Hello?" Leanne's voice squawked through the wall, distorted by the speaker.

"Hi, it's me, Marcy."

There was a pause and then the blast of sound that let you know the door was momentarily unlocked. Marcy grabbed the handle and tugged it open. She took her shoes off outside Leanne's apartment.

"Is it okay that I'm here?" Marcy said. "I don't have to stay."

But Leanne walked over to her with her arms out. Marcy

stepped into them and Leanne kissed the top of her head, hugging her tight.

"What the fuck is happening in the world?" Leanne said. "Are you hungry? I have some soup heating up."

"I did the study, Leanne." Marcy was surprised that she had tears in her eyes.

"I don't care, it's your life," Leanne said. "Have some soup."

AFTER A WEEK at Leanne's she went home to pick up some of her things. The loft was a mess. Sharon and Kathleen were both stoned and in their pajamas.

"How are you?" Sharon asked Marcy.

"I'm okay. I'm just getting some stuff to bring over to Leanne's. She got laid off and she's alone at her place. I don't want to leave her there, so I think I'll stay there for a while."

"Totally," Sharon said.

"She could come here," Kathleen said. "You should both stay here, we can watch movies and stuff."

"Yeah." Marcy hadn't thought of that. "Yeah, maybe we will."

"You should come back." Kathleen got up and stirred something on the stove.

"Probably I will, sometime soon." It was hard to imagine convincing Leanne to come stay in the loft. Leanne didn't like staying at Marcy's under the best circumstances and she wouldn't want to feel trapped there.

Marcy went to her room and filled her knapsack with clothes. She took some of the books she'd been reading and her drawing things. She was rushing because, for some reason, being in her own bedroom made her feel guilty. She was afraid of imposing on Sharon and Kathleen's cocooned privacy, even though they'd done nothing to make her feel unwelcome. She sat on the bed for a moment with her bookbag hanging open and appreciated being all alone with the door closed.

WEEKS WENT BY in Leanne's dark apartment. Marcy played an online scrabble game with Hannah. Leanne made elaborate meals every day for a stretch and then they ate takeout over and over. Marcy did hate speech sorting and workplace safety video captioning. The mental health gig was on hold again, but it didn't matter because soon she'd be receiving the money from the study. She found that she could sort and caption while stoned so she abandoned her rule of only smoking weed in the evenings. The days started slurring together even more intensely than before. Each morning in bed she or Leanne refreshed the rising number of infections and deaths and read the numbers to each other. In that first strange month they didn't fight at all.

THE NEWS HAD suggested monitoring your temperature for symptoms of the virus so Marcy went to the pharmacy down the block and bought a digital thermometer. The man behind the counter was wearing a paper mask.

Marcy walked by the gym where she'd taken spin classes and saw through the window that all the equipment was gone. Now the only piece of furniture in the enormous room was the front desk with the sign-in binder still open on the counter. She wondered whether the butchy, tattooed

spin instructor she'd loved was making videos in her basement or hosting classes online. Her phone buzzed in her
pocket, her mom. She'd been talking to her mom more
regularly since the lockdown had been announced.

"Marcy," she said. "I just read the news."

"Which news."

"They're saying they might close provincial borders. If
you want to get on a plane your father and I will help you
out."

"I'm okay. It's safe if you don't have to work. I work from
home."

"Marcy, that's ridiculous. You can't stay there. Why would
you?"

"I have a life here."

"We don't know how long this is going to be. It could be
like Italy up there. You know in Italy the doctors are having
breakdowns because they have to decide who to put on
ventilators? They don't have enough ventilators."

"I'm not coming home."

"Why would you want to be there instead of with
your family, I can't understand it. You can't even go out
anywhere."

"Because I live here." Marcy was searching for why. "All
my stuff is here."

"Your family might need you, did you ever think of that?"

"I think my phone's going to die."

"Okay, Marcy."

"No, really it is. I love you, Mom."

"Really?"

"I love you."

"Yeah, I love you too." Her mother hung up.

. . .

THE NEWS FLIP-FLOPPED about whether masks were helpful or not but Kathleen dropped a Ziploc baggy full of ones she'd sewn from old pillowcases into Leanne's mailbox. Marcy decided to wear one at the supermarket. She had been doing all the grocery shopping. It didn't make sense to go together because only ten shoppers were allowed inside PA at a time, and there was a massive line to get in. The one time they'd gone together Leanne had yelled at the woman in line behind them for not respecting social distancing. At the door a man in a white plastic jumper pumped hand sanitizer into waiting palms before admitting people into the store.

One night Hannah texted to ask if Marcy wanted to video chat. Leanne was in the bathroom rubbing peroxide through her hair. After the bleaching, they'd planned to tune in to a Twitch stream of the Wachowskis' *Speed Racer* that Leanne's co-worker was running.

"I'm going for a quick walk," Marcy called. She wasn't sure Leanne had heard her but she stomped into her shoes. Marcy sat on the curb outside the apartment in a big sweatshirt. She had three bars of internet. She pressed the little camera beside Hannah's name in her phone.

Hannah was on her couch wrapped in a fleece blanket. "Are you outside?"

"Yeah."

"I can barely see you," Hannah said. Marcy's image was pixelated from the lack of light.

"I wanted some privacy," Marcy explained. "But it's really good to see you. How are you?"

"I'm fine," Hannah said. "Like, I'm depressed obviously but I'm working from home. So I'm fine."

"Right, me too. I'm going to get paid from the study this week and I'm still doing captioning and stuff," Marcy said. "Leanne is trying to figure out how to get on the government benefit for service workers? Have you heard about it? They announced it the other day and said it's two thousand a month but there's no information on how to apply."

"Someone was telling me about it. Ashley, I think, because her mom works at a supermarket so she's not eligible because she's an essential worker, so she has to keep working. All she gets is the measly two-dollar raise," Hannah said. "You know what the other fucked thing is? If they know two thousand a month is the living wage, why are minimum wage and welfare so low?"

"I'm going to ask Sharon and Kathleen if they figured out how to apply."

"Yeah, good call. How are they?"

Marcy glanced over her shoulder at the house. "I haven't really been talking to them. I've been staying at Leanne's."

"How's that going? One sec." Hannah dropped her phone in her lap and leaned forward. The screen was momentarily filled with a blur of pink blanket. Hannah straightened up but left the phone in her lap, giving Marcy a view up her nose as she lit a roach. "Are you going to go home?"

"To my apartment, you mean?" Marcy said. She hadn't been wearing socks when she hurried outside and the cold was starting to make her ankles ache. "I don't know. I guess. Can you believe it's almost a month of this?"

"They're saying Quebec has some of the highest numbers. It could get worse than the States here. Oh, listen, you should come volunteer with me. Thursday evening at Strength Through Numbers, it's just handing out sandwiches and stuff. They really need people. I did it last week and it was so nice, it just felt really good to be around people."

"Okay, yeah!" Marcy said, excited by the prospect of spending time with Hannah. "I mean, I guess I have to talk to Leanne."

"I'm going Thursday around six thirty, I'll pick you up and we can bus down."

"I just have to check with Leanne, we haven't been seeing people at all," Marcy repeated. She was surprised to hear Hannah was using transit. "But yeah, message me. I should let you go. We're going to watch *Speed Racer*."

When the call ended Marcy saw it had been less than ten minutes. Inside the apartment, Leanne was still in the bathroom and Marcy could hear someone enthusiastically describing their home bleaching technique. Marcy followed the voice into the bathroom. Leanne was sitting on the closed toilet seat, she had a garbage bag with a head hole torn in it draped over her shoulders, and there was a smaller plastic bag flip-clipped to her head. Her phone was in a metal bowl on the edge of the bathtub playing a YouTube video.

"How's it going?"

"My scalp is burning." Leanne gestured to the phone. "This person says it's normal."

Marcy leaned in to kiss Leanne's face and the chemicals burned the inside of her nose.

"I was just talking to Hannah. She's been volunteering with Strength Through Numbers."

"Cool."

"Just like handing out sandwiches and stuff."

"Can you check the timer on my phone." Leanne held up her gloved hands.

"You have two minutes left." Marcy dropped the phone back in the bowl. "I was thinking I might join her next Thursday."

"Since when do you volunteer?"

"I used to do more of that kind of thing in St. John's. Well, Brit did a lot of that and I helped out sometimes."

"Your ex?"

Marcy nodded. She ran the tap in the sink, rinsing some thick, creamy chemicals down the drain.

"I think that's a seriously bad idea, Marcy. What if you get sick?"

"I think it's socially distanced, I mean it must be," Marcy said. "I could wear a mask."

"Hannah lives alone right? So she's not risking other people's lives with this decision."

The timer went off and Leanne ripped the bag off her head and stuffed it into the garbage, flip-clips and all. Her hair was white and clumped with the chemical cream. It made her eyes look even brighter green.

"I won't do it if you don't want me to." Marcy said. "Obviously."

"If you want to do that you can go stay at your place. You don't have to stay here." Leanne kneeled beside the bathtub, turned the tap and stuck her head under.

"Keep your eyes closed," Marcy squealed.

Leanne turned her head from side to side under the tap, rinsing the bleach out. Then she straightened and shook her wet hair, rubbing the back of her neck.

"I'm not going to do it," Marcy said.

Leanne stood up and put her arms around Marcy. "I'm sorry, it just freaks me out. What if you had to be in the hospital all alone and I couldn't come see you? That's scary. I don't think your mom would want you doing that."

Marcy thought about the crowded hospital wings. Even before the pandemic she'd heard stories about people having to sleep on cots in the bright and noisy hallways of the hospital for nights on end before seeing a doctor. And then there was the possibility of infecting other people. Kathleen's friend had gotten it early on, a guy their age, and weeks later he still felt winded from walking up the stairs to his place. She'd heard about the old people trapped in understaffed CLCss.

"You're right." Marcy squeezed Leanne tight, the bleach smell made her eyes water.

Leanne logged into Twitch. They'd missed the beginning and a chat was already running at lightning speed alongside the movie. Marcy texted Hannah.

I don't think I can make it thurs, let's chat again soon <3

THE MONEY FROM Leanne's settlement came in early April. She and Marcy watched through the small window above the sink as the van Leanne had purchased pulled into a parking spot behind the building. Leanne pulled the window open, snow was melting and the air smelled damp and fresh.

"It's fucking beautiful," Leanne said, and Marcy felt it too. The van was a baby blue rectangle with wheel-wells under the front seats and four huge windows in the back. The driver hopped out, a guy in his sixties dressed in denim pants and a denim jacket. All three of them waved to each other. Leanne took out her phone and e-transferred him. She yelled through the window screen, waving her phone, "Just sent the money!"

The man took out his phone. They all waited for the transfer to go through. Finally he called, "Keys are in the ignition!" and started walking down the alley.

Once he was out of sight Marcy and Leanne went around back to inspect the van. Leanne tugged the driver's door open and hopped in. She turned the key with the door still hanging open. "Oh my god, the gearshift is on the floor."

"Are you going to be able to drive that?" Marcy asked, marvelling at the steering wheel which was as big as a school bus's.

"Guess I'm about to find out."

"Now?"

"Yeah," Leanne laughed. She leaned over and unlocked the passenger door.

Marcy ran around and pulled herself up into the passenger seat. She liked the musty smell inside the van. She put her palms flat on the warm dash.

"Where should we go?" Leanne asked.

"Up the mountain?" Marcy suggested, falling back into her seat and rolling the huge window down. She savoured the sensation of turning the handle to lower the window — it was more satisfying than pressing an electric button.

"You got it, baby." Leanne wrenched the gearshift on the floor and drove them out onto Saint-Urbain. It was sunny and there were more people in the street than Marcy had seen in a long time. People biking and walking in pairs mostly, but some larger groups of teenagers.

At a stoplight she looked over her shoulder, taking in the back of the van. "There are seven seats back there!"

"I know — and room for bikes." Leanne smiled. "The seats come out too. I'm going to take them out for my trip."

Marcy hadn't believed in the trip. She hadn't believed the van would materialize. She was starting to understand how good Leanne was at getting the things she wanted.

Leanne glanced over at her. "You could come, you know. You're invited."

Marcy was grateful that the wind whipping her hair around was hiding her face. She didn't want to go with Leanne, and she didn't want to be left behind.

Leanne said, "We could just drive and explore, wander around in nature all day. Not be locked up in an apartment. You know numbers here are almost as bad as the States? Maybe worse now?"

"How long will it take you to get the van together?"

"I already put my notice in for the apartment. So I'm leaving July first, no matter what state it's in — but I think I can get it together by then." Now they were chugging slowly up the side of the mountain, Leanne reaching down to wrench the gearshift every so often. "It's mainly just building the bed. That's like an afternoon, tops. And then I have to get some camping gear together, mostly second-hand hopefully. I'm going to start planning the trip soon, there'll be a lot of improvising and like going with the flow, but I'm also going to do some planning."

"You didn't tell me that, about the lease."

"I did tell you, ages ago."

Leanne pulled them into a parking spot with a view of the city that stretched all the way to the Olympic Stadium and the water beyond it. There was a man leaning against the stone retaining wall with an open cooler and neat rows of clunky silver jewellery on a piece of cardboard at his feet. Two women approached and handed him fives that he slid into a leather fanny pack as they bent to take beers from the cooler.

"Our place is just there, see Jeanne-Mance?" Leanne was pointing out the windshield. Marcy looked at her end of the city, wondering if her own roof might be visible.

Leanne leaned across the wide space between their seats to squeeze Marcy's knee. "Do you want to come?"

"Things might be really different by then," Marcy said.

"Yeah, probably a lot worse," Leanne said.

BY MID-MAY IT was indisputably spring, you could leave the house without worrying about a jacket.

Marcy messaged Sharon and Kathleen to ask if they would be comfortable with her coming by to grab some of her summer clothes. She stopped in when they were out. The living room had been rearranged and one of the walls was painted a fresh salmon pink. In her bedroom most of the plants were dead. She tried to imagine what it would be like to sleep alone in her double bed. She stuffed her JanSport full of clothes and wrestled her bike out from the space between the bedframe and the wall. She rode home on flat tires.

Leanne was spending a lot of time in the alley behind the apartment working on the van. First, she carefully removed the seats so they could be reinstalled, then she started work on the bedframe. Sometimes she just lay on the corrugated plastic floor of the van looking at her phone or reading. There was a stack of books resting on the passenger seat and a box of granola bars in a net she'd attached to the ceiling.

"Imagining being on the open road?" Marcy asked one day.

"I can't wait to get the fuck out of here," Leanne answered without sitting up. "It's so claustrophobic in this city."

When she wasn't hanging around the van, Leanne made lists and calculations in a spiral-bound notebook, tapping the calculator app on her phone and jotting down her findings. When Marcy asked what she was working on, Leanne said, "I can't talk while I'm doing math."

One day, she left the notebook open on the kitchen table when she went to the bathroom and Marcy flipped through it. There were measurements for things Leanne wanted to build for the van, calculations about mileage and gas, lists of camping gear and meals to make on the road.

Marcy pictured stirring a pot of oatmeal balanced on a grate over a campfire, pulling the van over to skinny-dip, getting to appreciate the full force of the stars again. But there would also be moody mornings, waking up stiff in the dark van, the smell of shit and chemicals coming from the plastic toilet, Leanne grumpy after hours of driving. Plus, she didn't even know if she was invited anymore.

Leanne opened the bathroom door and kicked a pile of Marcy's dirty clothes out into the living room area. "Can you please not?"

Marcy stood. "Okay, jeez, you could just ask me to pick it up."

"There's dirty clothes on the bedroom floor too. I feel like I'm living with a teenager."

Leanne took her notebook and went back out to the van, slamming the door behind her. Marcy felt like she might cry until she looked at her phone.

A message from Hannah: *You know what I want to know? What evil shit is the government pushing through while all the news outlets are publishing endless articles about covid? Not saying they shouldn't be publishing covid stuff but I'm sure Legault, Trudeau etc will take advantage of people's attention being focused on the pandemic.*

And then a message Sharon had sent at one in the morning: *Have you heard of Club Quarantine? When are you coming home so we can dance together?*

Below the text was a photo of Kathleen in a long leather trench dancing in front of an image projected on the wall. There was a huge image on the wall of a stranger in a gold lamé bikini sitting on an exercise bike waving blurry hands above their head. A small square at the bottom of the screen showed their loft with Kathleen swishing her coat around in the foreground.

It was good to remember there were other people in her life. She could pack up her things and go back to her place right now if she wanted. But then, what if Leanne left the city without speaking to her? Marcy could easily imagine it.

ONE NIGHT LEANNE came in from hanging out in the van, a headlamp on her forehead casting a yellow beam around the apartment. Marcy was lying on the couch, playing online scrabble with Hannah.

"You know that thing is on?" Marcy put a hand over her eyes to shield them from Leanne's light.

Leanne pulled the headlamp down so it hung around her neck, a circle of yellow bouncing on her sneakers. "I need your help."

Marcy sat up. "Is everything okay?"

"I want to ask a favour."

Four bouncing bubbles on the screen meant that Hannah was about to post her next word but Marcy squeezed her phone and made the screen go black.

"It won't take long but it would be good to go now," Leanne said.

"Jesus, what?"

"You know that new condo by your place? I drove by this evening and they left a bunch of lumber out."

"You want to take it?" Marcy knew exactly the wood Leanne was talking about, she'd noticed it when she went to get her stuff from the apartment. The first sign that the construction surrounding her building had started up again.

"I can't lift it on my own," Leanne said.

They parked the van around the corner from the construction site and both wore the covid masks Kathleen had made them, to hide their faces from any cameras that might be trained on the site. Marcy's had a pattern of Care Bears on it, and it tied around the back of her head with loops of rainbow yarn.

A grid of rubbery orange safety fence separated the site from the sidewalk. Whatever was there before had been demolished. Three dumpsters filled with debris sat in the middle of the lot and new materials were stacked closer to the outside edge.

Marcy held up the bottom of the fencing so Leanne could crouch and crab-walk under it. Leanne quickly tugged boards off a massive pile of wood and slid muddy two-by-fours under the fence while Marcy kept watch. There was no one walking around the neighbourhood; everyone was inside making sourdough and video-chatting with their friends. Her building was just one block over. She imagined Sharon and Kathleen watching a movie on the projector with the couch throw over their knees. A car drove by and Marcy saw insulated DoorDash delivery bags stacked in the front seat. When Leanne passed the sixth board out, Marcy barked, "Okay, I don't think we can carry more than that."

Surprisingly, Leanne darted obediently out from under the fence.

They walked the boards around the corner facing each other. Marcy walked backwards with her legs bowed under the weight. Leanne guided them: "A little to the left, okay good, watch out, the curb!"

They parked the van out back with the stolen wood locked inside.

LEANNE USUALLY BROWSED iOverlander on her phone in bed, marking down the names of sites that interested her. Marcy would smoke weed until she fell asleep beside her with the lights on. They hadn't had sex since their drive up the mountain but after they got back with the wood Leanne pushed her up against the wall in the porch and started making out with her. It felt good. It had been ages since Marcy had even thought about masturbating when she was alone in the apartment. Now she was so wet her underwear was damp and the insides of her thighs felt slippery.

Marcy stuck her tongue into Leanne's mouth and Leanne sucked it hard, so hard it started to hurt and then it started to feel like Marcy's tongue might come off and slither down Leanne's throat and she'd never get it back. She slapped Leanne on the hip and Leanne let go of her tongue and took her by the hand and led her gently into the apartment. In the early days of the lockdown, before they completely stopped having sex, they'd mostly been making out with their respective vibrators between their legs, curling against each other when they came. Which was good in its own way. But on the night they stole the wood, Leanne got her leather harness and big purple dildo out of the bedside table. Marcy crawled onto the bed and flipped over onto her belly. Leanne pulled Marcy's sweatpants and underwear down to her knees, took her by the hips, and fucked her hard. Marcy came with her face in the pillow. Leanne collapsed on top of her and kissed the side of her face by her hairline.

When she woke up the next morning the apartment was empty. She looked out the kitchen window and saw Leanne out back in her sports bra and bike shorts, sawing up the wood they'd stolen the night before.

MARCY KNEW OTHER people were seeing their friends outdoors. Leanne's co-workers had messaged a couple of times and asked if she wanted to meet at the park beneath the underpass at Van Horne for picnics in the afternoon or beers in the evening. Leanne never went. Marcy thought it had more to do with her obsessing over the van and the trip than being afraid of getting or spreading the virus, but she kept her opinions to herself. When Kathleen texted to say some people from the building were meeting for a fire behind the shipping containers near their place, Marcy didn't mention it to Leanne. If she avoided having a real conversation about seeing friends it would be less of an overt betrayal when she met up with Hannah.

She had messaged Hannah the morning after the stolen-wood sex. She'd sat on the toilet with the bathroom door locked while she waited for Hannah to respond. They made a plan to meet at Laurier Park. The afternoon of the meet-up Leanne went to Home Depot to try to exchange her new circular saw because the cord sparked when she plugged it in. So Marcy didn't even have to make up an excuse about where she was going. She just unlocked her bike and climbed on and pumped her legs hard, cold handlebars pointed towards the park and Hannah. Even biking this short, flat distance after the long, sedentary winter made her butt hurt.

She saw Hannah at the intersection by the park and waved wildly to her. They rolled their bikes over the muddy ground to a picnic table, passing a children's play structure wrapped in flapping caution tape. They leaned their bikes at opposite ends of the table and sat across from each other. Hannah took a Tupperware container out of her messenger bag and peeled the lid off. There was a thick slice of cake inside coated in hot pink icing.

"I brought you a fork too," Hannah said, reaching into her bag.

"Did you make this?" Marcy was feeling overwhelmed with emotion. It felt so good to sit across from Hannah but it also made her realize how lonely she had been.

"Yeah." Hannah found the fork and wiped it on the front of her jacket.

"I didn't know you bake." Marcy speared a forkful of cake.

"I've been getting into it, like everyone else. The other thing I brought." Hannah held up a joint.

Marcy felt herself becoming giddy. "This cake is fucking amazing, it's moist and the icing is so thick and creamy."

"Do you want to smoke this?" Hannah asked.

"I mean I guess we shouldn't, technically." Marcy was taking another bite of the cake. "But we're already sitting here like this. I haven't been inside or even really outside with anyone besides Leanne in ages."

"Well I have," Hannah said, lighting the joint. "Volunteering. But I feel fine."

"I feel fine too," said Marcy, and after a pause, "but I guess some people are asymptomatic."

Hannah held the joint out to her, exhaling, "Up to you, no pressure."

Marcy took the joint and smoked it. When she finished the slice of cake she cleaned smears of icing off the sides of the container with her fingers. She and Hannah giggled as they watched an off-leash poodle squat on its haunches to shit.

"I think I feel differently than other people because I've been around people since the beginning with the volunteering," Hannah said. "It's like people who've had to work versus the people who've been able to isolate. Even though I'm mostly just alone in my apartment all the time. I don't know if I'd trade it though, I can't imagine what it's like to have roommates or live with a partner or whatever. You're still at Leanne's?"

"Leanne is leaving the city," Marcy said.

"Going where?"

"Just driving around in a van. She might not come back."

"Like a van-life kind of thing?" Hannah asked.

"I guess she does watch those videos," Marcy said. "She asked me to go with her."

"And you said no?" Hannah asked.

"If she asks me again, I might say yes."

"What about your roommates? Would you be able to do your job on the road?"

"I don't think I *should* say yes, but I feel like I might."

"Then don't. Stay here."

On the bike ride home, Marcy realized she had been hoping Hannah would beg her to stay, or demand she stay for her own good. Even though Hannah had said the magic words, it still disappointingly felt like her own decision.

When she got back to the apartment Leanne was in the back, lying on the roof of the van reading a book. Marcy opened the back door and called, "Did they take the saw back?"

Leanne answered without taking her eyes off the page, "Yep."

She never asked where Marcy had been.

LEANNE HAD PLANNED to make spaghetti for supper. She had started a big pot of tomato sauce with ground beef when she looked out the window and saw the front wheel of her bike had been stolen. Marcy could feel the immediate atmospheric shift of Leanne's mood changing but couldn't tell if Leanne was about to crash into tears or work herself up into a rage.

"They declared bike shops an essential service," Marcy said.

Leanne immediately called Right to Ride on Villeneuve and sprinted out the door still on the phone with them. She called, "Watch the sauce," before slamming the door shut.

Marcy felt the relief of having the apartment to herself and tried to think of what to do with the time. The roach she and Leanne had smoked as they watched *Seinfeld* the night before was still lying on the coffee table amongst some puzzle pieces. She kneeled and sparked the lighter. She hated the puzzle. It was an impressionist painting of a circus tent in burgundy and royal blue with smears of gold and electric green in 1,500 pieces. It was like a bruise smashed apart on the coffee table. Also, she was just bad at it.

After one puff she felt stoned and started sliding the green pieces together. Leanne might come back happy to have caught the store before they closed or she might be angry because of the theft. Marcy found a piece with a U-shaped opening and another with a tab that snapped right into it. The front door opened.

"I got it!" Leanne called. A cool breeze moved through the hall and made the wall hanging flutter. Leanne stood on the other side of the coffee table in her hiking boots. She was wearing a plaid jacket, her bleached hair ruffled from the wind, holding the wheel at her hip. Marcy thought she looked boyish and beautiful and also, thankfully, happy.

"Something's burning," Leanne said. "The sauce."

"I forgot." Marcy's finger was still holding the seam of two slime-green puzzle pieces together.

Leanne stormed to the stove and lifted the lid. The

burning smell intensified. She dropped the lid on the counter, sending drips of sauce all over the backsplash. She was still gripping the wheel tight in her other hand.

"Maybe it's just the bottom," Marcy said. "Maybe we can skim off the top."

"No, it's ruined," Leanne said. "You didn't smell that?"

"Just try tasting the top." Marcy gestured to the wheel. "Do you want me to put that away?"

Leanne didn't answer, dipped a wooden spoon into the sauce and tasted it.

"It's disgusting. It's burnt." But Marcy thought she heard some room for cajoling.

"Are you sure, can I try it?"

The pot bubbled and a drip of sauce leapt onto Leanne's pale-blue-and-yellow plaid. Marcy took a step towards Leanne at the same moment Leanne involuntarily swung her body away from the boiling pot and the wooden spoon slapped Marcy's face. It stung her cheekbone. She touched her hand to her face and found it wet. The scalding sauce from the back of the spoon coated her cheek. Leanne looked at her and scrunched her face into a sneer before turning and stomping away. The bedroom door slammed. Marcy wiped the sauce off her face with a flat palm that she rubbed on her pants. She turned the burner off.

She went to the bathroom and looked in the mirror. There was sauce on her neck, there were drips on her T-shirt and the big smear on her jeans. She wet a corner of the hand towel and rubbed her neck clean. The scratchy terry cloth felt good. She cleaned her whole face and then she looked in the mirror again. Her cheek was bright red. Maybe from rubbing with the scratchy towel or from the heat of the sauce but maybe from the impact of the spoon, it was impossible to tell.

She pulled her jacket off a hook by the door and felt in the pocket for a mask and a set of keys. Outside the cold stung her face, especially in the damp spot. She walked down Park. Usually she never walked that way but she was craving the ugliness of a rush of cars coming at her, the smell of exhaust in the damp air. She wanted to walk through the underpass and shiver at the pigeon wings beating around her.

She touched the tender spot on her cheek. It had been an accident, but the sneer meant it was deserved. She walked to Tim Hortons and ordered a small hot chocolate. Normally at this hour the place would be packed with people eating together. She wished she could sit at a table facing the door but instead she followed the arrows back out. The drink burned her tongue so that she could feel individual taste buds. The liquid was thin, sickly sweet, and a little bit salty.

A person with some self-respect would just go home to her own apartment. If she did that it would be days before Leanne forgave her. If she went back now and apologized, then maybe they could swing things around, hold each other through the night and have a nice morning together. It was true the burnt sauce was her fault and now there was no dinner. She loved waking up before Leanne and smoking a cigarette on the front step. She often made one cup of stovetop espresso for herself before Leanne woke up and then, close to nine, she made another cup for them to share.

She would wake Leanne by climbing under the covers and holding her warm body close. When Leanne accepted that it was time to wake up, Marcy would reach down the side of the bed for the second coffee. One of them would hold the hot cup as they took turns dipping their heads to suck coffee up, careful not to spill it on the covers. Often they would make a big breakfast with bacon or sausage and fry the eggs in the fat.

When she finished her hot chocolate she stuck a finger in the warm sludge at the bottom and sucked it clean. It was so sweet it made her throat itch. As she walked, Marcy pressed two fingers into the spot where the spoon had hit her face. Her skin was tight and sore but there wouldn't be a bruise, the pain didn't have that kind of depth. She walked fast to try to hold the heat of the hot chocolate in her belly.

She used her key to open the front door. Marcy could hear Sharon Van Etten playing in Leanne's bedroom. She knocked and there was no answer, so she knocked again. She heard the screech of Leanne's wheelie office chair — "What do you want?"

"Should we get some takeout?" Marcy said. "I can order us something."

She tried the knob, but it was stiff. Part of her had known it would be locked but the confirmation stung.

"I'm not hungry anymore," Leanne said.

In Marcy's family, fights ended when someone apologized and then the problem was erased. There were dramatic displays of rage: feet were stomped, dinners dumped in the trash, valuables thrown out the window. But you did not hold a grudge.

"What are you doing? Can I come in?" Marcy tried.

"Research for my trip."

"Can I come in?"

"Why?"

"To talk."

There was a pause and Leanne opened the door. "I think you should go home."

"I'm sorry about the sauce."

"I don't want to talk. It's not even about the sauce. I don't want to talk to you, okay? I just don't at all."

"Okay," Marcy said.

"I'm going to have to start emptying the apartment soon anyway. You should just take your stuff and go home." Leanne had crammed a bunch of Marcy's clothes into a plastic bag and now she dropped it in the hall.

For a moment they stood staring at each other in the doorway. Marcy had already humiliated herself so thoroughly, nothing could make it worse. So she said, "Are you sure?"

"Yes." Leanne shut the door.

"Leanne," Marcy said.

"I don't want to talk to you, can you give me some space please."

And then, just to make sure every single, tiny scrap of dignity left was scoured out of her, Marcy went to the kitchen, dumped the burnt sauce in the garbage, and cleaned the pot before leaving.

SHE WAS RELIEVED that Sharon and Kathleen were in their bedrooms when she came home. She could hear canned sitcom laughter on Sharon's side of their shared bedroom wall. Techno was thumping through the ceiling upstairs and, shockingly, she could hear many sets of feet moving around up there. People were still partying.

She turned on the humidifier and dripped lemon essential oil into it before turning out the lights. She focused very hard on not looking at her phone but her ears were aching for the sound of it vibrating. Eventually she summoned the will to reach down and squeeze the button on top that powered it down. It might be days before Leanne messaged her.

She got up and turned on the lamp on her dresser and leaned into the mirror to look at her face. There was no mark. When she pressed her fingers in hard she could still find a sore little puddle of tissue on the highest peak of her cheekbone. She dug in her sock drawer until she found a baggy of weed from the guy down the hall and made herself a limp joint. Once she was very stoned she pulled the covers over her head and fell asleep.

She woke up groggy and took a shower without turning her phone on. She decided to bike to the mountain and call Linda before her roommates woke up. She wasn't ready to explain to them or anyone else in the city why she was back in her own apartment. The sun had been up for an hour or two but the party upstairs had sustained itself through the night.

On the mountain she listened to an hour-long interview with Ashton Kutcher, preparing herself for the phone call. She stopped to watch a raccoon throw empty McDonald's containers out of a garbage can. There were un-masked police on horses plodding up and down the path. Marcy watched them stop two young women of colour in masks who were walking side by side, and interrogate them about whether they lived in the same household. She stood a few paces from them, trying to let the police know she was watching. After the girls took out their wallets and flashed

IDs, the cops finally let them go. A woman cop with a blond ponytail waved at Marcy and smiled.

They hadn't spoken since she left Montreal but Linda picked up on the second ring. First, Marcy told her almost everything she'd learned about Ashton Kutcher, how he'd been discovered by a modelling scout in a bar in the town where he'd grown up. He'd been working at a cereal factory with his dad but the scout convinced him to participate in a modelling contest at the local mall, and he won and left for the big city. With just his Boy Scouts bookbag and two hundred dollars, or a hundred dollars, it could have been three hundred dollars. Linda assured her she was getting the gist. And now Kutcher was a millionaire movie-star-art-collector-tech-investor guy. Marcy was surprised to feel a hot tear drip down her cheek.

"Art collector?" Linda said.

"Yeah, him and Brad Pitt are friends and they collect art together. Contemporary art. But like as an investment I think. And he said he only does roles that really interest him now."

"Huh, well there you go," Linda said. "And how are you?"

"Do you think he's handsome?" Marcy asked.

"Ashton Kutcher? I mean sure." Her tone said she knew Marcy had called for a reason but she wasn't going to rush her.

"Something kind of bad happened, I think," Marcy said.

A second, smaller raccoon was leaning against the outside of the garbage examining the bits of trash that fell over the lip of the can. It lifted a piece of shredded lettuce out of a Big Mac box between its leathery fingers and sniffed. Two teenage girls stopped to film the raccoons.

"Yeah?" Linda asked.

Marcy described the evening, the burned dinner, the spoon, her time in the cold with her Tim Hortons.

"It really was an accident," Marcy said. "But she was mad when it happened. It just felt bad."

"Yeah," Linda said.

"And I was stoned so I don't really know."

The first raccoon tumbled out of the garbage and snatched an empty fries sleeve from the smaller raccoon. He held it with both hands and stuck his snout deep inside.

"That's enough, feeling bad is enough. You don't need a reason, you don't need proof."

"It can be really lonely here," Marcy said.

"You could always come home," Linda said.

13

On the third night of sleeping alone above the chandeliers Marcy fell asleep thinking about Newfoundland. When she was a teenager, she'd hopped in a car with some older boys who were driving the Irish Loop to see the carcass of a whale that had washed up on the beach in Trepassey. They hotboxed the car as they sped along the dilapidated highway. They stopped for lunch at a fish and chips place, slamming together two small tables draped in vinyl at the back of the restaurant. The weed made Marcy ravenous and she ate two pieces of battered fish and a large fries with dressing and gravy. When she was done she leaned back in her chair and flaunted her bloated belly.

Just before reaching Trepassey, they'd pulled into the tall grass alongside an abandoned saltbox and crawled through a smashed window into the kitchen. An armchair had sunk through the wet ceiling and hung, caught in a tangle of cracked floorboards, above the kitchen table where a half-drunk bottle of whiskey and two glasses sat. It was Marcy who dared everyone to drink from the bottle. A calendar on the wall showed a picture of a red Cadillac above the date July 1994. It seemed possible the liquor had been sitting there for more than a decade. Marcy took the first swig, it burned but no differently than any other straight liquor. She found the detached, curved leg of a bathtub in the grass outside the house on the way back to the car and held it front of her crotch like a massive penis. She bowed her legs and waggled her metal cock at the boys and they laughed, slapped her on the back, and let her ride shotgun.

Marcy had watched barrens roll by through the windshield, wide-open stretches of land strewn with lichen-splattered boulders left behind by melting glaciers. There were no people on the beach in Trepassey, and even from the car the whale was enormous. It was on its side, its pale underside streaked with rusty yellows and oranges, and looked deflated. It didn't stink. When she breathed deep all she smelled was the usual briny smell of beach. She touched its spongy, pale skin. She didn't know what she'd hoped to feel when she saw the whale. She looked to the horizon behind it and the hugeness of ocean gave her a hit of vertigo — maybe that was the feeling she was craving. She and the boys gathered, lanky arms slung over bony shoulders for a photo with the whale's flopped-out fin. They all trooped back to the car. This time she was squished in the middle of the back seat between two sharp-hipped boys. They pooled their money at a gas station and bought a variety pack of fireworks. When the sun set they stopped at an empty schoolyard, got out, and blasted the sky. In less than an hour they hit an off-ramp then shot into downtown St. John's. Marcy hadn't expected to end up back in the city so soon.

"That's why it's called the Loop," one of the boys told her. "You end up back where you started." Slowing to match the pace of the downtown traffic was excruciating after speeding along the highway into the unknown.

On her sixth night in the apartment post-fight, Kathleen and Sharon invited Marcy to hang out in the parking garage beneath the building with some of their friends. They took folding camping chairs from the utility closet and a six-pack of beer.

"You could invite Hannah," Kathleen offered.

But Marcy stayed alone in the apartment and watched a reality TV dating show on the projector. The contestants spoke to each other through a wall. The goal was to get engaged without ever seeing your fiancé and then marry them on television. When enough time had gone by that it seemed unlikely Sharon and Kathleen would pop back up for a forgotten lighter or an extra chair, Marcy tried calling Leanne. She was going to beg her to take her on the road. She'd pack up what she needed and leave whenever. She was sure Sharon and Kathleen could find someone to replace her. The phone rang three times and then Leanne cancelled the call. Marcy sat for a moment staring at her phone screen. She thought about calling again but instead she pushed the phone down between the couch cushions.

Why had she called in the first place? It meant there must be some part of her that liked getting a strip taken off her and being ignored. She liked knowing she could take it. She believed the real her was small and hard and hidden, and she took pride in knowing she could protect it from any onslaught. Also, she deserved it.

. . .

MARCY MADE PLANS to meet Sharon, Kathleen, and Hannah downtown in the afternoon for the Black Lives Matter protest.

She had learned about George Floyd's murder from Instagram earlier that week when a friend in Minneapolis had posted about the protests happening there.

There were already hundreds of people downtown when she arrived at the corner of Sainte-Catherine and Saint-Dominique on her bike. On Sainte-Catherine they filled the sidewalks and the road as far as Marcy could see in either direction. There were children in strollers and on parents' shoulders, young and old people gathered behind painted banners and holding up signs:

BLACK LIVES MATTER

DEFUND THE POLICE

I CAN'T BREATHE

ASIANS AGAINST ANTI-BLACK RACISM

JE ME SOUVIENS
BONY JEAN-PIERRE
PIERRE CORIOLAN
NICHOLAS GIBBS

Most people were masked, so she found her mask in the back pocket of her shorts and put it on. She locked her bike to a pole and tried to imprint the spot on her brain so she could find it again later.

People were chanting, "Tout! Le monde! Déteste la police!" People leaned out the windows of buildings that towered above the crowds to join the chanting. Police helicopters chopped the air above the protestors. Marcy knew it was unlikely that she would find her friends, and she let herself be carried along by the enormous crowd for hours.

After a few hours police began shooting tear gas canisters into the crowd. Marcy saw blocks of cops in riot gear stomping into the crowds of unarmed people, protected by their weapons and Plexiglas shields and by the word POLICE on their bulletproof vests.

IN LATE JUNE, Jarry pool reopened with reduced capacity because of a heat wave. The pool was cleared every hour on the hour so that more people would have a chance to dunk under the cool water. When Marcy arrived a long line of people zigzagged around a maze of cylindrical orange pylons. Some chunks of the line had socially distanced gaps between groups of people but in other places everyone had impatiently bunched together.

Marcy joined the line behind a mom with a chubby toddler on her hip, inflatable water wings already slid on their arms. She was decadently eating up data, listening to a YouTube video of Mark Fisher lecturing about his book *Capitalist Realism*, another of Hannah's recommendations. She had three days left until the end of her billing cycle and she was only halfway through her data for the month because she'd spent so much time at home. Two teenage girls in peasant dresses joined the line behind her. Marcy looked around for Hannah, she checked her phone. No message. Her feet were sweating inside her sneakers.

At the front of the line she wrote her name and phone number on a clipboard. A teenage boy waved at a grubby bottle of hand sanitizer and she squirted a stream onto her palm. It was the very liquidy kind that smelled strongly of alcohol. The pool was packed. Four brown boys in the shallow end were taking turns standing on their hands and walking across the bottom. Two chubby white girls were whacking each other over the head with pool noodles. Socially distanced squares had been painted on the pool deck.

Marcy found a quadrant near the edge of the shallow end. She took off her sneakers first and then rolled out her towel. In her headphones Mark Fisher was talking about precarious employment, the attention economy, a book he recommended on how sleep was the last frontier of capitalism. A kid cannonballed off the diving board and Marcy heard children cheering overtop of poor, morose Mark Fisher. She pulled the headphones out to take her top off. She sat on her towel looking for Hannah. Outside the fence, the line had shrunk a little since she'd first arrived.

An old man was pushing an ice cream cart around the perimeter of the pool, jangling a bell on a string. Across the water a girl in a tie-dyed bikini was on her knees rubbing sunscreen onto her friend's back. Next to them a young guy in a straw fedora was rolling a cigarette in his lap. A man took a baby from a woman in a one-piece so she could slither over the side and into the pool. Once she was in she raised both arms and the man crouched and passed her the baby.

Marcy reclined on her towel and shimmied out of her

shorts. She closed her eyes and paid attention to how good the sun felt on her skin.

"Is this rectangle taken?" Hannah asked. She flapped a frayed green towel out next to Marcy. She lay down and took a notebook, a water bottle, and Casey Plett's *Little Fish* out of her bag.

Marcy heard a twanging. A middle-aged man had set up behind them. He was sitting in a plastic lawn chair and playing an acoustic guitar. Marcy had seen him outside the fence earlier, strumming as he waited in line. He said something in French when he saw Marcy turn around.

"Sorry?" Marcy asked.

The man pointed at his neck. "Your necklace is beautiful. I like it."

"Oh, thank you."

"Your necklace is pretty." He continued tapping his throat.

"Yeah, thanks."

Marcy turned back towards Hannah. She felt a blush burning on her cheeks.

"What?"

"He likes my necklace." Marcy said.

"Uh-huh," said Hannah. "Do you want some sunscreen?"

"No."

"No?"

"I don't really wear it. My dad doesn't believe in it, I never wore it growing up."

"What do you mean?"

"He said it's full of carcinogens. Like the chemicals are worse than the sun."

Hannah was rubbing thick white cream onto her nose. "Could be. You believe that?"

"I don't know," Marcy said. "He didn't believe in toothpaste either for a while."

"Toothpaste? Toothpaste is real."

"I feel like, is the planet even going to exist in the time it takes me to get cancer?"

Hannah shrugged. "Who knows."

Marcy held her hand out, palm up. "Okay, hit me."

Hannah and Marcy waited in a lineup of mostly children for a turn on the diving board. The sun was hot on the pool deck. Hannah stood with one foot on top of the other, switching the foot on the ground over and over to avoid burning the soles of her feet. Marcy stood on Hannah's cool shadow. She was trying not to think about Leanne loading up the van with everything that needed to be donated at Renaissance. The particle-board bookshelf empty on the sidewalk out front. She kept imagining Leanne packing her green canvas laundry bag with the clothes she was bringing on the trip. Marcy knew that Leanne rolled her T-shirts and underwear into tight cylinders to conserve space.

"This is how I like to get in," Hannah said as she climbed the ladder.

Marcy watched her fold her arms in front of her chest like someone in a coffin and step off the board. Hannah was under for a long time. Marcy watched her wobbly body glide under the string of buoys that marked the beginning of the shallow end. Then it was her turn. She bounced on the board and jumped with her knees up to her chest. When she hit the water her top rode up but she managed to wrestle it back on before her head broke the surface. As she was swimming towards the pool deck the lifeguard yelled a ten-minute warning about changeover time for the pool.

She and Hannah hauled their dry shorts on over their wet bathing suits and packed up their things. As they were leaving Hannah bought them two electric-green freezies from the old man with the cart. They sat in the shade of the pool change rooms under a tree with yellow trumpet-shaped flowers, and ripped the plastic tubes open with their teeth. Hannah lit a cigarette. A parade of wet people trampled past them on their way out of the pool. Hannah was saying her old boss from the bar had reached out to offer her shifts, since the possibility of bars reopening in the coming months had been floated in a recent press conference.

"It felt so fucking good to shut that prick down."

Marcy high-fived her.

"I was listening to this Mark Fisher lecture today," Marcy said. The neon green of the freezie washed over everything. All the people walking out of the pool were tinged with it, the water of the pool looked like a deadly chemical pit in a cartoon. A wall of bright green bounced brilliantly off the blue sky and made her eyes sting.

"Yeah?" Hannah said, and after a moment, "You were listening to Mark Fisher?"

"I don't feel good, I'm seeing something weird."

"What do you mean?" Hannah asked.

She tried to focus on Hannah but Hannah was wobbling again, like when she'd been gliding through the deep end. "I actually wanted to tell you something. Not a big-deal thing, just."

"Do you need water?" Hannah put a hand on her shoulder.

Marcy reached down and touched her damp suit, it was suffocatingly tight. She felt Hannah's metal water bottle in her hand and brought it to her lips. Warm water poured down her throat but also over her chin and chest. She felt it glugging out over her thigh.

"Jesus, Marcy," Hannah said. "You're freaking me out."

"I sort of fucked over my boss, before I left Newfoundland. I mean not even really because no one ever noticed. That I know of anyway. But I stole money." She could feel that she was swaying. She wasn't sure she was speaking out loud. "Sort of a pathetic amount of money. Like enough to get in trouble but not enough to really do anything besides buy a plane ticket. The worst part is I cheated on my girlfriend."

The green became so intense that it washed everything away. Something cold was sliding all over her face. Hannah's arms were around her. The green became watery and shapes emerged out of it. Hannah was holding her and rubbing the freezie package over her face.

"Marcy?"

"I'm okay." She could see again. Bright colours were forcing their way through the green. If she looked at the grey wall of the change rooms she could see the tint fading away. Finally she looked into the sky and it seemed to be a pure blue again.

"It's the heat," Hannah said. "You're okay. You're okay."

"I'm okay, I'm sorry. I have low blood pressure, this happens a lot."

"It's the heat," Hannah said again.

"I need to take this off." She plucked at the suit. "It's too tight."

"Let's get you home," Hannah said. "Can you stand up? I can get more water. I think there's a fountain on the other side."

"I think it's the heat." Marcy nodded.

"There's a heat warning," Hannah told her.

There were sticky green drips of melted freezie all over her. She was relieved to find it was easy to stand. She stood close as Hannah filled her steel water bottle from the fountain.

"Where did you get that?" Marcy asked.

"I found it beside a lake when I was hiking in B.C."

"I thought it looked fancy."

"The wilderness is full of expensive hiking gear abandoned by rich tech bros."

"Right, tech people love hiking," Marcy said. Even though her legs felt steady she braced herself against the wall. The cool cement felt good under her palm.

"Yes, that and finding themselves in the desert. Burning Man is all tech bros, I hear about it from my co-workers all the time." Hannah passed her the water and drinking it did feel good. She finished the bottle and handed it back to Hannah, who started filling it again.

"Everything was green."

"What?"

"When I passed out or whatever."

"That can happen, you blacked out."

"But green."

"Yeah." Hannah handed her the bottle.

"What if it's from the trial?"

"The birth control one? You're a hypochondriac. It's thirty-four degrees today. Have some more water."

They walked back through the park, past the strip of matching condos with the covered driveways. Marcy had seen people peeing there several times since public washrooms had been closed at the beginning of the pandemic. Then past the Hindu temple and through a little maze of side streets until they hit Jean-Talon. Dust swirled above four lanes of rushing traffic. They stood by the fish store with the hand-painted mermaids on the window. They were sirens, their chests thrust forward showing off the cleavage painted as a curved V between their clamshell bras. Inside, a man in a blue surgical mask was weighing a bag of scallops. When there was a break in the traffic the girls darted across to Marcy's building.

The guy who painted in a shared studio space on the second floor was smoking a cigarette on the steps.

"Look, there's people in there." He pointed at the towering office building across the street. For the first time they saw someone sitting at a desk below a glowing neon sign that read ENERGIZED. There was an enormous snake plant on the desk and for a moment it buzzed with the freezie green, but Marcy shook her head and it went back to normal.

"You know how much it costs to rent the hockey rink on the roof?" Marcy said.

"Did you know it's the Guru headquarters?" he said.

"The energy drink?" Marcy said.

"Headquarters?" Hannah asked.

The guy from the second floor finished his cigarette and flicked it over the rail onto a mangy shrub. "Okay, office, but I think they call it headquarters."

"No way, that's too ridiculous," Hannah said.

"I read a CBC article about how the rink is an example of new initiatives business owners are coming up with to try to lure people back to work. The whole building isn't Guru," Marcy said. "Just that chunk I think. Probably the rest will be tech start-ups or something."

All three of them watched as the Guru guy at the desk

stood and stretched his arms over his head and sat back down at his computer.

"I need water," Marcy said.

"Are your roommates going to mind me coming inside?" Hannah asked.

Marcy paused. "If you have it I have it. I drank from your water bottle."

"You were going to pass out."

"I don't think they're home now anyway."

"Okay." Hannah pulled open the big glass door.

Inside the apartment, Marcy and Hannah lay on the floor because it was cooler and they were exhausted.

"Are you going to be okay if I leave? You're feeling okay?" Hannah asked.

"Did you hear what I said at the park about stealing the money?"

"You stole money from your work. I heard."

"Do you think that's bad?"

"Do you?"

"Not really. The owner is just some guy who owns two condos and a big pickup. Like I said, I don't think anyone even noticed. But it was impulsive and stupid. I did a few things like that. I cheated on my girlfriend."

"You were being self-destructive."

"Yeah, maybe. And inconsiderate, and selfish with the cheating. But I'm trying to be different now, I want to be different."

"How?"

"What?"

"Like, different how?" Hannah was looking up at the ceiling.

"You think it's bad?"

"All that stuff is situational."

"What stuff?" Marcy asked.

"Stealing, cheating, lying. The context matters." Hannah sat up and looked Marcy in the face. "I can't tell you if it's wrong."

She felt cold, ever since almost fainting she'd been clammy and goose-pimpled.

"I guess I needed to get out of that situation. So in a way I don't regret any of it. But I could have done it better. More honourably," Marcy said.

"You're feeling more honourable?" Hannah smirked, she was calling Marcy pretentious.

"No."

"I'm genuinely asking," Hannah said.

"Yeah, I don't." Marcy rubbed her hands over the bumps on her forearms. "But I am trying to be less impulsive I guess."

"Well, good. I only befriend people with at least a little dishonourable streak." Hannah stood. "I'm going to go home. Make sure you stay hydrated."

After she was gone Marcy hauled herself onto the couch and fell asleep.

THE DAY LEANNE left the city, she drove by Marcy's apartment at six in the morning. Marcy looked out her bedroom window and saw piss-yellow sunlight pooling on the roof of the van. Marcy rushed over the stairs in her flip-flops. She climbed up into the passenger seat of the van. Through the windshield she could see the front door to her place; the van's back window was crowded with everything Leanne hadn't gotten rid of or left behind. The sun was rising on the skeleton of an office building being erected across the street. Jackhammers were pounding, plumes of steam rose from behind a plywood barrier and tickled the sky.

"What about if I come meet you in a few weeks?" Marcy asked. "I could get a bus."

"You have to come now, otherwise we'd have to quarantine separately," Leanne said. "If you really want to come, I'll wait for you to pack a bag."

They made out in the front seat as construction workers passed the windows on their way to the site, the parking brake jabbing Marcy right between the ribs.

"I'm going to stay."

Later (Epilogue)

Marcy woke up on the couch as the sun was setting on the little sliver of mountain that was visible from the kitchen window. Sharon was at the table, looking at her phone and taking bites from a banh mi still half inside a plastic bag.

"Have you seen the video of the John A. Macdonald statue?" Sharon said.

"I have no idea how long I've been asleep." Marcy walked to the sink and poured some water into a tall plastic glass with THE GLITZ on the side.

"You have to see this, it's incredible."

Marcy stood behind Sharon and watched the video over her shoulder. The looped footage showed a red cord wrapped around the enormous bronze statue of the founder of the residential school system being pulled taut. Beneath the pedestal, people with umbrellas circulated, chanting, "No justice, no peace! Abolish the police!" John A. Macdonald began to tip and people made room, the statue flipped in the air and was decapitated when it hit the ground, the head bounced and people cheered. Marcy and Sharon watched the video again and again, gasping in awe each time the head detached in a cloud of dust, followed by a burst of celebration from the crowd.

MARCY BIKED TO meet Hannah at a splash pad in Outremont, a part of the city she'd never been to before. She arrived early and sat on the top of a bench, her feet on the seat. She was wearing cut-offs and a windbreaker with a hot-pink spandex tank top underneath. There were rips in the shirt that showed her cleavage and stomach but if she wanted she could keep the jacket zipped, it was cool enough.

Marcy leaned over and hit the big rubber button that was supposed to make the splash pad gurgle to life, but nothing happened. Turned off for the night. A figure rode up to the bench and skidded her brakes.

Hannah swung one long leg over her bike frame and stood in front of Marcy, catching her breath. The streetlamp above the splash pad illuminated her flushed cheeks. She was wearing a flouncy, see-through, long-sleeved purple top with wide-legged black jeans. The straps of a collection of small bags criss-crossed her chest. She untangled the bags one at a time and dropped them on the shiny concrete floor of the splash pad.

"I ordered these pasties in deep lockdown. I knew there would be an occasion to wear them one day and here it is," she said, opening her arms wide. There was a heart-shaped cow-print sticker covering each of her nipples, and her smile was enormous. Marcy hopped off the bench and stepped into Hannah's open arms. Hannah hugged her tight.

"Those are amazing," Marcy said into her shoulder. "The pasties."

"I'm so glad you're coming." Hannah released her. "I can't wait to dance. With other people. With lots of other people."

Marcy's brakes were still shitty — it took two or three blocks to come to a complete stop. She'd smoked a few puffs of a loosely rolled joint with Sharon before leaving the house and traffic always made her nervous when she was high. The neighbourhood changed as they went through it, the apartment buildings got wider and taller. The road they were biking on split into four lanes. Hannah pulled into an empty oncoming lane to avoid a car backing out of an angled spot in front of a pharmacy. Marcy thumped up onto the sidewalk and just skirted the car's hood.

She thought she'd made the safer choice but realized too late the little parking lot was raised. She squeezed the brakes hard and managed to slow before sailing off a three-foot drop. Somehow she landed and stayed on the bike. She pedalled and careened back into the traffic, following Hannah's glowing lilac top between the cars.

She'd been in mid-air for a moment, and she might have flown face first over the handlebars into the asphalt. Instead she was following the lighthouse of Hannah's see-through shirt into the night, unscathed.

Hannah kept looking over her shoulder to make sure Marcy was still with her. Marcy followed her off the busy road onto a quiet and dark incline. The hill stretched on and on, getting steeper and darker.

"Up here?" Marcy asked.

The buildings on either side shrank and eventually became houses and grew farther and farther apart. Soon there were driveways.

"Yeah," Hannah said.

"All the way?" Marcy asked.

"Yeah."

"Should we walk a bit of it?" Already Marcy's legs were aching.

"Let's see how far we get."

Marcy pumped her legs hard and she could feel all the different muscles.

"Let me check the map." Hannah pulled over, rested one foot on the curb. Marcy's brakes wheezed and she waddled over to Hannah with the bike between her legs. They were stopped in front of a bungalow with a dry front yard. Marcy could see someone inside the lit-up window holding their phone at arm's length and smiling into it.

"Just checking the map," Hannah said, gazing into the light of her phone.

The waistband of Marcy's jeans and the armpits of her jacket were soaked with cooling sweat.

After a while Hannah said, "Hmmm." And then, "Okay yeah, so . . . okay. We're going the wrong way, but at least it's going to be downhill now." Then she swung one of her zippered pouches around to the front and opened it. "Let's do some drugs."

Marcy huddled in close with the bike between her legs. Hannah pinched the opening of a baggy.

"I want just a little bit," she told Hannah.

"This much?" Hannah asked.

"Is that a little bit?"

"Yeah, I think so, that seems good to me."

Marcy leaned in so close their heads were almost touching, to accept a dusty white shard.

"You need some water?" Hannah asked.

"I got some." She swung her own knapsack around and took out her plastic water bottle with the chewed-up nozzle.

They flew down the hill and pedalled alongside the traffic on the busy four-lane road. They pedalled out of the residential neighbourhood and into an industrial zone.

Hannah looked over her shoulder and said, "Marcy, we're re-emerging."

"We're back in the land of living," Marcy said as they passed empty warehouses on either side of the street.

"Almost," Hannah said.

"Almost back in the land of living," Marcy called ahead but her words were lost in the backdraft of a car.

Eventually the address from the instructions brought them to a Simon's warehouse and they pedalled behind it. Two people Hannah recognized were stumbling around on a muddy path between the back of the building and a tall chain-link fence. Hannah waved and dismounted, Marcy following her lead.

"Holy shit I haven't seen you in forever," Hannah said. "You're going to the party? Is it this way?"

"I don't know, seems like it." A girl with long, skinny dreadlocks held up her phone, showing a map on the screen. "I can't hear anything though."

The four of them listened intently for a moment but all they heard was faraway cars.

"We'll find it," Hannah laughed.

They all complimented each other on their outfits before continuing along the path. They came to a break in the fence, where there were already four or five bikes locked on. Marcy and Hannah added theirs to the line. There was a concrete barrier just like the instructions said and some-one had set up a stepladder, its legs sinking into the muddy ground.

Their small group hopped the fence and made their way through the field. Marcy had heard it was an abandoned landing strip. She hadn't expected it to be so huge, she hadn't expected the trees, she hadn't expected to be able to see stars. They arrived at a table where someone was sitting in the dark with a metal cash box.

"Ten dollars please unless you e-transferred, if you e-transferred just carry on through, it's an honour system folks, we're just trying to pay queer people like yourself, you e-transferred okay, away you go, no stamp, just carry on through, it's an honour system. Ten bucks please. Dix dollars, s'il vous plaît, merci."

Marcy and Hannah and Hannah's friends paid and continued on. The field was ringed with a dark forest, the centre full of beaten-down grass. The instructions had said uneven terrain and the terrain was uneven. In some places long chunks of runway stuck up out of the damp ground.

Marcy stumbled in a muddy rut and Hannah caught her by the arm and steadied her. Giddiness surged in her chest. She had to harness the feeling, stay on the right side of the feeling, not let it splash out into something scary.

"Hold my hand," Hannah said.

Marcy held Hannah's cool fingers. "You can see stars," she said.

Someone was DJing at a set of turntables between two big speakers. Marcy had seen Al's DJ alias on the flyer but they weren't on until later. A small spaced-out crowd was dancing. They wore baggy clothes with lots of straps. Someone had a knapsack that was a floppy teddy bear with a zipper sewn in his side, the kind Marcy had coveted in sixth grade. Her outfit wasn't quite right but Marcy unzipped her jacket anyway and the cool breeze felt good on her bare skin.

There was a tent set up at the far end of the field with a cooler on a folding card table where you could refill your water bottle, and an open box of untouched protein bars. People were just starting to arrive and joined the early dancers.

Marcy and Hannah danced on the outside of the crowd, swinging their limbs wide. Sometimes people came into their orbit and Hannah hugged them and introduced them to Marcy. Everyone smiled big smiles, they hugged her with loose arms over her shoulders. They offered her gum and water. Several times Marcy took water from a stranger's bottle and she also let people she'd never met drink from hers.

In her regular life, pieces of hate speech often clattered unexpectedly into Marcy's mind and stayed for hours. It felt like water in her ear or dirt in her eye. While she was dancing Marcy got a flash, not of any specific phrase but just of the way the screen burned her eyes after a few hours. She breathed in deep and smelled the damp grass and the trees and the bodies in motion, and then she was free of it.

The crowd grew around her. Sometimes Marcy and Hannah drifted apart and then they'd find each other again and hug. Marcy looked at the way other people were dancing and tried to emulate them, just for fun, to see if she could. Then she slipped back into her own dance, what her body did on its own. The way Marcy danced was she held the straps of her bookbag and jutted her hips right and left, her shoulders took turns rolling forward and back and her neck felt loose.

A voice came over the sound system. "The cops are outside but they don't know what's going on yet. Tell your friends not to come, tell them the party is shut down. The cops see a bunch of freaks like you walking around outside but they don't understand what's going on yet. Please no one leave, we don't want them to find the entrance."

Marcy and Hannah moved deeper into the crowd, closer to the speakers. The music was louder here, Marcy felt it in her muscles, they jutted and lolled of their own accord. She chewed the gum furiously. The beat changed and people around her started jumping and she did too. She recognized the blond mulleted person from the pinata party at NDQ. That party felt like years ago. They were dancing a few feet from her. What she recognized first was the way they moved. Marcy had never seen them dance before but their distinctive gait was in all their motions. Their face came into focus and Marcy grabbed Hannah's sheer sleeve.

"I know that person," she said urgently. "They're Leanne's friend."

"You want to say hi?"

"No, I don't think so." She wanted to be alone with Hannah in the sea of bodies and she didn't want to think about life outside of this moment.

The sky turned navy and the outline of the trees stood out against it in more detail. It seemed like hours had passed since the announcement about the cops. Worms of pink cloud stretched along the horizon. The music changed again, Marcy swayed, her legs were starting to be tired, but every now and then the drugs swooped a feeling up through her chest, a jet of joy.

Then the voice came over the speakers again. "Okay, everyone needs to leave, please leave. The cops are here. Everyone leave."

She looked for Hannah, and there she was, right beside her. A wave of police were coming through the trees at the back of the field. The dancers spread wide and some of them started moving towards the hole in the fence they'd come through to get in.

"Okay, we gotta go," Hannah said with flight-attendant calm and a smile.

Marcy looked back to see what was happening with the cops but she could only see the parade of people gathering behind her. There was a murmur of concern for the organizers and equipment.

"Not too fast," Hannah told her. "Let's just stay here, kind of in the middle of the crowd."

There was a bottleneck at the opening in the fence and some people were trying to scale it but mostly people were just trooping slowly through. Marcy saw Leanne's friend again as they waited for their turn to pass through the opening in the chain-link. This time they smiled at each other.

A police car was at the edge of the parking lot with the lights going. A cop stood with an elbow on the roof and shouted at people in a bored way. The crowd split apart on the other side of the fence, moving through the parking lot and out into the road in small groups. People on bikes looped back and forth alongside their friends.

Marcy closed her fist around the key to her bike lock, feeling the familiar scuffs in the plastic that covered the top of it. After climbing through the fence, she and Hannah crouched and freed their bikes from the fence.

Another police car came down the road with a cop leaning out the window yelling, "On circule, on circule, on y va," from the window. Marcy and Hannah coasted through constellations of ravers on foot with Hannah pausing to ask friends and acquaintances if they were going anywhere now. The sky was lightening, the moon was still visible but it was becoming easier to see the faces of people around them.

Acknowledgements

Firstly, an enormous thank you to my editor, Melanie Little, who has taught me countless invaluable lessons about story-telling. I feel so lucky to have gotten to work with you not once, not twice, but three times!

Thank you to everyone at House of Anansi Press for believing in this book and to the Canada Council for the Arts and ArtsNL for financial support that made it possible to complete this project.

Thank you to my family, Lisa Moore, Steve Crocker, Emily Amaral, Jared Amaral, Leo Amaral, Theo Crocker, Lynn Moore, Bob Howard, Libby Moore, Wanda Crocker, Sue Crocker, Tom Crocker, Lisa Mesher, and Shannon Mills for being a bunch of fun-loving freaks who've always made me feel supported in life and in creative pursuits.

Thank you to my girlfriend, Destiny Rosenberg, for reading and writing with me and for filling my life with music at the exact moment I need to hear it. It's a pleasure and an inspiration to be around someone so intensely dedicated to her craft, who approaches life with infectious kindness and vivacious energy.

Thank you to Rhys Alden, Ky Brookes, Emily Fearon, Brendan Drouillard, Jenn Ruskey, Johanne Sloan, Aaron Vansintjan, Esther Wade, and Kelly Zwicker for making me feel at home in the big city.

To friends who inspire me all the time with their work, many of whom have generously read and responded to bits and pieces of this novel: Ellen Adams, Sarah Burgoyne, Xaiver Michael Campbell, Carmella Grey-Cosgrove, Prudence Gendron, Jessica Gibson, and Devin Shears.

© Alex Stead

EVA CROCKER grew up in KTAQMKUK (Newfoundland) and currently resides in TIOHTI:ÁKE (Montreal). Her debut novel *All I Ask* was longlisted for the 2020 Giller Prize and won the 2020 BMO Winterset Award. Her short story collection *Barrelling Forward* was shortlisted for the Dayne Ogilvie Prize for Emerging LGBTQS2+ Writers and won the Alistair MacLeod Award for Short Fiction and the CAA Emerging Author's Award.